Paul Doherty was born in Middlesbrough and educated at Woodcote Hall. He studied History at Liverpool and Oxford Universities and obtained a doctorate at Oxford for his thesis on Edward II and Queen Isabella. He is now Headmaster of a school in North-East London and lives with his wife and family near Epping Forest.

By Murder's Bright Light

Paul Doherty

headline

First published in 1994
by HEADLINE BOOK PUBLISHING

First published in paperback in 1994
by HEADLINE BOOK PUBLISHING

8

ISBN 978 0 7472 4461 5

Printed and bound in Great Britain by
CPI Antony Rowe, Chippenham, Wiltshire

HEADLINE BOOK PUBLISHING
A division of Hodder Headline PLC
338 Euston Road
London NW1 3BH

To John Brunton of Nottingham
– many thanks

PROLOGUE

The great storm that had ravaged the south coast of England had now swept over the northern seas towards the ice lands where men, clad in deerskins, lit fires to nameless gods. The monkish chroniclers from London to Cornwall commented in detail how the storm was God's judgement on a sinful kingdom. Indeed, God's anger had been more than apparent in the last few months. A great French fleet under its pirate captain, Eustace the monk, had pillaged and plundered towns along the south coast. At Rye, in Sussex, the villagers had fled for sanctuary to their church. The French privateers had simply locked them in then burnt the place to the ground; they ignored the cries of those within as they loaded stolen carts with the silver objects, tapestries and food-stuffs looted from the ransacked houses.

The French fleet had withdrawn. Now London and its defences rested quietly as bleak autumn turned into freezing winter. Ships rode at anchor in the Thames, straining at their hawsers, their seamen resting and revelling in the city, leaving only skeleton crews on board to cry out the hours. But one ship, the big cog *God's Bright Light*, was silent. The lantern high on its mast winked and blinked in the cold, grey

1

light of dawn. The ship moved and creaked, floating gently to and fro on its anchor rope in the black, sluggish Thames. The cranes along St Paul's Wharf opposite the ship were silent, the warehouse doors shuttered and padlocked. Only the occasional cat, foraging for fat-bellied mice and sleek rats, padded across the coils of oil-soaked ropes, the stacks of wood and the great hooped barrels of salt left there.

For the mice and rats it had been a night of plunder as they moved from the mounds of refuse and slipped under the doors of warehouses to nibble at sacks of grain and large, juicy hams wrapped in linen cloth. Of course, the vermin had to run the gauntlet of legions of cats who also hunted there. One rat, more daring than the rest, scuttled along the wharf, slithered down the wet, mildewed steps and swam out, its oily body bobbing on the river, towards the anchor rope of the *God's Bright Light*. The rat was a keen hunter, so skilled and sly that it had survived three summers and grown grey around the muzzle. Cautiously it crept up the rope, using its small claws and tail, and slipped through the hawsehole on to the deck. There it paused, raising its pointed head to sniff. Something was wrong – its keen nose caught a sweaty odour mingled with perfume. The rat tensed, the muscles in its small black body bunching high in its shoulders. Its jet-black button eyes peered through the mist that trailed like a ghost around the deck; its ears strained into the silence, listening for the gentle swish of a cat's tail or the harsh creak of timber as some other predator stalked the boards. But it saw or heard nothing untoward and began to edge forward. Then it stopped abruptly as it heard noises – the bump of a boat as it pulled alongside, followed by the sound of human voices. Recognising danger, it turned, went back to the hawsehole and scurried down the anchor rope. It slipped quietly into the water and swam back to shore and the waiting jaws of a mangy tomcat.

It was a small bumboat that had disturbed the rat; the voices were those of a sailor and his companion, a young doxy from the fishmarket just outside Vintry. The sailor was trying to persuade the prostitute, her blonde hair already soaked by the river mist, the garish paint on her face now running, to climb the rope ladder. He swayed drunkenly and rather dangerously in the boat.

'Come on,' he slurred. 'Up you go! And, when you have pleasured me, you can have the rest! Each will pay a coin.'

The girl looked up at the precarious rope ladder and swallowed hard. The sailor had already been generous, paying her a whole groat. Now he had brought her back here for more tumbles with him and those poor unfortunates who had been left on guard as the ship's watch. She watched him twirl a piece of silver in his fingers.

'Marry and be damned!' she cursed, using her favourite oath. She grasped the rope ladder and, with the sailor behind her pushing his hands up her skirts to urge her on, clambered over the bulwark and on to the deck. The sailor followed, tumbling alongside her, breathing heavily in a mixture of curses and subdued giggling. The girl got up.

'Well, come on!' she whispered. 'Business is time and time is money. Where shall we do it?'

Her thin arms encircling the sailor's waist, she

pressed her body against his and began to move. The sailor grinned and grabbed the girl's dyed hair, pulling her head against his chest. He was torn between the excitement in his loins and, beneath the befuddlement from the ale, a nagging suspicion that all was not well.

'The ship's too quiet,' he muttered. 'Bracklebury!' he called. 'Bracklebury, where are you?'

The girl squirmed. 'Are you are one of those who like someone to watch?' she whispered.

The sailor smacked her on the bottom and stared into the misty darkness.

'Something's bloody wrong!' he muttered.

'Oh, come on!'

'Piss off, you little tart!' He pushed the girl away and, holding on to the bulwark to keep himself steady, staggered along the deck.

'Christ have mercy!' he breathed. 'Where is everybody?' He looked out over the ship's side, ignoring the whore, who sat huddled at the foot of the mast quietly grumbling, and stared across the misty river. Dawn was about to break; along the river he could see other ships and glimpse figures moving about on their decks. The cold morning air cleared the ale fumes from his mind.

'They have gone,' he whispered to himself.

He stared down at the dark, choppy waters of the Thames then looked back along the deck. The ship's boat was still lashed to the deck. Ignoring the pleadings of the doxy, who still crouched at the foot of the mast, he ran to the stern castle and pushed open the cabin door. The oil lantern hanging on its heavy hook was still glowing merrily. Inside everything was

4

undisturbed, all clean and neatly in order. The sailor stood stock-still, legs apart, letting himself roll with the gentle movements of the ship; he listened to the spars and timbers creaking and recalled the ghostly tales he and his companions had exchanged in the midnight watches. Was this the work of some magic? Had Bracklebury and the other two members of the crew been spirited away? They had certainly not left the ship in any natural way – the boat was still there and the freezing water would scarcely tempt even the most desperate sailor to swim for the pleasures of the city.

'Bracklebury!' he shouted, coming out of the cabin. Only the ship creaked and groaned in reply. The sailor looked up at the masthead, glimpsing the tendrils of mist swirling there.

'What's the matter?' the doxy wailed.

'Shut up, you bitch!'

The sailor walked back to the ship's side. He wished he had never returned.

'*God's Bright Light*!' he mocked under his breath. 'This ship's cursed!'

Captain Roffel had been a devil incarnate; even the sailor, hardened as he was by years of bloody fights at sea, had felt a flicker of pity at Roffel's ruthless despatch of French prisoners. But now Roffel was dead, taken short by a sudden illness. His corpse, wrapped in oilskins, had been sent ashore; his soul probably went to hell. The sailor shivered and turned to the doxy.

'We'd best raise the alarm,' he said, 'for what good that may do. Satan's visited this ship!'

CHAPTER 1

'I accuse Eleanor Raggleweed of being a witch!'

Sir John Cranston, coroner in the city of London, moved his massive bulk behind his high, oak table. He ground his teeth in silent fury as he gazed at the vixen-faced housewife from Rat-Tail Alley who stood pointing dramatically across the small chamber in the London Guildhall.

'She is a witch!' Alice Frogmore repeated. 'And this' – she pointed, equally dramatically, at the great fat toad squatting patiently in a metal cage on the floor – 'is her familiar!'

Cranston folded his hands across his enormous belly. He glared at the grinning scribe and smiled with false sweetness at Alice Frogmore.

'You have made your allegation.' He looked at the frightened Eleanor. 'Now, please produce the proof!'

'I have seen her!' Alice trumpeted. 'I have seen her in her garden at night, feeding her foul familiar with the sweetest bread and freshest milk. I have seen her talk to it and my husband also has proof!'

'Step forward, Master Frogmore!' Cranston boomed.

The man shuffled to stand by his wife. She, Cranston privately considered, looked more of a toad than the creature squatting in the cage: Alice Frogmore had

7

little piggy eyes, almost hidden by rolls of fat, and her short squat arms hung determinedly either side of a rather bloated body. Cranston gazed at Master Frogmore. He hid a smile as he wondered how the two fared in bed, for Master Frogmore was thin as an ash pole, with straggly white hair, protruding teeth and the frightened eyes of a hunted hare.

'Well, fellow,' Cranston barked. 'Have you seen anything?'

'Yes, your excellency.'

'"My lord coroner" will do.'

'Yes, your excellency, my lord coroner.'

Cranston's eyes darted to Osbert the scrivener, whose shoulders were beginning to shake with laughter.

'Be careful, Osbert!' Cranston whispered. 'Be very, very careful!' He stared at Frogmore. 'Well, what did you see?'

'It was on Walpurgis Night.' Frogmore's reedy voice dropped most dramatically. 'The time of the Great Sabbat for witches. I saw Mistress Raggleweed go into the garden, light a candle and feed her hideous visitor from hell.'

'How do you know about Walpurgis Night?' Cranston interrupted, a look of mock innocence on his face. 'You seem to know a great deal about witches, Master Frogmore?'

The man just hunched his shoulders.

'And, more importantly, what were you doing spying on Mistress Raggleweed in the first place?'

'I was in the garret of my house, mending the shutter on a window.'

'In the dead of night?' Cranston roared.

'My wife told me to.'

Frogmore edged behind his wife, whose head was pushed forward, mouth set, cheeks bulging. Cranston wondered whether she was preparing to spit at him.

'I need more proof than this,' Cranston rasped. He scratched his bald pate, the cheery look disappearing from his merry face and ice-blue eyes. He glared at Alice Frogmore, whom he was beginning to name to himself 'Mistress Toad'.

'Sometimes,' the woman shouted back, 'that toad enters my garden and each time ill-fortune befalls me!'

'Such as?' Cranston's tone carried a warning. He felt beneath the table for his wineskin.

Mistress Frogmore, however, had the bit between her teeth. She misinterpreted the hard look on the fat coroner's face – she took it for that of a severe judge. It wasn't – it was that of a coroner who desperately wanted a goblet of wine or a blackjack of sack in the Holy Lamb of God before he hastened home to play with his twin boys and tease his wife, the blessed Lady Maude.

'Well?' Cranston growled.

'On one occasion the milk turned sour.'

'And?' Cranston whispered between clenched teeth.

'On another occasion I fell off a stool.'

'It's a wonder you found one to bear your weight!' Cranston commented under his breath.

Osbert looked up, his face a mask of concern.

'My lord coroner, I missed that.'

'I won't miss you if you don't shut up!' Cranston growled back. 'I've had enough!' He banged the table and turned to Eleanor Raggleweed. 'What defence do you offer?'

'Sir John, I am innocent!'

Cranston glared at the toad. 'Is this creature yours?'

'Yes, my lord coroner,' she squeaked.

'And has it been on the Frogmore property?'

'Yes, my lord coroner.'

Cranston glared at the toad. 'So, it is guilty of trespass?'

'Yes, my lord coroner.'

'Why do you keep it?'

'My husband was a gentle man. He found the toad when it was small and we've always kept it.' Mistress Raggleweed's tired face forced a smile. 'I live alone, sir. It's all I've got. It's a friendly creature.'

Cranston glared at her from under his bushy white eyebrows.

'Have her stripped!' Mistress Frogmore broke in. 'Let us search for the marks of a witch! For the extra teat with which she suckles her familiar!'

Cranston brought one heavy fist down on the table.

'Quiet!' he bellowed.

'She's a witch!' Alice Frogmore insisted.

'Fined two pennies for contempt of court!' Cranston roared.

'But, my lord coroner—'

'Fined two pennies for contempt of court!' Cranston yelled.

He could see the bailiffs standing near the door beginning to shake with laughter. Cranston took the wineskin, drank a generous mouthful from it, pushed its stopper back and re-hung it on its hook on the side of his table. He glared at Eleanor Raggleweed.

'Are you a witch?'

'My lord coroner, I am an honourable widow. Ask Father Lawrence.' The woman turned and pointed to the white-haired priest standing with the bailiffs. 'I go to church on Sundays and three times in the week.'

The gentle-faced priest nodded as the woman spoke.

'So, why did the Frogmores bring this allegation?' Cranston asked.

'Because they have always contested the rights to a small plot of land behind my house. They drove my husband to an early grave with their wrangling and bickering.' The woman's voice dropped to a murmur. 'I am frightened they will kill Thomas!'

'Who the hell is Thomas?' Cranston roared.

'The toad, my lord coroner.'

Suddenly the little yellow-green monster in the cage shifted its fat, swollen body and emitted the most powerful croak. Osbert's head went down on the table; he was shaking with laughter so much he could no longer write. Mistress Frogmore immediately sprang forward.

'See!' she shouted. 'The toad talks to her!'

'Fined one groat!' Cranston bellowed.

He wiped the sweat from his brow and quietly thanked God that Brother Athelstan, his personal clerk, was not here to witness this but was safely ensconced in his parish church of St Erconwald's across the river in Southwark. By now Athelstan would have collapsed to the floor, hysterical with laughter. Cranston glared at the toad, which seemed to have taken a liking to him, for it jumped forward, croaking loudly in recognition.

'This has gone far enough!' Cranston murmured. 'Osbert,' he whispered, 'if you don't sit up straight, I'll fine you a noble and have you in the Fleet prison for a week!'

The scrivener, biting his lips to keep his face straight, picked up his quill. Cranston clicked his fingers, summoned the priest forward and pointed to the huge bible chained to a heavy lectern on the side of his table.

'Raise your hand, Father, and take the oath!'

The priest obeyed.

'Keep your hand there!' Cranston ordered. 'Now, tell me, Father, about Eleanor Raggleweed.'

'A kindly woman,' the priest replied. 'Good and true, Sir John. Her husband fought in your company of archers, when you served Sir John Chandos and Prince Edward.'

Cranston sat back in his chair and his jaw dropped as he suddenly remembered Raggleweed, a master bowman, a merry chap, honest, brave and true. He looked back at the old priest.

'And these allegations?'

'Before Christ and His mother, Sir John, arrant lies!'

Sir John nodded and motioned for the priest to stand back.

'This is my verdict. First, you, Mistress Alice Frogmore, are guilty of contempt of court. You are to be fined four pennies. Secondly, you, Mistress Alice Frogmore, have wasted the time of this court, so you are to be fined another four pennies. Furthermore' – he glared at the hate-filled face of the fat woman – 'you are bound over to keep the peace between yourselves and Mistress Eleanor Raggleweed, your neighbour. What do you say?'

'But that toad came on our property!' she whined.

'Ah, yes.' Cranston turned to Eleanor Raggleweed. 'Eleanor Raggleweed, your toad who is called Thomas' – Cranston fought to keep his face straight – 'is guilty of trespass. You are fined the smallest coin of the realm, one farthing.'

Eleanor smiled. Cranston glared at the toad, which now croaked merrily back.

'You, Thomas the toad, are made a ward of this court.' He glared at the Frogmores. 'So, if anything happens to it, you will have to answer!'

'This is not fair!' Frogmore whined. 'I will appeal.'

'Piss off!' Cranston roared. 'Bailiffs, clear the room!'

Eleanor Raggleweed picked up the toad and joined the priest, who gently murmured his congratulations. The Frogmores, with crestfallen expressions, dug into their purses and reluctantly handed over their fine to Osbert. Cranston rested his head against the high-backed chair and rewarded himself with another generous swig from the wineskin.

'Devil's bollocks and Satan's tits!' he breathed. He looked at the hour candle on its iron spigot. 'It's not yet ten in the morning and I'm already tired of this nonsense.' He glanced swiftly at Osbert. 'Have you ever heard such rubbish?'

Osbert licked his thin lips and shook his head wordlessly. He always liked to be scrivener in Sir John's court; the fat, wine-loving coroner was known for his bluntness and lack of tolerance of fools as well as for his scrupulous honesty.

'Never once—' Osbert told his chubby-faced wife and brood of children, 'never once have I seen Sir John swayed by fear or favour. He's as true as an arrow shot from a bow.'

The scrivener stretched over and picked up a greasy roll of parchment. He loved studying the coroner's moods.

'Well, Sir John, you are going to enjoy this next one.'

'Tell me,' Cranston growled.

'Well, Rahere the roaster owns a cookshop in an alleyway off Seething Lane. Next door is his rival, Bernard the baker. There's little love lost between them.'

'Yes?' Cranston snapped.

'Rahere had new latrines dug.'

'Well?'

'Bernard maintains that, out of spite and malice, Rahere had them dug so that all the refuse from them drained into the cellar of his bakery.'

'Oh, fairy's futtocks!' Cranston breathed. 'Always remind me, Osbert, never to eat in either place.' He smacked his lips and thought of the gold-crusted quail pie that the innkeeper's wife at the Holy Lamb of God was preparing for him. 'Must I hear the case now?'

The scrivener mournfully shook his head. 'I fear so, unless there's other pressing business.'

Cranston leaned his elbows on the table and rested his fat face in his podgy hands.

'Ah well!'

He was about to roar at the bailiffs to bring the next litigants in when there was a thunderous knocking on the chamber door. Edward Shawditch, under-sheriff to the city, swept into the room, his lean, pock-marked face red with fury. Cranston noticed that Shawditch hadn't shaved; his chin was marked by sharp hairs. His small green eyes were red-rimmed from lack of sleep and his lips twisted so sharply Cranston wondered if he was sucking on vinegar. The under-sheriff removed a gauntlet and combed back his sweat-soaked red hair.

'A word, Sir John.'

You mean a thousand, Cranston thought bitterly. 'What is it, Shawditch?' He respected the under-sheriff as a man of probity, but the fellow was so officious and so churlish in his manner that he put Cranston's teeth on edge.

'Two matters, Sir John.'

'Let's take one at a time,' Cranston barked.

'Well, there's been a burglary, another one!'

Cranston's heart sank.

'The sixth,' Shawditch declared flatly.

'Whose house this time?'

'Selpot's,' Shawditch replied.

'Oh, God, no!' Cranston breathed. Selpot was an alderman, a high-ranking member of the Tanners' Guild. 'Not his house in Bread Street?'

'You are correct.'

'And the same pattern as before?'

'Yes, exactly the same. Selpot is absent with his wife and children visiting friends in Surrey, or so his steward says. He probably went to cheat a farmer out of a pile of skins. Anyway, Selpot left his house in charge of his steward.' Shawditch shrugged. 'You'd best come and see for yourself.'

Cranston pushed his chair back, donned his thick beaver hat and clasped his sword belt around his ponderous belly. He grabbed his heavy military cloak and followed Shawditch out of the chamber. At the door he turned and smiled gleefully at Osbert.

'The day's business is adjourned,' he said. 'Either that or you can move it to another court.'

The coroner and the under-sheriff went out into the freezing morning air and up Cheapside. The muck and filth coating the cobbles was now frozen hard. The houses on either side of the thoroughfare were half-hidden by a rolling mist which deadened the din and clamour. Everyone was garbed from head to toe, the rich in woollen robes and cloaks, the poor in a motley collection of rags, as protection against the freezing mist.

An old beggar woman, crouched in the corner of an alleyway, had frozen in death in that posture. Now her corpse was being awkwardly lifted on to a cart, pulled by oxen whose heavy breath rose like steam. Behind the cart a group of children, impervious to the tragedy, used sheep bones to skate over the hard-frozen sewers and cesspools. A group of young men, dressed in a strange garb fashioned out of pieces of rags sewn together, sang a carol about Christ being born again in Bethlehem. Further down Cheapside, a bagpiper blew shrilly before the stocks where the petty criminals would stand for a day, hands and heads locked, to receive abuse and thrown refuse as well as suffer the frozen chill of a hard winter's day. A Franciscan, a leather bucket of warm water in one hand, a soft rag in the other, gently wiped the faces of this day's prisoners and offered them sips from a large bowl of heated posset. One of the prisoners was crying with the cold. Sir John stopped. He looked at the chapped faces, noticing the blue, high cheeks of one pinch-featured pickpocket and the tears rolling down the face of his rat-faced companion. He started to move on.

'Cranston, for the love of Christ!' the pickpocket shouted. 'Oh, please!'

Cranston stopped and looked at the supervising beadle. Shawditch, impatient, walked back.

'What's the matter, Sir John?'

Cranston beckoned the beadle forward. 'How long have they been here?'

'Four hours, Sir John.'

'Release them!'

A chorus of praise broke out along the stocks, benedictions being called down on Sir John and his progeny to the forty-fifth generation.

'You can't do that,' the beadle spluttered.

'Can't I?' Cranston winked at the under-sheriff who, despite his flinty exterior, was a compassionate man. 'Do you hear that, Master Shawditch. The word "can't" is used against the city coroner and his under-sheriff.'

Shawditch poked the beadle in the chest, dug into his purse and pushed a coin into the man's hand.

'You'll not only free them, my fat friend,' he rasped, 'but, for the love of Christ, you'll buy them something hot to eat.' He nodded his head towards the carol singers. 'Soon it will be Advent, Yuletide, the birth of Christ. For his sake, show some mercy!'

The beadle took his heavy bunch of keys and began to free the prisoners, who rubbed their fingers and faces. The smiling Franciscan waddled up.

'May Christ bless you, Master Shawditch.'

'Aye,' the under-sheriff mumbled. 'May Christ bless me. Now, Father, you make sure that the beadle spends my money well. Come along, Sir John.'

The under-sheriff walked on, Cranston hurrying behind him.

'They say you are a bastard,' Cranston murmured. 'Though a fair bastard.'

'Aye, Sir John, and I have heard the same about you.' Shawditch looked over his shoulder, back at the stocks. 'I thought as much.'

'What?'

'That bloody pickpocket has just filched my coin from the beadle!'

Cranston grinned and held a gloved hand up against an ear which was beginning to ache in the stinging cold.

'Too bloody cold for anything,' he murmured as they turned into Bread Street.

'Not for the burglars,' Shawditch replied.

He stopped before a tall timber-framed house, well maintained and newly painted. Cranston stared appreciatively at the gaudily painted heraldic shields above the door.

'Selpot must have sold a lot of skins,' he commented.

'Aye,' Shawditch replied. 'Including those of many of his customers.'

They knocked on the door. An anxious-faced steward ushered them into a small comfortable parlour and pushed stools in front of the roaring fire.

'You want some wine?' He looked at Shawditch.

'This is the city coroner, Sir John Cranston,' the under-sheriff told him. 'And you, I forget your name?'

'Latchkey, the steward!'

'Ah, yes, Master Latchkey.'

'We'll have some wine,' Cranston trumpeted. 'Thick, red claret.'

He looked around the small room, admiring the gleaming wainscoting, the rich wall-hangings and a small painted triptych above the fireplace. Bronze hearth tools stood in the inglenook and thick woollen rugs covered the stone floor.

'I am sure Master Selpot has some good burgundy,' he continued, threateningly.

Latchkey hurried across to a cupboard standing in the window embrasure and brought back two brimming cups.

'Well, tell us what happened.' Cranston drained the wine in one gulp and held his hand out for a refill. 'Come on, man, bring the jug over! You don't happen to have a spare chicken leg?'

The fellow shook his head dolefully, then refilled Sir John's cup before telling his sorry tale – his master was absent from the city and, on the previous night, some felon had entered the house and stolen cloths, precious cups and trinkets from the upper storeys.

'And where were you and the servants?' Cranston asked.

'Oh, on the lower floor, Sir John.' The man gnawed at his lip. 'You see, the servants' quarters are here, no one sleeps in the garret. Master Selpot is insistent on that. I have a small chamber at the back of the house, the scullions, cooks and spit boys sleep in the kitchen or hall.'

'And you heard nothing?'

'No, Sir John. Come, let me show you.'

Latchkey promptly led them on a tour of the sumptuous house, demonstrating how the windows were secured by shutters that were padlocked from the inside.

'And you are sure no window was left open?'

'Certain, Sir John.'

'And the doors below were locked?'

'Yes, Sir John. We also have dogs but they heard nothing.'

'And there's no secret entrance?'

'None whatsoever, Sir John.'

'And the roof?'

Latchkey shrugged and led them up into the cold garret, which served as a storeroom. Cranston gazed up but he could see no chink in the roof.

'How much has gone?' he asked as they went back downstairs.

'Five silver cups, two of them jewelled. Six knives, two of them gold, three silver, one copper. A statuette of the Virgin Mary carved in marble. Two soup spoons, also of gold. Five silver plates, one jewel-rimmed.'

Shawditch groaned at the long list.

Downstairs Cranston donned his beaver hat and cloak.

'Could the servants have done it?' he asked.

Latchkey's lugubrious face became even more sombre.

'Sir John, it was I who discovered the thefts. I immediately searched everyone. Nothing was found.'

Cranston raised his eyes heavenwards, thanked the steward and, followed by an equally mystified under-sheriff, walked back into the freezing street.

'How many did you say,' Cranston asked. 'Six since Michaelmas?'

Shawditch glumly nodded.

'And where's Trumpington?'

Shawditch pointed along the street. 'Where he always is at this hour, in the Merry Pig.'

Stepping gingerly round the piles of refuse, they

made their way down the street: they turned up an alleyway where a gaudy yellow sign, depicting a red pig playing the bagpipes, creaked and groaned on its iron chains. Inside the taproom they found Trumpington, the ward beadle, stuffing his face with a fish pie, not stopping to clear his mouth before draining a blackjack of frothy ale. He hardly stirred when Cranston and Shawditch announced them-selves; he just gave a loud belch and began busily to clean his teeth with his thumbnail. Cranston tried to hide his dislike of the man. He secretly considered Trumpington a pig, with his squat body, red, obese face, quivering jowls, hairy nostrils and quick darting eyes under a low forehead, always fringed with dirty yellow hair.

'There's been a robbery!' Trumpington announced.

'Yes, the sixth in this ward!' Cranston snapped.

Trumpington cleaned his mouth with his tongue and Sir John, for the first time in weeks, refused an offer of a drink or a morsel to eat.

'It's not my fault!' Trumpington brayed. 'I walk the streets every night. Well, when it's my tour of duty. I see nothing amiss and the robberies are as much a mystery to me as they are to you, my fine fellows.'

Cranston smiled sweetly and, placing his hands over Trumpington's, pressed firmly until he saw the man wince.

'You never see anything amiss?'

'Nothing,' the fellow wheezed, his face turning slightly purple at the pressure on his hand.

'Well.' Cranston pushed back his stool and lifted his hand. 'Keep your eyes open.' He tugged at Shawditch's sleeve and they both left the taproom.

'A veritable mystery,' Shawditch commented. He glanced warily at Cranston. 'You know there will be the devil to pay over this.'

Cranston waited until a group of apprentices, noisily kicking an inflated pig's bladder down the street, rushed by whooping and yelling. Then he thought aloud. 'Six houses. All in this ward. All belonging to powerful merchants but, with their owners away, occupied only by servants. No sign of forced entry, either by door or through a window. Robbery from within?' He shook his head. 'It is impossible to accept collusion between footpads and the servants of six different households.' He blew out his cheeks, stamping his feet against the cold. 'First there will be murmurs of protest from the city council. Then these will grow to roars of disapproval and someone's head will roll. Eh, Shawditch?'

'Aye, Sir John, and it could be mine. Or yours,' he added flatly. 'When there's a breakdown in law and order, God knows why, they always think that punishing some city official will make matters better.'

Cranston clapped him on the shoulder. 'You have met Brother Athelstan?'

'Your clerk? The parish priest of St Erconwald's in Southwark?' Shawditch nodded. 'Of course. He is most memorable, Sir John, being as different from you as chalk from cheese.'

Shawditch smiled as he recalled the slim, olive-skinned Dominican monk, with his jet-black hair and the smiling eyes that belied a sharp intelligence and ready wit. At first Shawditch had considered Athelstan to be secretive, but he had realised that the Dominican was only shy and rather in awe of the mountainous Sir

John with his voracious appetite and constant yearning for refreshment.

'What are you smiling at?' Cranston asked crossly.

'Oh nothing, Sir John, I just . . .' Shawditch's words trailed away.

'Anyway,' Cranston boomed, turning to walk down the street, 'Athelstan is always saying if there's a problem there must be a solution, it's just a matter of observation, speculation and deduction.'

Cranston hopped aside, with an agility even Thomas the toad would have admired, as an upper window opened and a night jar of slops was thrown into the street. Shawditch was not so lucky and his cloak was slightly spattered. He stopped to shake his fist up at the window, then moved as quickly as Cranston as it opened again and another night jar appeared.

'There should be a law against that,' he grumbled. 'But you were saying, Sir John?'

'Well.' The coroner tugged his beaver hat firmly over his large head. 'Question, how does the footpad get into the houses? Secondly, how does he know they are empty?'

'As to the second question, I don't know. And the first? Well, it's a mystery.'

'Have you checked the roofs?' Sir John asked.

'Yes, Trumpington summoned a tiler, the fellow inspected the roofs and found nothing amiss.'

They reached the corner of Bread Street. Cranston was about to go when Shawditch plucked at his sleeve.

'I said I had two problems for you, Sir John. The second is more serious.'

Cranston sighed. 'Well, not here.'

He led the under-sheriff up Cheapside and into the

welcoming warmth of the Holy Lamb of God. He roared at the landlord's wife for his capon pie and bowls of claret for himself and his friend. Once he had taken his first bite, he nodded at the under-sheriff.

'Right, tell me.'

'You know the king's ships have been at sea against the French?'

'Aye, who doesn't?' Cranston munched at his pie.

John of Gaunt, pestered into action by parliament, had at last assembled a flotilla of fifteen armed ships to carry out reprisals against French privateers in the Channel as well as surprise attacks on towns and villages along the Normandy coast.

'Well,' Shawditch continued, 'some of the flotilla are berthed in the Thames opposite Queen's hithe, among them the cog *God's Bright Light*.' Shawditch sipped at his wine. 'The ship was commanded by William Roffel. It returned to port two days ago, after capturing and sinking a number of French vessels. Roffel, however, on the return voyage, caught a sudden sickness and died. His corpse was taken ashore. The crew were paid their wages and given seven days' shore leave. Now, last night, the only watch left on the ship was the first mate and two other sailors. One in the bows and one at the stern.' Shawditch gnawed at his lip. 'A lantern was left on the mast and the ship was in earshot of others riding at anchor.'

'What happened?' Cranston interrupted him impatiently.

'Just before dawn a sailor came back with his doxy. They climbed on board and found the ship deserted – no first mate, no watch.'

'So?'

'Well, no one had seen anyone leave or approach the ship, although it's true there was a thick river mist that night. But that's only half the mystery, Sir John. You see, an hour before the sailor returned, in accordance with the admiral's instructions, the watch on board the neighbouring ship, the *Holy Trinity*, asked if all was well? A voice from the *God's Bright Light* replied, using the established password.'

'Which was?'

'The glory of St George.'

Cranston sat back. 'So, what you are saying is that nothing apparently untoward happened on board this ship? The watch even responded with the correct password to the neighbouring vessel?'

'Aye, and then passed it on to another ship, the *Saint Margaret*,' Shawditch answered.

'And yet,' Cranston continued, 'a short while later the ship is found deserted. No trace whatsoever of the first mate or the rest of his watch, two able-bodied sailors?'

'Exactly, Sir John.'

'Could they have deserted?'

Shawditch pulled a face.

'And there was no sign of violence?'

'None whatsoever.'

'Anything stolen?'

Shawditch shook his head.

'Well! Well! Well!' Cranston breathed. 'I wonder what Athelstan will make of this?'

'God knows!' Shawditch replied. 'But the mayor and council demand an answer.'

CHAPTER 2

Brother Athelstan sat at the table in his kitchen in the small priest's house of St Erconwald's in Southwark and stared moodily into the fire. He'd celebrated morning Mass. He'd cleaned the church with the help of Cecily the courtesan and talked with Tab the tinker about mending some pots. After that he had said goodbye to the widow Benedicta, who was going to spend a few days helping a relative across the river who was expecting a baby.

Athelstan got up and went to stir the porridge cooking in a black cauldron above the flames. He looked over his shoulder at Bonaventure, the big one-eyed tomcat, who was sitting patiently on the table, daintily washing himself after a night's hunting in the alleyways around the church.

'It will soon be ready, Bonaventure. Some hot oatmeal with a little milk, spice and sugar. Benedicta herself prepared it before she left. It will taste delicious. For the next week we will break our fast like kings.'

The cat yawned and stared arrogantly at this strange Dominican who constantly talked to him. Athelstan wiped the horn spoon, put it back on its hook, stretched and yawned.

'I should have gone to bed myself,' he murmured. Instead he had climbed the tower of his church to study the stars, watching in awe the fiery fall of a meteor. He walked back to the table, sat down again and sipped his watered ale.

'Why?' he asked Bonaventure. 'Tell me this, most cunning of cats. Why do meteors fall from heaven but not stars? Or,' he continued, seeing he had the cat's attention, 'are meteors falling stars? And, if they are, what causes one star to fall and not another?'

The cat just blinked with its one good eye.

'And the problem becomes even more complicated,' Athelstan explained. 'Let me put it this way. Why do some stars move? The constellation called the Great Bear does but the ship's star, the North Star, never?'

Bonaventure's reaction was to miaow loudly and slump down on the table as if desperate at the long wait for his morning dish of oatmeal. Athelstan smiled and gently stroked the cat's tattered ear.

'Or should we ask questions?' he whispered. 'Or just gaze in admiration at God's great wonder?'

He sighed and returned to the piece of parchment he had been studying the evening before. On it was a crude drawing of the church. The parish council, in their wisdom, had decided that on their saint's day they would produce a mystery play in the nave of the church. Athelstan was now drawing up a list of the things they'd need. Thomas Drawsword, a new member of the parish, had agreed to refurbish a large wagon which would act as the stage, but they would need more. Athelstan studied his list:

Two devils' coats
Two devils' hoods
One shirt
Three masks
Wings for the angels
Three trumpets
One hell's door
Four small angels
Nails
Last, but not least, a large canvas backcloth

The play was called *The Last Judgement* and already Athelstan was beginning to regret his enthusiasm for the venture.

'We are going to be short of wings,' he muttered, 'and we can't have one-winged angels.' He groaned. All this was nothing to the arguments over who would play the different characters. Watkin the dung-collector insisted on being God, but this was bitterly disputed by Pike the ditcher. The civil war had spread to their children, who were quarrelling over who would act the roles of the four good spirits, the four evil spirits and the six devils. Watkin's large wife, who had the brassy voice of a trumpet, had declared that she would be Our Lady. Tab the tinker was threatening to withdraw from the pageant if he was denied a principal role.

Huddle the painter, although aloof from these squabbles, presented problems of his own. He was having some difficulty in painting a convincing hell's mouth. 'The front of the cart must be raised, Father,' he insisted, 'so that when the damned go through the mouth of hell, they disappear downwards.'

Athelstan threw his quill down on to the table.

'What we need, Bonaventure,' he declared, 'is Sir John Cranston. He has agreed that his twin sons, the little poppets, can stagger about as cherubims and Sir John would make a marvellous Satan.'

Athelstan paused and stared up at the blackened timbered ceiling. Cranston! Athelstan had visited him only three days ago, had sat in his huge kitchen while the two poppets chased around, shrieking with laughter. They had hung on to the tails of the great Irish wolfhounds Cranston had, in a fit of generosity, taken into his house. Despite the uproar, the coroner had been in good spirits. He was involved in the minutiae of city government, though he had issued a dire prophecy, aided by generous cups of claret, that some dreadful homicide, some bloody affray, would soon be upon them. Athelstan could only agree; life had been rather quiet and sweet since he and Sir John had been involved in the business of the Guildhall some months previously.

Athelstan warmed his fingers in front of the fire. He was glad winter was approaching. The harvest had been good. The price of corn and bread had fallen, easing some of the seething discontent in the city. The prospect of revolt had receded, though Athelstan knew it was just hiding, like seeds in the ground, waiting to sprout. Athelstan sighed, he could only hope, pray and do his best.

'Come on, Bonaventure,' he said. 'Let's eat.'

He took two large bowls from the shelf over the fireplace, ladled into them hot, steaming dollops of oatmeal and took them to the buttery. Following Benedicta's instructions, he sprinkled each bowl with cinnamon and sugar and went back into the kitchen. One bowl was placed before the hearth for the ever-hungry cat. Athelstan blessed himself and Bonaventure, took up his horn spoon and began to eat the nourishing, boiling-hot oatmeal. He had finished his bowl, or was letting Bonaventure do it for him, when he heard the clamour outside – the sound of running footsteps and a voice screaming, 'Sanctuary, Christ have mercy!'

Athelstan hurried out of his house and round to the front of the church. A young man, white-faced, eyes staring under a shock of blond hair, gripped the great iron ring of the church door.

'Sanctuary, Father!' the man gasped. 'Father, I claim sanctuary! In the name of God and his Church!'

'Why?' Athelstan asked.

'Murder!' the young man replied. 'But, Father, I am innocent!'

The priest studied the man carefully: his thick, serge jerkin, hose of bottle-green wool and leather boots were all coated in muck and ordure.

'Father!' the man pleaded. 'They'll kill me!'

Athelstan heard the sound of running footsteps and the faint cries of pursuit further up the alleyway. He took out his keys and unlocked the door. The fugitive dashed up the darkened nave and through the new rood screen carved and erected by Huddle. He clung to the corner of the altar and once again shouted.

'I seek sanctuary! I seek sanctuary!'

Athelstan, followed by an ever-inquisitive Bonaventure, walked up after him. The man now sat with his back to the altar, legs out, fighting for breath as he wiped his sweat-soaked face on the sleeve of his jerkin.

'I claim sanctuary!' he gasped.

'Then, by the law of the Church, you have it!' Athelstan replied softly.

He turned at the clamour behind him. A cluster of dark figures, armed with staves and swords, stood just inside the church.

'Stay there,' Athelstan called. He went out through the rood screen. 'What do you want?'

'We seek the murderer, the assassin, Nicholas Ashby,' a voice growled.

'This is God's house,' Athelstan replied, coming forward. 'Master Ashby has claimed sanctuary and I have given it according to canon law and the custom of the land.'

'Bugger that!' the voice replied.

The figures walked up the nave. Athelstan hid his own panic and stood his ground. The group, wearing the stained red and white livery of some lord, were led by a burly, bewhiskered man. They advanced threateningly towards him, swords drawn, staves in their hands. Athelstan studied their buff jerkins, tight hose, protuberant codpieces, the sword and dagger sheaths hanging on their belts and the way they trailed their cloaks. He recognised them as bully-boys, the hired thugs of some powerful lord. He held a hand up and they stopped only yards away.

'If you go any further,' he said quietly, 'you have broken not only man's law but God's. You are already committing sacrilege' – he pointed to the drawn swords – 'by coming into God's house with such weapons.'

The leader stepped forward, sheathing his sword, as to Athelstan's relief, did the rest.

'What's your name?' Athelstan asked.

'Mind your own business!'

'Very well, Master Mind-my-own-business,' Athelstan continued. 'If you don't leave this church, I'll consider you excommunicated on the spot. Felons, condemned to hell fire.' Athelstan glimpsed the sullen, arrogant faces of the others. He was pleased to see some of them show a flicker of fear.

'Come on, Marston,' one of them muttered to the leader. 'Let the little turd hide behind the skirts of a priest! He'll have to leave some time!'

Marston was full of bravado. He walked slowly forward, hands on hips, and pushed his face close to Athelstan's.

'We could kick the shit out of you!' he hissed. 'Drag that little turd out, kill him and deny anything happened!'

Athelstan stared coolly back, even though his stomach was heaving. He was tempted to quote Cranston's name, for he didn't like the smell of sour sweat and stale perfume that came from this bully. He prayed Watkin the dung-collector or Pike the ditcher would make an appearance. Then he smiled, remembering that God helped those who helped themselves.

'Stay there,' he commanded. Turning, he walked back through the rood screen.

'Oh, please don't!' Ashby whispered. 'They'll kill me!'

Athelstan picked up the heavy bronze cross from the altar. He winked at Ashby and walked down the nave carrying the cross before him. The smirk faded from Marston's face.

'What are you going to do?'

'Well,' Athelstan answered him, 'first, I am going to

33

excommunicate you with this crucifix. Then, if you come any closer, I'm going to use it to crack you on the noddle!'

Marston drew both sword and dagger. 'Come on!' he hissed. 'Try it!'

'Now, now, my buckos! Lovely lads all!'

Sir John Cranston, swathed in his great military cloak, swept up the nave through the group, knocking them like ninepins left and right. He shoved Marston aside, stood by Athelstan and lifted his wineskin to his mouth. He smacked his lips as the wine disappeared down his throat. Marston and the others stepped back.

'Who are you, you big fat turd?' Marston asked. His sword and dagger came up.

Cranston, his arms folded across his chest, walked slowly towards him. 'Who am I?' he whispered in a sweet, almost girlish voice.

Marston looked puzzled – but only briefly, for Cranston hit him full in the face. His large, ham fist crashed into the man's nose and sent him sprawling back among his companions, blood spurting out, drenching moustache, beard and the front of his jerkin. Marston wiped his face, looked at the blood and, roaring with rage, lunged at Sir John. The fat coroner, moving as nimbly as a dancer, simply advanced towards him, stepped quickly aside and stuck out one fat leg. Marston went flat on his face, sword and dagger spinning from his hands. The coroner, tut-tutting under his breath, picked the man up by his greasy black hair, jerked his head back, marched him along the nave and flung him down the steps of the porch. Then he turned to the others.

'I will count to ten,' he threatened.

By the time the coroner had reached five the rest of Marston's group were standing like frightened boys around their leader. They stared up in awe at the great cloak-swathed figure standing, legs apart, on the church steps. Marston, his face covered in blood and bruises, still had fight left in him. Sir John waggled a finger warningly.

'You asked who I am. And, now you have left the church, I'll inform you. I am Sir John Andrew Patrick George Cranston, personal friend of the king. I am coroner of this city, law officer, husband to the Lady Maude and the scourge of thugs like you. So far, my buckos, you have committed a number of crimes. Trespass, blasphemy, sacrilege, attempting to break sanctuary, attacking a priest, threatening a law officer and, ipso facto' – Cranston hid his smile – pro facto, et de facto, guilty of high treason, not to mention misprision of treason. I could arrest you and you'd stand trial before the King's Bench at Westminster!'

The change in Marston was wonderful to behold. He forgot his blood and bruises, his mouth gaped open and his arms hung limply on either side of his body as he stared fearfully at the coroner.

'Now, my lads.' Sir John tripped down the steps of the church, Athelstan following him. 'Tell me what happened, eh?'

Marston wiped the blood away. 'We are the retainers of Sir Henry Ospring of Ospring Manor in Kent. Our master was staying at the Abbot of Hyde inn in Southwark whilst journeying into the city.'

'Oh, yes, I have heard of Ospring,' Cranston said. 'A mean-spirited, tight-fisted varlet I gather.'

'Well, he's dead,' Marston went on. 'Stabbed in his

chamber by the murderer now sheltering in that church.'

'How?'

Marston licked his lips, feeling the lower one tenderly because it was beginning to swell.

'I went up to the chamber this morning to rouse Sir Henry. I opened the door and my master lay sprawled in his nightshirt, on the floor, the blood pumping out of him. Ashby knelt above him grasping a dagger. I tried to arrest the bastard but Ashby fled through the window. The rest you know.'

'The Abbot of Hyde inn?' Cranston queried. 'Well, let's see for ourselves.' He turned to Athelstan. 'Lock the church, Father. Let's visit the scene of the crime.'

Athelstan did what he asked. Cranston strode off up the alleyway, leaving the rest to hurry behind him. They found the Abbot of Hyde a scene of chaos and commotion – slatterns crying in the taproom, other servants sitting around looking white-faced and terrified. The landlord was gibbering with fright. He bowed and scraped as Cranston made his entrance and demanded a tankard of sack. Draining it immediately the coroner swept up the broad wooden stairs. Marston hurried before him along the passageway to show him the murder chamber.

Cranston pushed the door open. Inside all was confusion. Sheets had been dragged from the great four-poster bed, half-open coffers lay overturned and a cup of spilt wine was nestling among the rushes on the floor. What caught their attention, however, was the corpse lying near the bed, its arms spread wide, its thin hairy legs pathetic as they peeped out from beneath a cream woollen nightshirt. The dagger in the man's chest was long and thin and driven in to the hilt. The blood had splashed out in a great scarlet circle. The corpse's face, lean and pointed like that of a fox, still bore the shock of death in its open, staring eyes. From a corner of the gaping mouth ran a now dry trickle of blood.

'God have mercy!' Athelstan whispered. 'Help me, Sir John!'

Together they lifted the corpse on to the bed. Athelstan, ignoring the blood spattering the white hair, knelt down and spoke the words of absolution into the man's ear, sketching a benediction in the air.

'*Absolvo te,*' he whispered, '*a peccatis in nomine Patris et Filii.* I absolve you from your sins in the name of the Father and of the Son.'

Cranston, more practical, sniffed at the wine jug and, whilst the friar performed the last rites, walked around the chamber picking up pieces, handling cloths, sifting among the rushes with the toe of his boot.

'Tell me again what happened,' Cranston muttered over his shoulder to a now more subdued and respectful Marston.

'Ashby is Sir Henry's squire. He'd just returned from a sea voyage on the *God's Bright Light.*'

Cranston turned his face away to hide his surprise.

'Sir Henry was coming to London to meet Roffel, the ship's captain.'

'Do you know that he's dead too?' Cranston snapped the question.

Marston's eyes rounded in surprise. 'You mean Roffel—?'

'Yes, he's been dead two days. Taken ill on board

37

ship. By the time they reached the port of London, he was dead.' Cranston nodded at Athelstan's surprised face. 'That's why I came to Southwark. Not only did Roffel die in rather mysterious circumstances but last night the first mate and the two men on watch aboard the *God's Bright Light* disappeared. However, let's leave that.' He turned back to Marston. 'Continue.'

Marston scratched his head. 'Well, Sir Henry was coming in to have words with Captain Roffel. He always stayed here and took a barge down-river to meet the captain.' Uninvited, Marston slumped down on a stool. 'This morning I came to arouse Sir Henry. The door was off the latch. I pushed it open. Ashby was by the corpse, his hand round the hilt of a dagger. Then' – Marston pointed to the open window – 'he fled. The rest you know.'

'Was the window closed last night?' Athelstan asked.

'Aye, closed and secure.'

Athelstan pulled a sheet over the corpse and closed the curtains around the four-poster bed.

'Why should Sir Henry be visiting a captain of a fighting ship?' he asked.

'I can answer that,' Cranston replied. 'The exchequer is almost empty. Great landowners and merchants like Sir Henry agree to fit out the ships. In return, they not only receive royal favour but a percentage of any plunder taken. Isn't that right, Marston?'

The henchman nodded.

'A lucrative trade,' Cranston continued evenly, 'which ensures that the captains not only defend English shipping but constantly search for well-laden French ships or the occasional undefended town along the Seine or the Normandy coast. Sometimes they even turn to piracy against English ships.' Cranston took his beaver hat off and rolled it in his large hands. 'After all, if an English ship goes down, it can always be blamed on the French.'

'Sir Henry was not like that,' Marston snapped.

'Aye,' Cranston said drily. 'And cuckoos don't lay their eggs in other birds' nests.'

The coroner paused at a tap on the door. A young woman entered, her face as white as a sheet, her corn-coloured hair loose. She was agitated, her fingers lacing together, and she played nervously with the silver-tasselled girdle around her slim waist. Her red-rimmed eyes flitted to the great four-poster bed. Marston rose as she entered.

'I am sorry,' she stuttered. She wiped her hands on the tawny sarcanet of her high-necked dress.

Athelstan strode across the room and took her hand. It was cold as ice.

'Come on,' he said softly. 'You had best sit down.' He took her gently to the stool Marston had vacated. 'Do you wish some wine?'

The young woman shook her head, her eyes still fixed on the great four-poster bed.

'It's Lady Aveline, Sir Henry's daughter,' Marston explained. 'She was next door when Ashby was in here.'

Athelstan crouched down and stared into Aveline's doe-like eyes.

'God rest him, my lady, but your father's dead.'

The young woman plucked at a loose thread on her dress and began silently to cry, tears rolling down her cheeks.

'I don't want to see him,' she whispered. 'I can't bear to see him, not in a nightshirt soaked in blood.' She looked at Marston. 'Where's Ashby?'

'He's taken sanctuary in a church.'

Suddenly there was a commotion in the passage outside. The door was flung open and a tall woman with steel-grey hair swept into the room. Behind her followed another woman, rather similar in appearance but more subdued. Both women wore heavy cloaks with the hoods pushed back. The innkeeper followed, waving his hands in agitation.

'You shouldn't! You shouldn't really!' he spluttered.

'Shut up!' Cranston roared. 'Who are you?'

The first and taller of the two women drew her shoulders back and looked squarely at Sir John.

'My name is Emma Roffel, wife to the late Captain Roffel. I came here to see Sir Henry Ospring.'

Cranston bowed. 'Madam, my condolences on your husband's death. Was he a sickly man?'

'No,' she replied tartly. 'As robust as a pig.' She narrowed her eyes. 'I know you. You're Cranston, Sir John Cranston, coroner of the city. What has happened here? This fellow' – she indicated the innkeeper – 'says Sir Henry has been murdered!'

'Yes,' Athelstan tactfully intervened, seeing the look on Cranston's face. 'Sir Henry has been murdered and we have the culprit.'

Emma Roffel's face relaxed. Athelstan studied her curiously. She was rather pretty, he thought, in a tired-looking way. He was always fascinated by women's faces and Emma's struck him as a strong one, with its high-beaked nosed and square chin. Its pallor emphasised lustrous dark eyes, though these were now red-rimmed and tinged with shadows. She let her cloak fall open and he glimpsed her black widow's weeds. She smiled at Athelstan.

'I apologise for my entrance but I couldn't believe the news.' She pointed to the other woman, quiet and mousey, standing behind her. 'This is Tabitha Velour, my maid and companion.'

Aveline still sat on the stool, her face white with shock. Emma Roffel went over and touched the girl gently on the shoulder.

'I am sorry,' she murmured. 'Truly sorry.' She glanced up at Cranston. 'How did this happen?'

'Stabbed by his squire,' Cranston said. 'Nicholas Ashby.'

Emma Roffel pulled her face in surprise.

'You find that difficult to believe, madam?' Athelstan asked.

The woman pursed her lips and stared at him. 'Yes,' she said slowly. 'Yes, I do. Ashby was quiet, more of a scholar than a soldier.'

'But he sailed with your husband?'

Emma Roffel smiled cynically. 'God forgive me and God rest him but Sir Henry was a suspicious man. Yes, squire Ashby was often sent by his master to make sure his investment gained a just return.'

'And you came here to inform Sir Henry of your husband's death?'

'Yes, yes, I did. But there's little point,' she said with a half-smile, 'for I suppose they can talk to each other now.'

'Madam,' Cranston barked, 'I need to talk to you about your husband's death!'

'Sir, you can. I live in Old Fish Street off Trinity on

the corner of Wheelspoke Alley. But now I must go. My husband lies coffined before the altar of St Mary Magdalene. Sir John, Father.' And Emma Roffel spun on her heel, leaving the chamber as dramatically as she had arrived.

'What will happen now?' Marston grated.

Sir John walked slowly over to him. 'Ashby can have sanctuary for forty days. After that he has two choices – he either surrenders himself to the king s justice or he walks to the nearest port and takes ship abroad. If any attempt—' Cranston glared at Marston. 'If any attempt is made to take him by force from St Erconwald's, I'll see the perpetrators dangle on the end of a noose at Smithfield! Now, I suggest you look to your master's corpse and secure his belongings. I want the dagger removed and sent to my office at the Guildhall.' Cranston turned to where Aveline sat. 'Madam, please accept my condolences. However, I must insist that you stay here until my investigation is finished.' Then, gesturing to Athelstan, Cranston left.

'What's this business about the ship *God's Bright Light*?' Athelstan asked once they had left the Abbot of Hyde's courtyard.

'As I said,' Cranston answered between swigs from his wineskin, 'the ship's at anchor in the Thames. Last night the first mate and two other members of the crew disappeared whilst on watch. We also have the strange business of Captain Roffel's death. The murder of Sir Henry Ospring and the flight of Nicholas Ashby have muddied the waters even further.' He popped the stopper back in and hid the wineskin beneath his cloak. 'I am hungry, monk.'

'I'm a friar and you're always hungry, Sir John,' Athelstan replied. 'So, you came to collect me, to go where?'

'Downstream to the good ship *God's Bright Light.* The admiral of the eastern seas, Sir Jacob Crawley, is waiting to grant us an audience, but' – Cranston sniffed the air like a hunting dog – 'I can smell pies.'

'Round the corner,' Athelstan said wearily, 'is Mistress Merrylegs' pie shop. She's the best cook in Southwark.'

Cranston needed no second bidding and was off like a greyhound. A short while later, as he and Athelstan fought their way back through the thronged, narrow streets of Southwark, Cranston chomped greedily on one of Mistress Merrylegs' rich, succulent beef pies.

'Lovely!' he breathed between mouthfuls. 'The woman's a miracle, a genuine miracle!'

Athelstan smiled and stared around. Now and again he shouted greetings to members of his parish. Ursula the pig-woman was sitting on a stool in the doorway of a house, her large pet sow crouched beside her. Athelstan could have sworn the sow smiled back at him. Tab the tinker was beating out pots on an anvil just inside his shop. Athelstan would have liked to have stopped but Sir John pushed his way, true as an arrow, through the crowd, returning with vigour the usual cat-calls and good-natured abuse.

'Father! Father!' Pernell the Fleming, her hair dyed a grotesque red, bustled up in a shabby black dress, a necklace of cheap yellow beads around her scrawny neck. Pernell reminded Athelstan of a rather battered crow.

'Father, can you say a Mass?'

A thin, dirty hand held out two farthings. Athelstan closed the fingers of the hand gently.

'A Mass for whom, Pernell?'

'For my husband. He died sixteen years ago today. The Mass is for the repose of his soul.' The woman smiled in a display of yellow teeth. 'Oh yes, Father, and in thanksgiving.'

'For his life?'

'No, that the old bugger's dead!'

Athelstan smiled. 'Keep your pennies, Pernell. I'll say a Mass tomorrow morning. Don't you worry.'

They turned off the alleyway into St Erconwald's church. Athelstan unlocked the door and, with Cranston beside him greedily licking his fingers, walked down the nave and through the rood screen to find Ashby curled up fast asleep on the altar steps.

'On your feet, lad!' Cranston growled, kicking the young man's muddy boots.

Ashby woke with a start, his eyes full of panic.

'Have they gone?'

'Yes, they've left.' Athelstan sat down beside him. 'Don't worry about that. But they will be back. They might not invade the church but they will certainly keep a watch. So, if I were you, my lad, I'd stay where you are, at least for the time being.'

'What will happen now?' Ashby asked anxiously.

Cranston took a swig from his wineskin, then thrust it at Ashby. 'Well, you can stay here for forty days. Once that's up you either surrender to the sheriff's officers or, dressed in the clothes you're wearing now, walk the king's highway to the nearest port, carrying a cross before you. If you drop the cross, or leave the highway, Marston and his men can kill you as a wolfshead.' Cranston took the wineskin back. 'Marston and his gang will probably follow you all the way. Unless they have powerful friends, very few sanctuary men reach port.'

Ashby's head drooped.

'Did you kill him?' Athelstan asked abruptly.

'No!'

'But you had your hand on the dagger when Marston entered the chamber?'

'Yes.'

'Why?'

'I went in, I saw my master lying there, I . . . I tried to pull the dagger out.'

'Strange,' Cranston mused. 'You tried to take the dagger out? Was it yours?'

'No, no, it was Sir Henry's own!'

'But instead of screaming "Murder!" and looking for help,' Athelstan put in, 'you tried to remove the dagger from the dead man's chest?'

Ashby looked away, licking his lips. 'I'm telling the truth,' he muttered. 'I went into the room. I saw my master's corpse. I tried to take the dagger out. Marston came in and I fled.'

'Well, tell that to the king's justices,' Cranston said merrily, 'and you'll soon find yourself on your way to the scaffold.'

Ashby crossed his arms and leaned back against the altar.

'What can I do? If I stay, I hang. If I flee, I die anyway.'

'And there's another matter,' Cranston told him.

'You seem mixed up in a great deal of murder, my lad. Do you know anything about the death of Captain William Roffel?'

CHAPTER 3

Athelstan went across to his house and brought back a bowl of oatmeal, two blankets and a bolster. He returned for a napkin, a bowl and a pitcher of water so that Ashby could wash himself. Then Cranston began his questioning.

'You are Sir Henry Ospring's squire?'

'Yes, Sir John,' Ashby replied between mouthfuls of oatmeal.

'You also sailed on the *God's Bright Light* with Captain Roffel?'

'Aye. Sir Henry financed most of the crew's wages and brought the armaments for the ship. In return he drew fifty per cent of all profits.'

'And you were sent to keep an eye on things?'

Ashby smiled sourly. 'You could say that. I left on the *God's Bright Light*—' Ashby screwed his eyes up. 'What date is it today?'

'It's the feast of Simon and Jude,' Athelstan replied. 'The 28th October.'

'Well, we left the Thames two days before Michaelmas, so it would have been on the 27th September. The weather was good, the winds fair. We took up a position between Dover and Calais and began to attack the occasional merchant ship. The plunder was

47

good and we soon had our hold full of foodstuffs, wine and cloths, not to mention the occasional precious object.'

'What was Roffel like?' Athelstan asked.

'A hard man, Father. A good sailor, but brutal. He always attacked, never allowed an enemy to surrender. Fishing smacks, galleys, wine ships from the Gironde. The pattern was always the same. We would pursue, pull alongside and the archers would loose. After that a boarding party would cross and—'

'And?'

Ashby looked down at the floor.

'And?' Cranston repeated.

Ashby muttered something.

'Speak up, man!'

'There were never any prisoners. Corpses would be thrown overboard. Captured vessels of poor quality would be sunk. The others would be towed back to the nearest English port.'

'Did anything untoward happen? Anything at all?'

'Yes, on about the 11th October we captured a small fishing smack which had been trying to slip from one French port to another. I think it was heading towards Dieppe, but the wind blew it out to sea. We attacked and the ship was sunk. Nothing untoward except—' Ashby put the bowl down and wiped his lips on the back of his hand. 'Captain Roffel seemed pleased, very pleased. You know, like a cat who has stolen the cream. Usually Roffel was a taciturn man, but I saw him walking on the poop and he was clapping his hands. It was the only time I ever heard him sing.'

'And then what?'

'A few days later he took to his cabin, complaining of stomach pains. However, the hold was full of booty so we put into Dover. I took Sir Henry's share and came ashore. After that the *God's Bright Light* put back to sea under Hubert Bracklebury, the first mate.'

'Did Roffel send any letter ashore to Sir Henry?'

'No, none whatsoever. They were business partners rather than friends. Sir Henry provided the money, Roffel did the pillaging.' Ashby kicked the bowl with his foot. 'They were murderers. Ospring was a devil from hell, he squeezed every penny from his tenants. He didn't give a fig about God or man.'

'Is that why you killed him?'

'No,' Ashby replied. 'I did not kill him.'

Athelstan got up and looked at Cranston. 'Sir John, we have learnt enough here.'

Cranston sighed and lumbered to his feet. Athelstan pointed to a large niche in the sanctuary.

'Rest there,' he said. 'You have some ale and a blanket and bolster. When I return I will make you more comfortable.'

'Father, is there anything I can do?'

Athelstan grinned and pointed to two heavy wrought-iron candlesticks on the altar.

'Yes, you can clean those and trim the wicks of the candles.' He looked down at Ashby. 'You have a dagger?'

Ashby smiled and patted it.

'Well, I would consider it a great favour if you could also scrape the candle grease from the floor. I will see you on my return.' He pointed to Bonaventure sleeping at the base of the pillar. 'And, if you get lonely, talk to the cat. He's not a great conversationalist but he's a wonderful listener.'

Athelstan followed Sir John out of the church.

'Stay there, Sir John.'

Athelstan checked the stable. Old Philomel stood leaning against the stable wall, happily chewing on a bundle of hay. The priest patted him gently on the muzzle. Philomel snickered with pleasure and snatched another mouthful whilst Athelstan hastened to his house. He collected his cloak and the leather bag that contained his writing instruments, then he and Sir John strode down to the quayside. It was now past midday. The skies were overcast but the streets and alleyways were as frenetic as ever. Children ran screaming around the stalls. Beggars whined for alms. Hucksters, their trays slung around their necks, offered ribbons, pins and needles for sale. Athelstan glimpsed Cecily the courtesan standing outside a tavern door.

'Go to the church, Cecily!' Athelstan shouted. 'We have a visitor.' He tossed a coin, which she deftly caught. 'Buy him one of Mistress Merrylegs' pies!'

They passed the stocks, strangely empty. The commissioners of gaol delivery would not meet for another week; when they did, the stocks would be full of a week's harvest of villains. Bladdersniff the ward bailiff, drunk as a lord, was sitting at the foot of the stocks chatting to Ranulf the rat-catcher, who kept stroking the pet badger that now followed him everywhere. Athelstan had even glimpsed it in church, the creature's little muzzle peeping out from beneath Ranulf's tarred, hooded cape. Both men shouted greetings. Athelstan replied, surprised that

Sir John was so strangely quiet – usually the coroner commented on everything and everyone as they walked through the streets. Athelstan caught Cranston by the arm.

'Sir John, what is wrong?'

Cranston took another swig from his wineskin and smacked his lips. He wrinkled his nose at the foul fish smell from the nets laid out to dry on the quayside.

'I don't know, Brother. This whole business is rotten. Ospring and Roffel were two murderous bastards and got what they deserved.' He belched noisily. 'But the disappearance of the watch from the *God's Bright Light*, Roffel's strange sickness and the unexplained stabbing of Sir Henry – it all adds up to nothing.'

'Did you notice something strange about Ashby?' Athelstan asked.

Cranston grinned wickedly and touched Athelstan gently on the tip of his nose with his finger. 'You are a cunning, conniving priest, Athelstan. I have learnt a lot from you. What's that saying you sometimes quote? "Four things are important: the questions you ask, the answers you receive and . . ."?'

'". . . the questions you don't ask and the answers you don't receive",' Athelstan filled in. 'Never once did Ashby try and explain how Sir Henry died. He protested his innocence but gave us no information whatsoever. All he says is that he came into the room, saw the corpse and had his hand on the dagger when Marston interrupted him.'

'And what else, my dear monk?'

'Friar, Sir John, friar. Well, the lady Aveline, in better days at least, must be a lovely, comely woman.'

'And?'

51

'Never once did our young squire ask after her?'

Cranston sniffed. 'You think there's something wrong?'

'Of course there is.'

'Ashby's protecting someone?'

'Perhaps.'

'Aveline?' Cranston asked.

'But why should she kill her own father?' Athelstan sighed. 'We are going to have to choose our moment and ask that lovely lady a few pertinent questions.'

Cranston gripped Athelstan by the shoulder. 'The whole business stinks like a manure heap at the height of summer. But, come on, let's see this bloody ship and the mysteries it holds.'

They went down to the quayside steps. Athelstan glimpsed one of his parishioners, Moleskin, an old, wiry man, forever smiling, who boasted he could pull the fastest skiff on the Thames. He waved Athelstan and Cranston over and led them down the slippery steps. Within minutes, arms straining, muscles cracking, he was pulling them out across the choppy, misty Thames, past Dowgate to where the fighting ships were anchored opposite Queen's hithe. The river mist was still thick, cloying, shifting ghost-like above the river. Occasionally Moleskin pulled in his oars as other skiffs, barges and bumboats plied their way down-river. Now and again the mist broke and they glimpsed fat-bottomed Hanseatic merchantmen making their way to the Steelyard. Cranston leaned over and gave Moleskin directions. The man grinned, hawked and spat into the river.

'You just keep your eyes on the river, Sir John.'

Cranston peered over his shoulder. Suddenly the

mist shifted. A big cog loomed above them.

'To the right! No, I mean to your left!' Cranston shouted.

The oarsman grinned, and skilfully guided his craft under the stern of the ship, on which Cranston glimpsed the name *Holy Trinity*. Then they came alongside another ship, its timbers painted black, its mast soaring up into the mist as it gently bobbed on the Thames.

'This is the one!' Cranston shouted.

Moleskin brought his small craft alongside. He yelled at Sir John to sit down before he put them all in the Thames, then, standing up, shouted, 'On deck! On deck!'

Athelstan, gazing up, saw a man come to the side, a lantern in his hand.

'Who's there?'

'Sir John Cranston, coroner of the city, and his clerk, Brother Athelstan. Sir Jacob Crawley is expecting us!'

'About bloody time!' the voice bawled back.

A piece of netting was thrown over the side of the ship, followed by a strong rope ladder. Moleskin brought the skiff closer in. Sir John grabbed the ladder and heaved himself up as nimble as a monkey. Athelstan followed more gingerly, helped by a smirking Moleskin.

'Take it carefully, Father,' the boatman advised. 'Don't look down, just take your time.'

Athelstan did, half-closing his eyes. As Sir John lurched over the bulwark the ladder swayed and Athelstan clung on for dear life. He moved upwards, then Cranston's strong hands lifted him by the arms and dragged him on to the deck rail with as much dignity as a sack of oatmeal. Athelstan unslung his leather bag from around his neck, then lurched as the ship moved. He would have been sent sprawling if Cranston had not held on to his arm.

'It takes time to get your sea legs,' Cranston said. 'But stand with your feet apart, Brother.'

Athelstan obeyed, blinked and stared around. The deck was cluttered with leather buckets, coils of rope, some sacks, balls of iron and two braziers full of spent charcoal. Athelstan glimpsed figures moving about in the mist. He looked to his left, down the deck towards the stern castle, then to his right where the forecastle rose up. A sailor, naked except for a pair of breech clouts, the same man who had first greeted them, studied Athelstan carefully.

'You must be freezing,' Athelstan commented. 'No shirt.'

'Aye, I am that, Father. But you had best come. Sir Jacob Crawley is fair bursting with anger.'

He led them along the deck and knocked at the door in the stern castle.

'Piss off!' a voice shouted.

The sailor shrugged, grinned over his shoulder and opened the door. He ducked as a tankard was thrown at his head.

'Sir Jacob, Sir John has arrived.'

Cranston, grinning from ear to ear, brushed by the sailor.

'Jacob Crawley, you dirty old sea dog!'

Athelstan followed cautiously. The cabin smelt musty and sweet. The man who half-rose from his chair at the table to greet Cranston was white-haired, small, lithe, and brown as a berry. He was dressed in a dark blue cloak tied around the middle with a silver belt. A cap of the same colour, with a feather stitched in the brim, lay on the table. Crawley grasped Cranston's hand, beaming from ear to ear, and poked him gently in the stomach.

'More of you than before, Sir John?'

'Then all the more for the Lady Maude to hang on to when the going gets rough!'

Both men bellowed with laughter. Crawley shook Athelstan's hand, patting him absent-mindedly on the shoulder. He indicated two empty stools at the table and Cranston and Athelstan joined the men already crammed around it. Crawley introduced them to the others: Philip Cabe, second mate; Dido Coffrey, ship's clerk; Vincent Minter, ship's surgeon; and Tostig Peverill, master-at-arms. A motley lot, Athelstan thought, in their sea-stained clothes – lean, hard-faced men with close-cropped hair, weather-beaten faces and unsmiling eyes. They sat, ill at ease, and Athelstan sensed their dislike and impatience at being kept so long.

'We have been waiting for hours,' Cabe snapped, his leathery, horsey face full of disapproval.

'Well, I'm bloody sorry, aren't I!' Cranston shouted back. 'I've been bloody busy!'

'Now, now.' Crawley clapped his hands like a child. 'Sir John, some claret?'

Cranston, of course, accepted with alacrity.

'Father?'

Athelstan smiled and shook his head. He unpacked his writing bag and laid out ink horn, quill and parchment. He stared around the low, crowded cabin, noticing the cot bed in one corner. He felt rather dizzy, especially when the ship moved and creaked as if the whole world was about to roll. Once Cranston had drained his cup, and Crawley had just as quickly refilled it, the king's admiral of the eastern seas leaned forward and belched.

'How many years, Sir John?'

'Sixteen, sixteen years since we chased the French off the seas and now the buggers are back!'

Athelstan moved his arm and nudged Sir John – a reminder that this was business, not some drinking contest between old friends. Cranston coughed.

'Master Cabe,' the coroner began, 'you are now the senior surviving officer of this unhappy ship. I understand Captain Roffel was taken ill and had died by the time the ship dropped anchor in the Thames?'

'Yes. On the 14th October the captain complained of pains in his belly. He said it was like fire.'

Cranston turned to Minter. 'Did you examine Roffel?'

'Yes, I did. I thought it was some form of dysentery – violent cramps, putrid faeces, high fever, sweating.'

'And what did you prescribe?'

'I concocted some binding ointment, but nothing worked. By 20th October, Roffel was delirious. He died the night before we sailed up the Thames.'

'Do you think he was poisoned?' Athelstan asked.

He studied the ring of faces in the flickering light of the single lantern. Minter's vinegarish features broke into a crooked smile.

'Oh yes, Father, he was poisoned. But not,' he added hastily, 'as you think. Belly cramps, stomach bile, dysentery, inflammation of the bowels and rectum are common on ships. Rats shit on our food, the water's brackish and the biscuits have more weevils than flour.'

'How many people died on this voyage?'

'Two. The captain and the cook, Scabgut.'

'What did the latter die of?'

'He suffered from similar cramps. But there's usually a death on every voyage – if it's not the food, then a man falls overboard.'

'So,' Cranston intervened, 'there was nothing suspicious about Roffel's death?'

'Nothing whatsoever. Though he did have his own supply of wine.'

'But I drank from that as well,' Coffrey the clerk intervened.

'In which case,' the surgeon concluded, 'Captain Roffel ate and drank nothing we didn't.'

'We understand,' Athelstan said, 'that Captain Roffel was a hard man?'

'Like flint,' Cabe replied. 'Hard as rock. He had a stone for a heart.' He smirked. *'God's Bright Light!* What a name for the devil's own ship!' He lifted a hand. 'Oh, don't get me wrong, Roffel was successful. We always came back with our holds full of treasure. But we took no prisoners. Roffel always made sure of that.'

'And Ashby?'

'No bloody use at all!' Peverill the master-at-arms snorted. Athelstan caught the jeering note in his voice.

'A landsman if there ever was one. Sir Henry Ospring always insisted that he joined us for at least part of the voyage. No bloody use, was he?'

A murmur of approval greeted his words.

'Sick as a dog he was,' Cabe added. 'He hated ships and he hated the sea. I think that's why the old bastard sent him. Captain Roffel was always taunting and making fun of the lad.'

'And Ashby hated Roffel?' Cranston asked.

'No, he didn't hate him, he despised him. Almost as badly as he did Sir Henry Ospring.'

'Well, it may come as news to you,' Cranston said 'but Ospring's dead and Ashby's in flight.'

His words created little surprise and the coroner quickly gathered that both Roffel and his patron Sir Henry Ospring had been hated as iron-hard taskmasters.

'But Ashby had left the ship before Roffel died?'

'Yes, he landed at Dover on 19th October. Our holds were full of booty and Sir Henry's estates lie two miles to the north of the port. Ashby took his master's portion, a very generous one too, and left.'

'And Roffel was sickly then?'

'Yes, he had been for some days, Sir John.'

'We have questioned Ashby.' Athelstan ignored Cranston's warning look. He wanted to shake the hardened contempt of these sailors. They sat as if they couldn't give a damn about the mysterious death of their captain or the disappearance of three of their shipmates. 'Ashby maintains that, after you took a small fishing smack which was slipping between French ports, Roffel seemed especially happy. Is this true?'

Athelstan looked around the group. He caught the hooded look in Cabe's and Coffrey's eyes; even Peverill seemed a little discomfited – his expression shifted momentarily and his lips tightened. Men who had been sitting at their ease now shuffled their feet. Both Cranston and Crawley sensed the change of mood.

'What is this, eh?' the admiral asked. 'What's this? A ship?'

'As the good Father says,' Cabe replied, measuring his words, 'the captain was very happy after the taking of the French ship. We found some wine aboard, some very good claret. There's still some left.'

'Is that all?' Athelstan asked.

'Yes,' Cabe snapped. 'Why, should there be more?'

'Let's move on.' Athelstan smiled faintly. 'The ship dropped anchor two days ago.'

'Aye.'

'And what happened then?'

'Well,' Peverill intervened. 'My archers were paid off and given shore leave. We unloaded most of our plunder, what was left after Ospring had taken his portion. Sir Jacob here sent down the wagons.'

'It's taken to a warehouse,' Crawley explained, 'and guarded until it's sold. I collect the proceeds. Some goes to the crew, with a large portion for the captain, some to the exchequer. Of course, Sir Henry, if he had been alive, would have received his portion.'

'Go on,' Athelstan urged, looking at Cabe.

'Well, the crew were given shore leave. We began to check the ship for damage done, repairs to be made, stores to be bought.'

'And Roffel's body?'

'Oh, the first mate, Bracklebury, took that ashore at first light – that and the captain's personal possessions. He handed them over to his widow.'

'Were there any visitors during the day?'

'I came on board,' Crawley replied, 'for the usual inspection and routine questions.'

'You were not upset that you'd lost a good captain?'

Crawley shrugged. 'He wasn't a good captain, Father. He was a good seaman. Personally, I couldn't stand him. I know, I know, the man's dead, God rest him, but I'll say it now, I did not like him!'

'Then in the afternoon,' Cabe quickly picked up the conversation, 'as is the custom, some whores came on board.' He looked away sheepishly. 'You know how it is, Father? Men at sea for some time, especially the young ones, if they don't get their greens, they desert.'

Cranston coughed. 'And the whores did their business?' he asked.

'No,' Cabe replied tartly. 'They stood in the stern and sang carols!' He caught the warning look in Cranston's eyes. 'Of course they did, but we had them off the ship before darkness fell, when most of the crew left.'

'Were there any other visitors?'

'Bernicia,' Minter the surgeon said with a smirk.

'Who's she?'

Now even Crawley was smiling.

'Well, come on man, share the joke!'

'She's a whore, Sir John. Well, Roffel's mistress. A pretty little thing. She has a house in Poultney Lane near the Lion Heart tavern. She didn't know that Roffel was dead.'

'And?'

'When we told her the captain was dead, coffined and sent to his wife, she started blubbing. We let her stay for a while in the captain's cabin, smacked her bottom and sent her ashore. No more bloody fingers for her.'

'What do you mean, bloody fingers?' Cranston asked.

Cabe leaned forward, out of the shadows.

'When we took ships, Sir John, we were always in a hurry. We boarded them, despatched the crew, grabbed the plunder, sank the ship and left. Roffel always scrutinised every corpse for valuables, particularly rings. If they didn't come off fast enough, he hacked the fingers off. He thought it was a joke. He used to give the rings, fingers still in them, to Bernicia his doxy.'

Athelstan looked away in disgust. He had heard about the war at sea, bloody and vicious on both sides, but Roffel seemed the devil incarnate. No wonder his wife could hardly be described as the grieving widow.

'And after Bernicia had left?' Cranston asked.

'Everything was done. Bracklebury fixed the watch – himself and two other reliable fellows. We had our purses full of coins, so we took a bumboat and went ashore.'

'Wasn't the watch rather small in number?' Cranston asked.

'Not really,' Crawley said. 'The ships are moored in line on the Thames. An officer and at least two men should stay on each vessel, one at the stern and one in the bows.' His eyes fell away.

'But not really enough?' Cranston insisted.

'This is the devil's own ship, Sir John,' Coffrey said. 'We wanted to get off. Especially after . . .'

'After what?' Athelstan asked quietly.

'Children's nightmares.' Crawley laughed. 'I've heard of this.'

'During the afternoon,' Cabe explained, 'when the day began to die and the mist started rolling in, some of the men said the ship was haunted by Roffel's ghost.' He shrugged. 'You know sailors. We're a superstitious lot. They talked of feeling cold, of an unseen presence, of scrabbling noises from the hold. They put this to the mate, he asked for two volunteers to stay, the rest of us went ashore.'

'So, after dark,' Athelstan said, 'there was only the mate and two of the watch? Did anyone here approach the ship?'

There was a chorus of denials.

'But we keep in contact,' Crawley explained. 'On every hour, when the candle flame reaches the ring, the password is sent along from ship to ship by speaking trumpet. On the half-hour, a shuttered lantern on each ship sends three quick flashes of light as a sign that all is well.'

'So.' Athelstan stretched. 'Further up the river you have the *Holy Trinity*. The watch on that ship would pass the message to the *God's Bright Light*. A password on the hour, a lantern flashing every half-hour?'

Crawley nodded.

'And was this done?'

'The watch on the *Holy Trinity* did it.'

'But did the *God's Bright Light* pass it on to the *Saint Margaret*?'

'Oh yes,' Crawley replied. 'That's where the mystery comes in. You see, Father, the *Holy Trinity* is my own ship. I let my men go ashore and I myself commanded the night watch.'

'And the messages were sent from you?'

Crawley nodded. 'At five o'clock I sent on the password, through a speaking trumpet. At half-past five the lamp winked three times.'

'And at six?'

'Ah, there were no more messages. One of the crew returned with a whore. He found the ship deserted and raised the alarm. He forced the whore to help him and rowed, with her screaming and shouting, over to my ship. I and my two men went aboard. It was like a ghost ship. The cabin was tidy, the decks in order, nothing amiss. The lantern on top of the mast was still burning as was the shuttered lantern in its recess outside the cabin door. No mark of violence, nothing missing.'

'So' – Athelstan picked up his quill to make a few more notes – 'let us say this sailor returned fifteen minutes after the last message was sent and fifteen minutes before the password. According to his story and to yours, Sir Jacob, in that time three able-bodied sailors disappeared from this ship?'

'It would appear so.'

'And the ship's boat wasn't missing?'

'No!' Crawley snapped his fingers. 'You might as well question the man yourself.'

Cabe went out and returned with the monkey-faced fellow who had first greeted them; he told his story in a strange, sing-song accent and it agreed exactly with what Cranston and Athelstan had already been told.

'As you approached the ship,' Athelstan asked, 'did you notice anything untoward?'

'No, Father.'

'And once on deck?'

'Quiet as a grave.'

Athelstan thanked him and the fellow left.

'Could someone have come aboard by boat?' Cranston asked. 'And left again after inflicting some terrible damage?'

'Impossible,' Cabe replied. 'First, the watchers on the other ships would have seen it.'

'There was a river mist,' Cranston pointed out.

'No.' Cabe shook his head. 'Even if you were half-asleep you'd hear the splatter of the oars, the boat bumping alongside. Secondly, any approaching boat would have been hailed. Thirdly, Bracklebury would have fought any boarders. The sound would have carried and the alarm raised. None of this happened. Everything was in order. Even the galley. We haven't touched it.'

'There's one possibility,' Cranston suggested. 'Maybe the mate and the two sailors abandoned ship? Swam to the shore and disappeared?'

'Why should they do that?' Cabe asked. 'And if they did, someone on the other ships would surely have seen them.'

Coffrey spoke up. 'This is the devil's ship, Sir John. Many of the men think Satan came aboard to claim Roffel's spirit for his own and took Bracklebury and the others with him!'

Athelstan shivered; even by these cynical, hardened men, Coffrey's pronouncement was not disputed.

CHAPTER 4

Cranston and Athelstan brought the meeting to an end and the seamen went back to their duties. The admiral took Cranston and Athelstan around the ship, showing them the broad deck, the cavernous, smelly hold partitioned into sections, the primitive living quarters of the crew and archers, the storage space for weapons and the small, fetid galley. Everything was clean and in order, though Athelstan flinched as the occasional dark, furry rat scampered across the deck or scurried along the timbers.

'Was anything amiss when the ship was inspected?'

Crawley shook his head. 'Not even in the galley. The cups were cleaned and the fleshing knives back on their hooks.' Crawley rubbed the side of his face. 'It was as if a devil had climbed on board and simply swept all three sailors away.'

'And there's been no sign of them since?'

'None whatsoever.'

Crawley took them back on deck and summoned a bumboat. The coroner and Athelstan took their leaves and clambered down, Sir John muttering that he was no wiser than when he arrived.

'Where to now?' Athelstan asked, settling himself in the stern next to Cranston.

As they were rowed back across the choppy Thames towards Queen's hithe the coroner studied the darkening sky.

'It's late,' he murmured, 'but perhaps we should inspect Captain Roffel's corpse before the requiem is sung and he is committed to the grave.'

Cranston and Athelstan found the church of St Mary Magdalene on the corner of Milk Street cloaked in darkness. The parish priest, Father Stephen, had been asleep in his chair before a roaring fire in the presbytery. He greeted them owl-eyed, his aged face heavy with sleep, but he greeted them kindly. He held up the lantern and peered at the coroner.

'God bless my tits!' he said. 'It's Sir John!'

Cranston shoved his face closer. 'Why, it's Stephen Grospetch!'

The two men shook each other warmly by the hand.

'Come in! Come in!' the priest invited. 'I have heard of your exploits, Sir John, but you are too busy for old friends.'

Cranston tapped him affectionately on the shoulder and smacked his lips.

'Yes, Sir John, I have some claret.' Grospetch pulled two stools before the fire. 'Sit down! Sit down! Father Athelstan?'

The priest gripped Athelstan's hand as the coroner finished his introductions.

'Well, well, well, Cranston and a Dominican. You always told me you didn't like friars, Sir John.' Father Stephen winked mischievously at Athelstan.

'You are a lying mongrel!' Cranston answered, pretending to be cross. He eased himself on to a stool, spreading his great hands before the flames. Father Stephen bustled about bringing cups of claret. Athelstan thought it was a miracle he didn't trip, for the room was shrouded in darkness, except for the single candle on its spigot and the light from the roaring fire.

The old priest sat in his chair. He toasted Cranston and Athelstan, slurping merrily from his wine cup.

'This priest,' Cranston explained, turning to Athelstan, 'was chaplain in the retinue of the Prince Edward. He could say the quickest Mass and sometimes had to. The French were bastards' – the coroner glowered – 'they never gave us time to finish our prayers.'

For a while Father Stephen and Cranston exchanged pleasantries and news of old comrades. Then the old priest put his cup on the floor and rubbed his hands.

'Right, Sir John. You are not here to kiss my lovely face. It's business isn't it?'

'Captain William Roffel,' Cranston replied.

'Gone to God,' the priest said. 'And where to next is up to the good Lord.'

'Why do you say that, Father?'

'Well, he was in my parish yet I never saw him or his wife darken my church. She came to see me yesterday. She wanted a Christian burial for her husband and paid a fee for a Mass to be said. Last night, I received the corpse, all encased in its cedar coffin. It now lies before the high altar and will be buried tomorrow.'

'So you know nothing about the Roffels?'

'Not a thing. The wife was calm. She claimed other business had kept her from attending our church.'

'So, she wasn't the grieving widow?'

'Now, Sir John, don't be harsh. She was very agitated.' The old priest shrugged. 'But I get many such requests. And you know canon law? Unless a person has been publicly excommunicated, Christian burial must be provided as speedily as possible.'

'And did she hire mourners? You know, people to keep vigil.'

'She and her maid attended when the corpse was received into the church. They went away. Mistress Roffel returned just before midnight and I allowed her to stay there until dawn this morning.'

Cranston looked over the old priest's shoulder and winked at Athelstan. But Father Stephen was quicker than he seemed and caught the glance.

'Come on, you old rogue, what do you want?'

'Father, is it possible for us to look at the corpse?'

The priest rubbed his lips. 'It's against canon law,' he replied slowly. 'Once a corpse has been sheeted and coffined—'

'God would want it!' Athelstan broke in quietly. 'Father Stephen, on my oath as a fellow priest, terrible crimes may have been committed.'

'You mean Roffel?'

'Yes,' Athelstan replied brusquely. 'He may have been murdered.'

Father Stephen stood and picked up his cloak. He lit a lantern and shoved it into Athelstan's hand.

'As soon as I clapped eyes on Cranston,' he grumbled, 'I knew it was bloody trouble.'

Returning the banter, Cranston and Athelstan followed the priest out into the cold, wind-swept churchyard. Father Stephen unlocked the church door and they entered. Athelstan later swore that he would never forget the scene awaiting them. The nave of the church was black and cold. The lantern's flickering light made it all the more eerie as they walked up towards the sanctuary. They all stopped, Cranston cursing, as a loose window shutter banged shut.

'That shouldn't happen,' Father Stephen whispered. He took the lantern from Athelstan, walked past the pillars and into the transept. He stopped and looked up at where the shutters clattered against the stonework.

'I closed these,' Father Stephen explained over his shoulder, his words ringing hollow through the church. 'There's no glass here, so anyone can get in.'

Athelstan walked over. He took the lantern and held it close to the ground.

'Well, whether you like it or not, Father, you have had unexpected visitors. See, the mud-marks and scraps of dried leaf?' He moved the lantern. 'Look, a faded footprint.'

'Oh, no,' Father Stephen moaned. 'Oh, don't say they've rifled the sanctuary again!' His face looked ghostly in the lantern light. 'Or worse,' he whispered. 'The lords of the crossroads, the black magicians, are always searching for sacred vessels to use in their blasphemous rituals. Come on! Come on!'

They hurriedly walked up the church, Athelstan's sandals slapping against the paving stones, and went through the rood screen.

Not as grand as mine, Athelstan thought, but then quietly prayed for forgiveness for such childish thoughts. Father Stephen edged slowly forward, the circle of light from the lantern preceding him.

'I can see nothing wrong!' he exclaimed.

Athelstan glimpsed the faint outline of the coffin and the six great purple candles surrounding it. They walked nearer. Athelstan gasped – the coffin still lay on its trestles but the lid was thrown back. The casket was empty, its white linen lining gleaming in the poor light.

'Hell's tits!' Cranston breathed.

Father Stephen hurried towards the altar where he scraped a tinder to light candles. Athelstan stared around the sanctuary.

'Oh, Lord, look at that!' Cranston muttered.

Athelstan followed his pointing finger. Sitting sprawled in the heavy, ornate sanctuary chair was the corpse of Captain Roffel. His throat had been slashed and someone had daubed in blood on a piece of parchment pinned to his chest the word ASSASSIN.

When Father Stephen saw it, he was so overcome that he sat on the sanctuary steps and sobbed. Cranston and Athelstan took two of the candles from the altar and walked gingerly towards the ghastly corpse, which slouched grotesquely in the high-backed chair. The pennies had been removed from Roffel's eyes, which were now half-open. The jaw strap had been removed and the wound across the neck was a dull scarlet gash. Cranston looked at the scrap of parchment and realised that the perpetrator of this blasphemy had used his finger to draw the letters. He and Athelstan, seeing how Father Stephen was so overcome, moved the corpse gingerly back into the coffin. Cranston whispered he had seen worse in France when he helped fill the burial pits. Athelstan,

70

however, despite his attendance at many deaths, trembled at how cold the corpse felt, half-expecting it to come back to life. They arranged the corpse as decently as possible in the coffin. Only then did Athelstan study the hard face, high cheek bones, thin, bloodless lips and narrow, skull-like head of Captain William Roffel.

'Dreadful in life, dreadful in death,' Athelstan muttered.

He sketched a blessing above the corpse and, without further ado, undid the points on its jerkin. He pushed back the cambric shirt and studied the torso carefully. Someone had punctured the belly so it would not swell but Athelstan also saw tell-tale dull, reddish blotches. The friar smiled in satisfaction and, with a sigh of relief, asked Cranston to help him with the coffin lid.

Cranston pointed to the piece of parchment.

'Shouldn't we remove it?'

Athelstan shrugged. 'God forgive me, Sir John, but I see little point. It tells the truth. Captain Roffel was the devil's own man. His corpse was disturbed and his throat cut as an act of vengeance.' Athelstan replaced the lid on the coffin. 'But I tell you this, he was murdered. His belly bears the tell-tale signs of poison.'

They made sure the church was secure and took a still-trembling Father Stephen back to his house. Athelstan poured him a goblet of wine, made sure he was settled and then joined Cranston outside.

'My bloody wineskin's empty!' the coroner snapped. 'I don't care what you say, Athelstan, I definitely need refreshment after that.'

The friar linked his arm through the coroner's and

led him back to the now deserted Cheapside, steering him carefully around mounds of refuse, and into the Holy Lamb of God. Two sips of claret and Cranston relaxed, beaming around at the rest of the customers.

Athelstan was more sombre. He gripped the fat coroner's wrist. 'We know Roffel was murdered, but by whom or why or how is a mystery. We must also face the possibility that the first mate and his two companions may have suffered a similar fate.'

'Do you think Ospring's death is connected with this?'

Athelstan shook his head. 'No, no, Ospring's was a crime of passion. A murder committed without a second's reflection. There's a mystery there but the mystery we must resolve, Sir John, is what happened during that voyage – how three able-bodied sailors disappeared from their ship at night even though, according to the admiral himself, signals were being sent from the *God's Bright Light* until only minutes before that sailor and his girl came back on board.'

'Well, you're the student of logic,' Cranston grumbled. 'What are the possibilities? We are told no boat was seen going towards the ship.'

'What about swimmers?' Athelstan asked.

Cranston shook his head. 'Imagine, Brother, let us say even a party of six to ten. They reach the ship, clamber on board without the watch noticing, despatch three men without raising any alarm. They leave no mark of violence before disappearing over the side. Yet we have no reason for why they came. No one sees them and the lights and the password are still passed on. I can think of only one possibility – those three sailors jumped ship.' Cranston blew his cheeks out.

'But two problems remain. No one saw them leave and the signals still continued. If they had left the ship, they must have done so at almost the same time as that sailor and his whore arrived, yet that would have been noticed.' Cranston shoved his cup away. 'I am tired, Brother.'

'Do you think we should go home?'

'No.' Cranston gathered up his cloak. 'We should make one more visit. Roffel's little whore or mistress. Perhaps she can cast some light on the gathering gloom.'

As Athelstan and Cranston refreshed themselves in the Holy Lamb of God, a man, garbed in black from head to toe, strode quietly along a passage in a house that stood on the corner of Lawrence Lane and Catte Street. He moved softly, the rags wrapped around the soles of his leather boots deadening any footfall. He gripped his leather sack and gazed intently through the eye-holes of his mask at the precious candlesticks he could glimpse on a table at the end of the passage, their silver filigree glinting through the darkness.

The thief smiled with pleasure. As usual, everything had been cunningly planned. The old fool Cranston would never discover how he was able to enter and leave these deserted mansions without any trace of forced entry. He reached the table, took the candlesticks and placed them carefully in his leather bag. Moving stealthily on, he was passing one of the rooms when its door opened. A young, sleepy-eyed maid came out. She must have sensed something wrong, for she turned and glimpsed the thief in the light of the candle she carried. She dropped the candle and opened her mouth to scream but the man sprang. He clapped his hands over her mouth and drove a thin, stiletto dagger straight into her chest. The girl's eyes widened with terror and pain. She struggled, but the thief had her pinioned against the wall. He brought the dagger out and stabbed once more. The girl coughed. He could feel her hot blood seeping through the glove on his hand. Then she sank against him and crumpled slowly to the floor.

Sir John and Athelstan tapped on the door of the house in Poultney Lane near the Lion Heart tavern. There was no response so Cranston rapped again. This time he was answered by the sound of running footsteps. A small voice asked, rather prettily, 'Who is it?'

'Sir John Cranston, coroner of the city, and Brother Athelstan his secretarius!'

Locks turned and bolts were pulled back. A young red-headed woman in a murrey-coloured dress came out to greet them. She held a horn lantern high and thrust her thin, pale face towards them.

'What do you want? What can I do?'

'You knew Captain William Roffel?'

The eyes, ringed with black kohl, blinked. Athelstan was fascinated by the brightly painted lips, garish against the pallor of the woman's skin.

'Your name is Bernicia?' he asked. 'Can we come in?'

The girl nodded and beckoned them forward, down the stone-vaulted passageway into a small, cosy parlour. She made them welcome, pouring two cups of wine whilst Cranston and Athelstan stared around the room. Everything was neat; small tables were polished and draped with linen cloths, the floor was covered with Ottoman rugs, on the hearth the fire tongs gleamed brilliantly in the light of the flames. The air was heavy with a musky perfume which mingled with the scent from the candles and small capped braziers standing in each corner of the room.

'You live in comfort, Mistress Bernicia?'

The young woman shrugged and smirked. Cranston peered at her closely. Her every movement was elegant. She flounced her hips as she walked in her high-heeled pattens. When she sat, crossing her legs, she pulled her gown further down but not so far as to hide the creamy whiteness of her petticoats and the scarlet and gold of her hose. She leaned forward.

'So, what can I do for you, sirs?'

Cranston thought how mellow and rich her voice was.

'You were...?' he began tentatively.

'I was William Roffel's paramour.' Bernicia held up a hand and sniggered softly behind beringed fingers. Her nails were painted a deep purple.

'Ah, yes!' Cranston's unease grew. 'And he visited you often?'

She spread her hands and looked around the room.

'Captain Roffel was generous for the favours I gave him.'

'And did you love him?' Athelstan asked.

Again the pretty snigger and the quick movement of her hand.

'Oh, Father, don't be ridiculous! How can you love someone like Captain Roffel? A blackguard born and bred! He was generous and I was available.' She pursed her lips. 'You know he was a defrocked priest?'

'What?'

'Oh, yes.' She laughed gaily. 'Roffel was once a curate in a parish near Edinburgh. He became involved in some trouble and had to leave his parish rather quickly.'

'What was this trouble?'

'I don't know.'

'And you met him where?' Cranston asked.

'In a tavern.'

'Which one?'

She shrugged. 'I don't know. I forget.'

'Did you ever meet his wife?'

'Oh Lord, that sour bitch. Never!'

'Did you give Captain Roffel anything before he left on his last voyage?'

'A nice, big kiss.'

'And are you suspicious about his death?'

'Oh, no, the evil bastard always had a weak stomach.' Bernicia shrugged. 'Now he's gone' – she fluttered her eyelashes – 'and I'm available again.'

'Do you know anything about his last voyage?'

'Nothing. I went on board the ship. They wouldn't even let me go to his cabin, so I came ashore.'

'Did Roffel have any enemies?'

Bernicia rocked with laughter. 'I think the question, Sir John, should be, "Did he have any friends?" He had enemies all along the river Thames. Roffel may have been one of the king's captains but he was also a pirate.' Bernicia lowered her voice. 'You've heard the stories, surely? Roffel was not above attacking any ship. Many a sailor's lonely widow curses him before she falls asleep at night.'

'Have you visited his coffin in St Mary Magdalene?' Athelstan asked. He, too, had caught Cranston's unease and was studying the woman carefully.

'No, I haven't and I don't intend to.'

Perhaps it was the way that she said it, moving her face sideways. Or perhaps, in the light of the fire, Cranston caught a glimpse of hair on her upper lip not quite covered by the white paste she had rubbed there. Suddenly the coroner leaned forward and grabbed her by the knee.

'Well, aren't you the pretty one?' he growled. 'What's your real name, Bernicia?'

She tried to struggle free. Sir John's hand went further up her thigh. He shrugged off Athelstan's warning glance.

'I have heard of your type,' he said. 'I wonder, if I kept moving my hand up to your privy place what I'd find, eh?' He placed his other hand gently on her rather flat chest, his fingers gently pressing back the muslin. 'Bernicia the whore,' he said softly, 'you're no woman. You're a man!'

Athelstan's jaw sagged. He gaped at Bernicia and then at Sir John. Bernicia tried to struggle free.

'The truth,' Sir John demanded. 'Otherwise I'll have the beadles brought in and have you stripped. You can't hide what God gave you!' He leaned forward and touched Bernicia's hair. 'I know where you met Roffel,' he continued. 'In the Mermaid tavern down near St Paul's Wharf. What's your real name? Come on, what is it?'

'My name is Roger-atte-Southgate.'

Athelstan could only keep gaping.

'I once served as a cabin boy with Roffel. I was, I am a woman in a man's body.' Bernicia looked into the fire. 'I used to envy the whores, the way they moved, the clothes they could wear, the excitement they aroused in the sailors. And then, one night, I discovered there were others like me.'

'If the sheriffs discover you,' Cranston warned, 'they'll burn you as a sodomite at Smithfield! Isn't that true, Father?'

Athelstan could only stare. He studied Bernicia more closely and caught the lost, despondent look in her eyes. Athelstan blinked. He still considered her a woman, whatever Sir John or she might say. He felt a wave of compassion. In his days in the novitiate, and in camps in France, he had met men who liked to be used as women, but never had he met one who dressed and acted the part so convincingly.

'Your secret is safe with us,' he said gently. 'Sir John and I are not here to inflict any pain, though you are involved in serious sin.'

'Am I, Father? Men like Roffel? I have known them as far as my memory stretches. They like to use me as a woman, so why blame me for what others made me? Oh, yes, there were priests too. They liked such strange bed sports.'

Athelstan held his hand up. 'I am not your judge nor your confessor.'

'Little point in that,' Bernicia interrupted. 'I have no need for either. There's no God and, if there is, he's forgotten all about us.' Bernicia moved on her chair. 'Roffel used to bring me precious trinkets – fingers with the rings still on them, once an ear with a small gold band in it. He used to sit where you are, Father, and boast about what he had done. How he would cheat his crew, his business partner Ospring and even his dull wife.'

'Did you return to the ship last night?' Cranston abruptly asked.

Bernicia looked away.

'Don't lie! Did you return?'

'Yes, I did. Well, at least, to the quayside. I wanted to see if Roffel had left any of his valuables. He always had a full purse and a little coffer full of trinkets. I thought the first mate might let me back on board.'

'Why only to the quayside?' Cranston asked.

'Well, there was no bumboat available to take me to the ship. I did hail it, though.'

'And what happened?'

'One of the watch must have heard me, for the first mate came.'

'What time was this?' Athelstan asked.

'Oh, it was about midnight. I thought it was safe then. The quayside is usually deserted by that time – all the revellers have gone home or are too drunk to care.'

'And what happened?'

'The mate came to the side of the ship. He was drunk. He just waved his cup at me and shouted, "Piss off!".'

'Strange,' Cranston mused. 'The nearest ship was the admiral's *Holy Trinity* and he did not tell us about any disturbance?'

'I have told you what I saw.' Bernicia pulled a face. 'But there was something strange.'

'What?' Athelstan asked.

'Well, I was on the quayside; it was deserted, cold and windswept. I realised how foolish I had been, even in going there. Now, as I turned away, I am sure I saw a figure move in the doorway of one of those warehouses.'

'You are certain?'

'Oh yes. There were the usual night sounds along the quayside – rats slithering about, the lapping of the water – but I heard a scrape as if someone had drawn a sword or was carrying some metal implement. I am sure whoever was hiding there was keeping watch and guard on the ship. I called out, but there was no response so I hurriedly left.'

'And that's all you saw or heard?'

'Yes, yes, it is.'

'Did you ever meet any of Roffel's crew?'

'Oh, only from a distance. When they accompanied the captain ashore, Roffel usually kept me away from them.'

'And Sir Henry Ospring?'

'No, though Roffel did receive letters from Ospring accusing him of embezzling some of the profits.'

'And Roffel's squire, a man called Ashby?'

Bernicia shook her head.

Cranston looked at Athelstan and raised his eyes heavenwards. He took a sip of the wine, but it tasted bitter to him. He pulled a wry mouth and got to his feet.

'So, you know nothing at all?'

'No, I don't. Sir John,' Bernicia pleaded, 'you will keep my secret?'

The coroner nodded.

'I have one final question.' Athelstan picked up his leather writing bag and cradled it against his chest. 'Tonight we visited St Mary Magdalene's church. Someone had broken in, plucked Roffel's corpse from his coffin, slit his throat and left him sprawling in the sanctuary chair. There was a piece of parchment pinned to his chest with the word "assassin" daubed on it in his own blood. Now, who hated the captain enough to do that?'

Bernicia sneered. 'Sir Henry Ospring for one.'

'He's dead, murdered too!'

Bernicia smiled. 'Roffel will be pleased to have company in hell.'

'Who else?' Cranston insisted. 'Whom did Roffel mention in anger or spite?'

'You should go back to the fleet, Sir John. Ask the admiral, Sir Jacob Crawley. Roffel always said he hated him.'

'Why should Roffel hate Crawley?'

'Oh, no, the other way round. Crawley couldn't stand the sight of our good captain. I think there was bad blood between them. Roffel once said Crawley had accused him of sinking a ship in which one of Crawley's kinsmen had been murdered. Roffel said he'd never drink or eat with the admiral and would always be careful never to turn his back on him.'

'In which case, mistress—' Cranston grinned sourly. 'Yes, I'll call you that. In which case, we bid you goodnight.'

Once outside the house Cranston gave vent to a belly laugh which rang like a bell through the narrow street. A householder opposite opened a window and shouted for silence. Cranston apologised, hitched his cloak about him and led Athelstan back into Cheapside.

'So, so, so,' he muttered. 'Here's another mystery. A man who dresses as a woman and claims to be the dead captain's whore.' He yawned, stretched and looked up at the night sky. 'Tomorrow we'll continue,' he said. 'They talk of the mysteries of the sea. But, mark my words, Brother, what happened on the *God's Bright Light* last night is a mystery that deepens by the hour.' He patted the friar on the back. 'Now, come on, Brother, I'll walk you back to London Bridge and tell you a very funny story about the bishop, the parson and someone very like our young Bernicia!'

CHAPTER 5

Athelstan celebrated his usual early morning Mass, surprised to see his sparse congregation graced by the presence of Aveline Ospring. She knelt by the rood screen, hands piously joined, but her eyes never left young Ashby, who was helping Crim the altar server during the ceremony. Once the Mass was finished, Athelstan hung up his vestments, cleared the altar and went out to find Aveline and Ashby sitting on the sanctuary steps quietly conversing.

'Do you want some breakfast?' Athelstan asked.

Ashby nodded. 'I am starving, Father. Is it possible to have a razor and some soap? Lady Aveline' – he patted the saddle bag – 'has brought me other necessities.'

Athelstan went across to his house. He built up the fire and, after giving the ever-hungry Philomel his morning meal of hay, washed his hands and took a tray of bread, cheese and wine back into the church. Ashby ate hungrily. Now and again Aveline, who looked more composed and certainly more radiant than on the day before, sipped from Ashby's cup or nibbled on the bread and cheese.

'I came to see that all was well,' she said shyly, looking at him from beneath long-lashed eyelids.

Athelstan nodded, then started as Bonaventure, who was sleeping by the pillars, suddenly stood up, back arching, tail high, as the door of the church opened. Marston entered and stood, arms crossed, staring down into the sanctuary. Athelstan ignored him and looked down at Aveline.

'My lady,' he said quietly, 'you are in the House of God, so you must not lie.'

Ashby choked on a piece of bread. Athelstan patted him vigorously on the back.

'It is barely dawn, my lady,' Athelstan continued drily, 'yet you, the daughter of the man Ashby has supposedly murdered, bring him supplies and whatever comforts he needs. Now you sit beside him on the altar steps sharing his food.'

Lady Aveline blushed crimson and glanced away.

'Do you love him?' Athelstan asked.

'Yes,' she whispered.

'And you her, young Ashby?'

The young man nodded and wiped his eyes, still streaming after his fit of coughing.

'Well, well, well!' Athelstan said. 'And I suppose you want to marry?'

'Yes,' they whispered in unison.

'Good!' Athelstan rubbed his hands together. 'However, Holy Mother Church teaches that before you can take the sacrament of matrimony you must confess and be shriven. Now, I can hear your confessions separately or perhaps together?'

The two lovers stared at each other.

Athelstan fought hard to hide his amusement. 'Good,' he said. 'You have no objections, so I'll proceed. Nicholas, you stand accused of the sin of murder, of slaying Sir Henry Ospring.' He spoke softly so that his words were not carried to where Marston stood at the back of the church. 'You didn't do it, did you?'

'I am innocent!' the young man whispered.

'Which,' Athelstan said, turning to Aveline, 'cannot be said of you.'

She looked up, her eyes rounded in shocked surprise.

'God forgive me,' Athelstan continued. 'But, Lady Aveline, I accuse you of your father's murder.'

The young woman's face turned white as chalk. She stood up, placing her fingers together in agitation.

'That's wrong!' Ashby hissed, but Athelstan pressed his fingers against the young man's lips. 'Don't lie in confession!' he said. 'Lady Aveline, please sit down.'

The young woman did so and Athelstan gripped her ice-cold hands.

'You did murder your father?'

'God forgive me, Father, yes I did. How did you know?'

Athelstan looked down the nave. Marston, who had apparently seen how agitated Aveline had become, now began to walk slowly forward. Athelstan rose and went to meet him.

'Can I help you?'

'I'm here to protect the lady Aveline from that murderer.'

'Lady Aveline is safe in my hands,' Athelstan replied.

'I am also here to see that bastard doesn't escape.'

'Don't swear,' Athelstan replied. 'Not in God's house.'

The man stepped back, crestfallen.

'Please wait outside,' Athelstan said. 'You may wait

on the steps. Be assured no one will leave this church without you knowing.'

Marston was about to object.

'Sir John Cranston would like that,' Athelstan added sweetly.

Marston shrugged and left, closing the door behind him.

Athelstan went back into the sanctuary where Ashby and Aveline were sitting, heads together, talking conspiratorially. Athelstan unceremoniously sat down between them.

'How, when, did you know?' Ashby asked.

'Oh, this morning during Mass,' Athelstan replied. 'It is a matter of logic. First, you were found with your hand on the dagger. Why? Because you were getting ready to pull it out. But why should you do that? It wasn't yours, it was, as you claimed, Sir Henry's. Yours is still in its sheath hanging on your belt. I noticed that yesterday morning. Secondly, if you didn't kill Sir Henry, then who did? Who had the right to approach such a powerful lord whilst he was still dressed in his nightshirt? Certainly not Marston. He made that very clear. So, if it wasn't you or Marston, who else? Now, when I arrived in Sir Henry's room, I discovered the window had been locked until you used it to effect your escape. Accordingly, I doubted if anyone had broken into the room. Moreover, Sir Henry was a powerful man and there was no sign of a struggle. To conclude, the murderer must have been someone who had every right to be close to Sir Henry. And who does that leave but you, Aveline?'

'Oh, my God, she'll hang!' Ashby whispered. 'No one would ever believe her story.'

'Let me try,' Athelstan replied. 'My lady?'

'Yes, I killed my father,' she replied. 'To be precise, he was my stepfather. My mother's first husband, my real father, was killed in the king's wars in France. At first, all was well. I was an only child. I think my mother regretted her re-marriage, but she died eight years ago. In the main, Sir Henry left me alone. He looked after me. I was spoilt, even pampered. But' – she began to play with the bracelet on her wrist – 'as I grew older, he began to take more notice of me. Nothing much at first, just asking me to sit on his knee while he stroked my hair. Sometimes he would touch me in a privy place and say it was our secret.' Aveline blinked to hold back her tears. 'I had everything,' she continued. 'Or everything except a maid. He wanted it that way. As I grew older his attentions became more demanding. I avoided him, though there were times I could not. On the evening before he died, as he sat at table at the Abbot of Hyde inn, he told me to come to him at first light because he wanted to give me something precious that had belonged to my mother. I should have known.' Aveline's lower lip quivered and her eyes brimmed with tears. 'He was filthy!' she whispered. 'Obscene! He tried to embrace me, place his hand on my breast. He claimed he had lain awake all night thinking about me. Then—'

Athelstan sensed Ashby's growing tension. He patted the girl on the wrist.

'Just tell me,' he said gently

'He said he hoped I was as good as my mother and tried to pull me across his lap. As he did so, I saw the hilt of his dagger sticking out from a pile of clothes on a chair. Everything moved so quickly. I grabbed the hilt, the next second the dagger was deep in his chest. He just stared at me as if he couldn't believe what had happened, then he slumped to the floor. I must have stood for some time just staring down. I thought it was a dream. I kept pinching myself to wake up. It was so clean, so swift, not even a speck of blood on my hands or clothes. I heard a knock on the door—'

'That was me,' Ashby interposed quickly. 'I was in the room next to Sir Henry's. I heard Aveline go down the passageway and the sound of a faint disturbance, of something falling. I went into Sir Henry's chamber. Only then did Lady Aveline tell me what had been happening.'

'I daren't say anything before,' the young woman whispered. 'Who would believe me? I knew Nicholas Ashby and I loved him but I kept everything a secret. Sir Henry would have killed us both.'

'I just pushed her out of the room,' Ashby continued. 'Once she had gone, I tried to pull the knife out, but Marston came, banging on the door.' Ashby nodded contemptuously down the church. 'He's all bluster. He could have stopped me but he just shouted "Murderer! Murderer!". I opened the window and fled.'

Athelstan rose. What Aveline had said did not really shock him. Time and again in confession he had heard the same sin in all its variations – brother and sister, father and daughter. It was the natural result of people living so close together. But who would believe Aveline? Sir Henry had been guilty of what the theologians called 'the great and secret sin', incest, much practised but never discussed. In a court of law it would look different. Some might even argue that both Aveline and Ashby were involved in killing Sir Henry for their own private ends. She must have known that Sir Henry would be against any such love match. Ashby had been found red-handed. If he kept quiet he would go to the gallows. If he tried to defend himself Aveline might well join him, pushed there by grasping relatives eager to get their share of Sir Henry's wealth.

Athelstan stood at the foot of the sanctuary steps, staring at the two anxious, white-faced lovers.

'Do you have any proof?' he asked.

'I thought you might ask that,' Aveline replied.

Before Athelstan could stop her, she unbuttoned the top of her dress and pulled it down. 'Only this,' she said. 'It came up later.' And Athelstan glimpsed the purple bruise on her milky-white shoulder.

'That's where Sir Henry gripped me,' she said, and, free of any embarrassment, pulled the dress back and re-tied the little thongs. 'Am I guilty of a great sin, Father?'

Athelstan stared at her now-covered shoulder. That bruise could never have been self-inflicted. He believed both she and Ashby were telling the truth. He sketched a blessing in the air.

'I absolve you,' he said. 'Though God knows what I am going to do now.'

'You could speak for us,' she said hopefully.

'Who would believe me?' Athelstan replied. 'And what you have told me is bound by the seal of confession. No, no. What I must do is ponder carefully and coolly on a solution to all this. Look, let us leave that for the moment. I wish to question you on other matters. Sir Henry provided monies for Captain Roffel and the ship *God's Bright Light?*'

Ashby nodded.

'And you joined the ship in September but left when it docked at Dover?'

'Yes.'

'During the voyage did anything happen?'

'I have told you, Roffel was the same. Dour and secretive, except after taking that fishing smack.'

'What else do you know about Roffel?'

'He drank a great deal.' Ashby smiled bleakly. 'Not just wine or beer like the rest of us. He drank wine and beer, of course, but he also had a special flask containing a very fiery drink, usquebaugh he called it. Before every voyage he would go ashore and have his flask filled at the Crossed Keys tavern behind a warehouse at Queen's hithe.'

'He filled it himself?'

'Oh, yes, Father. Where Roffel went so did that flask.'

Athelstan smiled as he thought of Cranston's wineskin. 'So, no one else was allowed to refill it?'

'That's what I said, Father. But we knew he drank from it. Well, not all the crew, but I did. His breath used to smell. He'd take it in very small doses. He once told me it was five times as powerful as any wine and kept him warm at night against the sea chill.'

'And Roffel was in good spirits at the beginning of the voyage?'

'Oh, yes. Sir Henry gave me a sealed package to hand to him, but I don't know what it contained.'

'Do you, Lady Aveline?' Athelstan asked.

'No, no, though my stepfather seemed very pleased with himself.'

'Then what?'

She shook her head. 'I don't really know.'

'I often took such packages,' Ashby interrupted. 'Roffel would read what was in them then toss them into the sea.'

'Wait!' Aveline leaned forward. 'Yes, now I remember. When the *God's Bright Light* began its voyage my stepfather was very, very pleased, but when Nicholas returned his temper changed. I heard him say that he didn't trust Roffel. He claimed the captain was cheating him. He was coming to London to confront Roffel when . . .' Her voice faded away.

'Is there anything else?' Athelstan asked.

She shook her head.

Athelstan crouched down and gripped her hand.

'You are now your stepfather's heir,' he said. 'Your secret is safe with me and I will think about what I can do. For the moment, however, you should return to the Abbot of Hyde inn. Go through your stepfather's papers, everything and anything. See if you can find anything that will give some hint, however faint, of the secrets he may have shared with Roffel.'

'How will that help us?' she pleaded.

'God knows!' Athelstan said. 'God only knows!' He genuflected before the altar. 'You may stay here for a while but, Master Ashby, on no account leave the sanctuary! I have your word on that?'

Ashby nodded just as the church door crashed open and Watkin the dung-collector rushed in.

'Father! Father! The cart's arrived!'

Athelstan, breathing heavily and slowly, prayed for patience.

'Good man, Watkin. Have the other door opened and bring it up into the nave.'

The dung-collector trotted off. The doors opened and, after a great deal of crashing and banging, a huge, four-wheeled cart pulled by Watkin and other parishioners rolled up a makeshift ramp on the steps and into the nave. Athelstan went down to help. His anger at being so rudely disturbed was soon dispelled by the good humour and generosity of his parishioners, who had left their trades to ensure that this cart arrived in time for their mystery play. Panting, shouting, sweating and shouting instructions to each other, the parishioners heaved the cart until it stood in the centre of the nave.

'There!' Watkin wiped the sweat from his face. 'There you are, Father. And,' he added quickly, his hairy nostrils quivering in the full fury of his self-righteousness, 'in the play, I'm going to be God, aren't I?' He lowered his voice. 'Pike can't be God. I am leader of the parish council.'

Pike the ditcher came round the cart. Athelstan sensed that, despite the impending marriage between Pike's son and Watkin's daughter, the old animosity between these two men was beginning to reappear.

'I heard that, Watkin!' Pike snapped. 'I'm to be God in the play!'

'No, you're not!' Watkin shouted back childishly.

Both men looked at Athelstan to arbitrate. The priest groaned quietly to himself.

'Well, Father?' Pike demanded. 'Who is God?'

Athelstan smiled. 'We all are. We are all made in God's image so, if we are like God, God must be something like us.'

'But what about the play?' Watkin insisted.

'Yes, what about it?' Hig the pig-man, square-jawed and narrow-eyed, came around the cart and stood beside Watkin. Hig worked in the fleshing yards and his brown gown was stained with offal and blood from the carcases he cleaned. He always wore the same gown and his thick hair was cut as if the barber had just thrust a bowl on his head and trimmed around it. Athelstan didn't like him. Hig was a born trouble-maker, very conscious of his rights and ever ready to shatter the peace of parish-council meetings by fishing in troubled waters.

'Hig, you stay out of this!' Athelstan warned.

The pig-man's close-set eyes narrowed.

'I know what we can do.' Athelstan looked at Watkin and Pike. 'As I said, we are like God. So, Watkin can be God the Father, I can play God the Son and you, Pike, dressed in a white gown with the wings of a dove attached to your back, can be God the Holy Ghost. Now, remember what Holy Mother Church teaches, there are three persons in God and all three are equal.' He lowered his voice and looked darkly at them. 'Unless you are going to contradict the teaching of Holy Mother Church?'

Watkin and Pike just stared open-mouthed, then glanced at each other.

'Agreed,' said Watkin. 'But God the Father always does more than God the Holy Ghost.'

'No, he doesn't.'

They both stamped off, merrily discussing the finer points of theological dogma. Athelstan heaved a sigh of relief. The rest of the parishioners milled around the cart, loudly talking to each other but never bothering to listen. Athelstan slipped out of the church and across to his house.

'Father, a word?'

Athelstan, his hand on the latch, spun around.

The two cloaked women must have walked over quietly. They stood, white-faced, staring at him.

'Emma Roffel.' She pulled back her hood. 'You remember me, Father?'

Emma's face was drawn and her grey hair was unruly, as if she had hardly bothered to finish her toilet. Tabitha Velour, standing just a pace behind her, looked similarly drawn and tired.

'You'd best come in.' Athelstan led them into the kitchen and sat them down. He offered some bread and wine but they declined. He sat at the head of the table, gently stroking a purring Bonaventure, who had jumped into his lap.

'Why are you here?' he asked Emma. 'I thought your husband was to be buried this morning?'

'He is to be, within the hour,' Emma replied. 'I'm here because of what happened at St Mary Magdalene church last night.' Her eyes widened. 'I had to ask you, Father. Have you found the culprit? Why should anyone do so disgusting a thing?'

'You have come across the river to ask me that?' Athelstan asked. 'Sir John and I did intend to visit you today.'

'I went to Sir John's house,' Emma said, 'but he was not there. He had been summoned to the Guildhall. I just want to know who did it.'

'Madam, we don't know who or why but your husband had few friends and many enemies.'

Emma sighed heavily.

'He was a hard man, Father.'

Athelstan peered at her. 'That's not really why you came,' he said. 'There's something else, isn't there?'

'I will speak for her.' Tabitha Velour leaned forward. 'When we went to St Mary Magdalene church this morning, Father Stephen was still very upset. He overheard you tell Sir John that Captain Roffel may have been poisoned. Is this true?'

'I think so,' Athelstan replied. 'Probably white arsenic. It's cheap and easy to obtain.'

'But how?' Emma Roffel asked. 'My husband was very careful on board ship, only eating and drinking what the crew did.'

'That's not quite true,' Athelstan said. 'Your husband was Scottish. He had a special flask which he filled at a tavern near Queen's hithe with a fiery Scottish drink called usquebaugh.'

Emma Roffel put her finger to her lips. 'Of course,' she whispered. 'Where he went, so did that flask.' She stared at Athelstan. 'But he always filled it at that tavern! He took it there himself, because he paid the landlord to import a special cask from the port of Leith in Scotland.'

'Did he always carry the flask around with him?' Athelstan asked.

'He never drank from it on land,' Emma answered. 'But at sea, always. He would never leave it in his cabin but carried it on his person.'

'And at sea, of course, he could not refill it,' Athelstan mused.

Emma suddenly stood up. 'Father, you must excuse us. The funeral Mass is at ten o'clock. There will only be the two of us there. We must go.'

'We may visit you afterwards?' Athelstan asked.

'Yes, yes,' she said impatiently and, followed by her maid, hurried out of the house.

Athelstan banked the fire. He collected the leather bag containing his writing materials, filled Bonaventure's bowl with milk and went out to saddle the protesting Philomel.

'Come on, old man,' he whispered as he gingerly heaved himself into the saddle. 'Let's go and see old Jack Cranston, eh?'

Philomel snickered in pleasure. The old destrier liked nothing better than butting the fat coroner's protuberant stomach or expansive backside. As they passed the church door, Athelstan glimpsed Marston and two other of Sir Henry's retainers lurking in the alley opposite. Athelstan did not stop. His parishioners had now spilled out on to the steps. Neatly divided into two groups, one led by Watkin and the other by Pike, they were fiercely debating whether God the Father was, in fact, superior to God the Holy Ghost.

Lord help us, Athelstan thought, perhaps I should be Three Persons in One and Watkin and Pike could be two of the archangels. He turned Philomel out of the church grounds and into the alleyway, smilingly sketching a blessing towards where Marston and his accomplices lurked. Then he forced his way through the smelly, noisy throngs in Southwark's narrow alleyways. Outside the Piebald tavern, two of his parishioners, Tab the tinker and Roisia his wife, were engaged in a bitter verbal battle, much to the delight of a growing crowd of onlookers. Athelstan stopped to watch and listen.

'We've been happily married for twenty years till this!' Roisia, red in the face, shouted at her husband.

'Yes,' Tab retorted. 'You've been happy and I've been married!'

This was too much for Roisia, who swung her tankard at Tab's head. He ducked and she went sprawling in the mud.

'Tab!' Athelstan shouted. 'Stop this nonsense! Pick Roisia up and go into the church! The cart for our pageant's arrived.'

Roisia, kneeling in the mud, caught her husband's arm.

'You're supposed to be St Peter!' she shouted. 'But Watkin will distribute the parts as he thinks fit.'

Husband and wife, now firm allies, headed off in the direction of St Erconwald's. Athelstan continued on his way, past the priory of St Mary Overy to the approaches of London Bridge. At the roadside the beadles were busy meting out punishments. Two dyers, who had used dog turds to make a brown dye that washed out in the first shower, were standing, bare-arsed, with only a scrap of cloth covering their privy parts, tied hand and foot to each other. They would stand there until sunset. The stocks and pillories were also full with the usual malefactors – footpads and other petty villains who regarded capture and a day's confinement as an occupational hazard. However, the death-cart had arrived and stood now beneath the high-beamed scaffold. A felon, the noose already around his neck, was proclaiming, to the utter indifference of the crowd, that he was an innocent man. The condemned man's face, almost hidden by his ragged hair and beard, was sunburnt.

When he saw Athelstan, he jumped up and down in the cart.

'There's a priest!' he shouted. 'There's a priest! I want to be shriven! I don't want to go to hell!'

Athelstan groaned as Bladdersniff the bailiff came towards him, his vinegarish face looking even more sour than usual.

'We haven't been able to find a priest to hear his confession,' Bladdersniff said. 'He killed a whore in a tavern brawl, was caught red-handed and spent the night in the compter drunk as a pig.' Bladdersniff clutched Philomel's reins and swayed dangerously.

You're none too sober yourself, Athelstan thought. He dismounted, threw the reins at Bladdersniff and climbed up into the death-cart. The condemned felon was pleased, whether at the postponement of his execution or at the appearance of spiritual comfort Athelstan could not decide. The black-masked hangman, Simon, who also worked as a scullion in Merrylegs's pie shop, pulled the noose from the man's neck, smiled through his executioner's mask at Athelstan, jumped off the cart and walked out of earshot.

'Sit down,' Athelstan said. 'What's your name?'

'Robard.'

'And where do you come from?'

'I was born in Norwich.'

'And how have you lived? What have you done?'

'Oh, I was a sailor, Father.' He pulled back the rags of his jerkin to reveal a shrivelled arm. 'That's until someone poured boiling oil over me.'

'Did you know Captain Roffel?' Athelstan asked.

'Captain Roffel!' Robard replied, his whiskered face

breaking into a gap-toothed grin. 'Yes, I knew him, Father – the biggest pirate this side of Dover. A real killer, Father.' Robard belched a gust of stale-ale fumes into Athelstan's face. 'He was also a bugger.' Robard looked apologetic. 'I mean in the real sense, Father. He liked little boys and pretty young men. Always touching them on the buttocks, he was. But he never touched mine, more's the pity. If he liked you, good rations always came your way.'

'Your confession,' Athelstan reminded him.

'Oh yes, Father.' The felon sketched the sign of the cross. 'Bless me, Father, for I have sinned. It's thirty years since I was shriven. I confess all.'

'What do you mean?' Athelstan asked.

'I confess all,' Robard declared. 'You name it, Father, I've done it. I have shagged women, boys and, on one occasion, even a sheep. I have stolen men's property, even their wives. I curse every hour I am awake. I have never been to church.' The man's eyes suddenly filled with tears. 'You know, Father, I have done bugger-all in this life. I have not done one good thing!' He blinked and looked at the friar. 'I have never shown any love but, there again, I've been shown bugger-all myself! I don't know my father. My mother dumped me on a church's steps when I was two summers old.' Robard licked his lips. 'Now I am going to die, Father. I have been in hell on earth, why should I spend the rest of eternity there?' His tears were coming freely now. 'I wish I could go back,' he whispered. 'I wish I could. There was a girl once, Father. Her name was Anna. She was soft and warm. I think she loved me.' He wiped the tears away from his face. 'I am sorry, Father.' The fellow licked dry lips. 'I'll never look at the sea again, or study the sky. Never feel a woman's soft skin or drink red wine. I've drunk good wine, Father. Christ, I need some now!'

Athelstan looked over his shoulder at Simon. 'Simon, get this man a drink, a good deep bowl of claret.' Athelstan fished in his purse and tossed a coin, which the executioner expertly caught. Athelstan pointed at the executioner. 'And one for yourself.'

Simon popped into the nearest ale house and returned with a two-handled hanaper brimming with strong Bordeaux. He handed it to Athelstan, who gave it to Robard, placing it carefully, for the man's hands were bound at the wrists.

Robard pushed it gently back. 'No, Father, you take a sip. Wish me well.'

Athelstan obeyed. 'I wish you well, Robard.'

Robard held the wine.

'Do you deserve to die?' Athelstan asked.

'Oh, yes, I killed the whore. She was laughing at my arm. Will I go to hell, Father?'

'Do you want to go there?' Athelstan replied.

'Oh no, Father.'

Athelstan murmured the words of absolution and made the sign of the cross slowly. 'You are absolved, Robard. The only people who are in hell are those who wish to be there.' Athelstan got to his feet. 'You may have lived a bad life but you will die a good death. Christ on the cross showed he was partial to penitent criminals. Now, drink the wine. Drink it fast. May God help you.'

Athelstan climbed off the cart and, as he passed Simon, the executioner, he gripped him by the arm.

'For the love of Christ!' Athelstan whispered. 'Let

him finish his wine, then make it quick!'

Simon nodded and Athelstan walked over to remount Philomel.

'Father!'

Athelstan looked back towards the scaffold. He kicked his horse forward and reined in next to the cart. Robard drained the hanaper.

'I said no one showed me any love. Bugger-all was the phrase I used.' The felon smiled. 'I was wrong. By what name are you called, Father?'

'Athelstan.'

'God be with you, Brother Athelstan.'

Athelstan turned Philomel away and urged him on. Behind him he heard the crack of Simon's whip and the creaking of the wheels as the horses pulled the cart from underneath Robard. He thought he heard the crack of Robard's neck as Simon pulled hard on the condemned man's legs.

'Oh, sweet Jesus,' he whispered to himself, 'have mercy on him and all of us!' He stared across the busy approaches to the bridge. 'But especially him! Especially him!'

CHAPTER 6

Athelstan knocked on the door of Cranston's house. He was immediately greeted by a raucous noise – the poppets screaming and Cranston's two great wolf-hounds, Gog and Magog, barking furiously. The door opened and Cranston's petite, pretty wife Maude came out, patches of flour on her cheeks and the sleeves of her dress. In each arm she held her beloved poppets Francis and Stephen, their little heads now covered in downy hair, their round, fat faces red and cheery. Behind her Boscombe the steward prevented the two great dogs from lunging at Athelstan and licking him to death.

'Brother Athelstan,' Lady Maude exclaimed, her face smiling in pleasure.

The two poppets strained towards him, clapping their fat hands and gurgling with glee.

'Come in, Brother.' Lady Maude stepped back.

Athelstan shook his head. 'Sir John's not at home?'

'He could be in the Holy Lamb of God,' Lady Maude replied sharply.

'Dadda.' One of the poppets strained forward, a fat, dirty finger pointing at Athelstan. 'Dadda.'

Athelstan seized the finger and squeezed it gently. The beaming baby burped.

'Just like his father!' Lady Maude declared.

'Dadda.'

Athelstan grasped the chubby little finger and stroked the other baby's head. 'Bless you both, bless you all.' He grinned. 'But I'm not your Dadda.'

'Dadda,' the baby repeated.

Athelstan, a little embarrassed, pointed at Lady Maude. 'And who's that?'

The baby stared at his mother and then back at Athelstan.

'Not Dadda.'

Athelstan laughed. He said he would search out Sir John and, leaving the confusion of Cranston's household behind him, pushed his way through the throng. He stabled Philomel in the Holy Lamb of God's stables and entered the taproom. Lady Maude was right. Cranston was sitting in his favourite chair, a tankard of ale in front of him, and staring mournfully into the garden.

'Good morrow, Sir John.'

The coroner, full of self-pity, looked at his secretarius, who slipped on to the bench opposite him.

'You are in poor spirits, Sir John?'

'Bloody murder!'

'You mean the business at Queen's hithe?'

'No, there have been burglaries in the streets around Cheapside. Always the same pattern. A deserted house is robbed but the felon leaves no sign of any forced entry or exit. Last night there was another one, in Catte Street. I have just been down to the Guildhall. A group of angry aldermen gave me and under-sheriff Shawditch the rough edge of their tongues!' Cranston drained his tankard. 'Anyway, what do you want, Brother?'

'Emma Roffel came to see me. She was shocked about what had happened to the corpse of her husband and by the rumours that he had been murdered. She's at the funeral now.'

'We'll deal with my troubles first,' Cranston muttered.

He grabbed his cloak and trudged out of the tavern across Cheapside, so sullen, he ignored the usual banter and good-natured abuse hurled at him.

'Sir John, is this so serious?' Athelstan asked, hurrying beside him.

'Never forget, Brother. The city council pays my salary. I am friendly to all of them but ally to none. Sometimes I think they'd like to remove me.'

'Nonsense!' Athelstan protested.

'We'll see, we'll see,' the coroner said dolefully. 'And how's your bloody parish?'

'My bloody parish is fine, preparing for the play.' Athelstan seized Cranston's sleeve. 'Sir John, pause a minute.'

Under his thick beaver hat, the coroner's fat, usually cheery face now looked so mournful that Athelstan had to bite his lip to hide his smile.

'Sir John, will you be in our play?'

He caught the flicker of amusement in the coroner's eyes.

'As what?'

'Satan.'

Cranston stared at him, threw his head back and roared with laughter. He clapped the friar so vigorously on the shoulder that Athelstan winced.

'Of course I bloody will! I'll even buy my own costume. Now come on!'

He led Athelstan up a lane and stopped before the main door of a grand four-storeyed house.

'Who lives here?' Athelstan asked.

'A big fat merchant,' Sir John replied. 'He made a fortune in the wine trade and is now absent from the city visiting friends and relations.'

Cranston hammered on the door. A pale-faced servant opened it. Sir John roared who he was and marched straight in. Shawditch was already in the large, white-washed kitchen questioning the servants, who sat, anxious-faced, around the great fleshing table. Cranston introduced Athelstan, who shook the under-sheriff's hand.

'Well, what happened?' the coroner snapped.

'The same as ever, Sir John, with one difference. Last night some footpad entered the house. God knows how – the doors were barred and the windows shuttered. He stole precious objects from the upper floors. Unfortunately a linen-maid, Katherine Abchurch, had fallen asleep in one of the chambers. She woke after dark, opened the door and surprised the intruder, who promptly stabbed her to death.'

'And then?'

'Disappeared leaving no trace of how he left or how he entered.'

Cranston nodded towards the servants. 'And you have questioned all of these?'

'They can all account for their movements. In fact, the steward here noticed Katherine was missing and went looking for her.'

Athelstan beckoned the under-sheriff closer. 'Is

there anyone here who had anything to do with the previous burglaries?' he asked.

Shawditch shook his head. 'No one.'

'And you are sure that all the entrances and exits were sealed?'

'As sure as I can be.'

'Ah well, let's see for ourselves,' Cranston said. 'Come on, Shawditch.'

The under-sheriff led them along a corridor and up a broad staircase where the oak gleamed like burnished gold. The walls were panelled and the plaster above them painted a soft pink. Heraldic shields hung there and, on one wall, the head of a ferocious-looking boar had been mounted on a wooden plaque. On the second floor just outside a chamber, Katherine Abchurch lay where she had fallen, a woollen blanket tossed over her. Athelstan looked around the corridor. He saw chamber doors, the staircase at the far end and a table with dusty rings on it.

'Something was stolen from here?'

'Yes,' Shawditch replied, then jumped at a loud knocking on the door downstairs.

'That will be beadle Trumpington,' he said. 'I'll tell him to wait below.'

He hurried down the stairs. Cranston and Athelstan pulled back the blanket and stared at Katherine's mortal remains.

'God save us!' Athelstan whispered. 'She's only a child.'

He saw the bloody puncture marks on the girl's dress and his heart lurched with compassion at the terror still frozen on her face. 'God rest her!' he said softly. 'And God punish the wicked bastard who did it!'

He replaced the blanket tenderly, covering the girl's face. 'My mind's a jumble of problems but I will do all I can to bring this assassin to justice!'

Shawditch rejoined them.

'Let's inspect the house,' Athelstan urged. 'Every floor, every room.'

'I have asked for all the chambers to be opened,' Shawditch said.

'Then let's begin.'

There was a look of cold determination on Athelstan's usually gentle face as he moved from room to room. It reminded Cranston of a good hunting dog he had owned as a boy. Athelstan's irritation at not being able to find any clue, however, grew as they reached the top floor.

'Nothing,' he whispered through clenched teeth. 'Nothing at all.'

They went into the garret, which was dark and chilling – only the beams and the tiles above separated them from the cold. Athelstan kicked among the rushes on the floor.

'No window. No opening.' He crouched down and felt the rushes. They were cold and damp to his touch. He walked into the corner of the room and felt the rushes there. He came back shaking his head. 'Let's go downstairs.'

They returned to the kitchen, where Trumpington the beadle was holding court before the great roaring fire.

'Sir John, Master Shawditch, have you found anything?' The beadle's eyes narrowed as he looked at Athelstan. 'Who's this?'

'Brother Athelstan, my secretarius,' Cranston replied.

Athelstan stared at the beadle. 'It's a mystery,' he said absent-mindedly. 'But you, good sir, could do me a favour.'

'Anything you ask, Father.'

'But, first, one question.'

'Of course.'

'You patrol the streets. You noticed nothing wrong?'

'Father, if I had I'd have reported it.'

Athelstan smiled.

'And the favour, Father?'

'I want you to get a tiler, a good man.'

'I've done that already,' Trumpington said.

'To check this house?'

'No, but he checked all the others and found nothing amiss.'

'Well, ask him to check again. See if any tiles have been removed. If he finds any aperture we have missed, report your findings to the coroner.'

'Is that what you want, Sir John?' Trumpington asked pointedly, throwing a look of disdain at the friar.

Sir John caught the tinge of contempt. 'Yes it is. And do it quickly!'

They made their farewells and left the house.

'Well, Brother, did you find anything?' Cranston asked. Athelstan saw the expectation in his and Shawditch's faces.

'Nothing, Sir John.'

Cranston cursed.

'There is one thing, though,' Athelstan said. 'Master Shawditch, a small favour?'

The under-sheriff looked at Cranston, who shrugged.

'It's nothing to do with this business,' Athelstan went

on, 'but could you ask the boatmen along the Thames if they took anyone out to the ship *God's Bright Light* two nights ago?'

'I'll do what I can, Father,' Shawditch replied and hurried off.

'What's that all about?' Cranston grumbled.

'Well, let me tell you.'

Athelstan pulled Cranston into a small alehouse. Sir John needed no second invitation to refreshment – he immediately began shouting for a cup of claret and a piece of freshly roasted capon. Athelstan sipped at his ale as he watched the food restore Sir John's good humour.

'First,' Athelstan whispered, leaning across the table, 'Aveline Ospring murdered her father. She told me under the seal of confession but has asked for our help.'

Cranston stared, his mouth wide open, as Athelstan described what he had learnt earlier in the day. The coroner threw the capon leg down.

'She'll hang,' Sir John muttered. 'Either she'll hang or he'll hang or they'll both hang. She can't prove what she said. What else, Brother?'

'Somebody boarded that ship,' Athelstan declared, 'and somehow killed those three men. But how and why I don't know. However, you heard what Crawley said? No one from the neighbouring ship, the *Holy Trinity*, saw or heard anything amiss and that includes Bernicia's shouting.' Athelstan angrily shook his head. 'Someone is lying, Sir John, and we must discover who. How do we know every sailor left the ship? There could have been someone hiding on board.'

'Oh, I see,' Cranston said sarcastically. 'And he killed

those three sailors with no fuss or trace, continued passing the signals and then disappeared into thin air, just like the felon robbing the merchants' houses?'

Athelstan smiled. 'No one disappears into thin air, Sir John, and that goes for the house we have just visited. I have a suspicion. No, no.' He held a finger up as expectation flared in Sir John's eyes. 'Not now. Let's deal with Roffel's widow. But, before that, do you know a tavern called the Crossed Keys near Queen's hithe?'

'Yes, the landlord's a relative of Admiral Crawley. An old seafarer. Why, what's the matter, Brother?'

Athelstan leaned his elbows on the table and put his head in his hands. 'Roffel used to buy usquebaugh, a Scottish drink, there. He kept it in a flask that he always carried with him. By the way, Sir John, have you noticed how Crawley's name keeps recurring? He disliked Roffel. We have only his word that no one approached the *God's Bright Light*. He must have heard Bracklebury shouting to Bernicia. And now his cousin owns a tavern where Roffel bought the usquebaugh that, I suspect, contained the arsenic that killed him.'

Cranston drained his cup and wiped his mouth on the back of his hand.

'Let's visit the tavern.' He tapped the side of his fleshy nose. 'Then we'll go to see someone else – a man who knows about what happens along the river because he earns his living from it.'

Cranston left some coins on the table and they strode out of the alehouse. It was beginning to rain. The streets were empty so they kept to the shadow of the houses to avoid the filthy puddles as well as to shelter from the rain.

'We should have brought the horses,' Athelstan grumbled.

'Shut up and say your prayers!' Cranston quipped back.

They found the Crossed Keys tavern nestling behind the warehouses. It was a sailors' haunt, filled with a babble of voices. Customers from every nationality thronged the taproom: Portuguese clad in gaudy clothes, their faces bearded and swarthy, silver earrings dangling from their ear lobes; Gascons, proud and argumentative; and Hanseatics, solemn-faced, sweating under their fur caps and cloaks. A salty, fishy odour mingled with strange cooking smells. Cranston licked his lips as a servitor pushed by him with a bowl of diced steak under a thick onion sauce. Athelstan wisely moved the coroner on through the noisy throng towards the landlord, squat and round as a barrel, who stood in front of a great fishing net pinned to the wall. The fellow kept surveying the taproom, shouting out orders to his sweat-soaked servitors. Athelstan could see he had spent his life at sea from his rolling gait and eyes creased after years of straining against the sun and biting wind. A merry-looking man, with his rubicund cheeks and balding head, he was mouthing a string of colourful oaths which made even Cranston smile.

'You are the owner?' Cranston asked, coming up in front of him.

'No, I am a peeping mermaid!' the fellow replied out of the corner of his mouth as he turned to shout orders into the kitchen.

'Jack Cranston's the name and this is my secretarius, Brother Athelstan.'

The coroner extended a podgy hand. The landlord grasped it and smiled.

'I have heard of you. I am Richard Crawley, one-time ship's master, now lord of all I survey. I know why you are here or can I guess? Roffel's death. God damn him!'

'You didn't like him?'

'Like my cousin, Sir Jacob, I hated Roffel's guts. He was a bad bastard and I hope he gets what he richly deserves, rotting in hell—' He broke off suddenly and shouted at a scullion. 'By a mermaid's paps! Hold that platter straight! You're listing like a scuppered ship!'

'Why did you hate him?'

'Why not? The same reason as Sir Jacob. I had a half-brother,' the landlord continued, lowering his voice, 'a good sailor, plying the cloth trade between the Cinque Ports and Dordrecht. His ship went down with all hands. Roffel was cruising in the vicinity at the time. He blamed the French. I blamed him.'

'But you did business with him?'

'Of course I bloody well did – and charged him highly for it. A Scotsman, he liked his drink, usquebaugh. I bought it in cask from Leith in Scotland and sold it at treble the price to that evil bastard. He always filled his flask before he left for any voyage. Roffel knew, to the last drop, how much he had left.'

'Do you have any of it now?'

'Yes,' Richard replied, 'and I'll finish it myself one day and toast his black soul with every drop.'

'May we see it?' Athelstan asked.

The landlord shrugged and, going back into the scullery, returned with a cask about a foot wide and a foot across with a small tap in the bottom. He took a battered pewter cup from the shelf, ran a few drops into it and handed it to Cranston.

'Taste that!'

Sir John did, drinking it down in one gulp while the landlord grinned evilly.

'Shitting ships!' Cranston exclaimed. His face turned puce and he coughed. 'Satan's balls! What in hell is that?'

'Usquebaugh, Sir John. Do you like it?'

Sir John smacked his lips. 'Hot,' he said. 'Strong at first, but it certainly warms the belly. How many barrels do you have of this?'

'Just the one cask.'

'And before he sailed on his last voyage Roffel filled his flask from it himself?'

'Oh, of course, he did. And then he drank some, a small cup.'

Athelstan, who was half-watching a Portuguese sailor feed his pet monkey, which was climbing all over his shoulders, looked at the landlord in surprise.

'He drank some here?'

'Oh, yes.' The landlord turned and glared towards the clamour from the kitchen. 'Sir John, if you have no more questions, I have a trade to follow.'

Cranston muttered his thanks and they left the tavern. Thankfully, the rain had stopped. The coroner gripped Athelstan's shoulder.

'It can't have been the usquebaugh can it, Brother? Or the flask?'

Athelstan shook his head. 'No, not if Roffel drank some here and suffered no ill effects.' He shook his head as he and the coroner trudged up the rain-soaked street.

'Aren't we going in the wrong direction, Sir John?

Shouldn't we be going to Roffel's house?'

'Ah, no, there's someone else.' Cranston stopped and took a generous swig from his wineskin. 'As I said, Brother, someone who knows and watches what goes on along the river.'

At the corner of the alleyway the coroner suddenly stopped and turned quickly. The two figures at the other end of the alleyway didn't bother to hide. Athelstan followed the coroner's gaze.

'Who are they, Sir John?' He strained his eyes. Dressed in brown robes, the figures looked like Benedictine monks. 'Are they following us?'

'They have been with us most of the time,' Cranston whispered. 'Let's leave them for a while.'

They walked on, across Thames Street, down towards Vintry, then turned right past the warehouses and along Queen's hithe towards Dowgate. A thick, cloying mist boiled over the river, hiding the ships that rode at anchor there.

'Where are we going?' Athelstan demanded.

'Patience, my dear friar. Patience!'

They walked along the quayside. Cranston peered into the dark corners then suddenly stopped.

'Come out!'

A ragged, hooded figure shuffled forward. As the man came closer, Athelstan saw the rags swathed across his face and around his hands and tried to hide his revulsion. The man moved in an ungainly shuffle and, as he did so, he rang a small bell.

'Unclean!' the ghastly figure croaked. 'Unclean!'

'Oh, bugger that!' Cranston retorted. 'I doubt if I'll catch leprosy!'

The man stopped a few paces from them. To

Athelstan he seemed like some apparition from hell, with the rags covering his face and hands, the dark cowl pulled well forward. Now and again tendrils of mist would drift between them.

'These are the gargoyles,' Cranston whispered. 'Cripples, beggars and lepers. They work for the Fisher of Men. They take corpses from the Thames, murder victims, suicides, those who have suffered accidents as well as drunks. If the man's alive, they earn tuppence, for murder victims three pence. Suicides and accidents only a penny.'

'You wish to meet the Fisher of Men?' the leper croaked.

'That's right, my jolly lad!' Cranston called back. And, taking a penny from his pocket, he flicked it at the man who, despite his disability, neatly caught it in one hand.

'Tell the Fisher of Men old Jack Cranston wants a word.' He pointed down the alleyway. 'I'll meet him in the alehouse there.'

'And what business shall I say?'

'The *God's Bright Light*. He'll know,' Cranston added to Athelstan. 'Nothing happens along the riverside without the knowledge of the Fisher of Men.'

The leper disappeared. Cranston led Athelstan down the alleyway into a small, smelly alehouse with only one window high in the wall. It was dark and dank, lit by smoky tallow candles and smelly oil lamps, but the ale was rich and frothy, the blackjacks clean and the tables and stools neatly wiped.

'You have met the Fisher of Men?' Cranston asked.

'Yes, you introduced us some months ago,' Athelstan replied.

Cranston stuck his nose into his tankard but his eyes never left the doorway.

'Here he comes.'

The doorway became black with huddled figures, cowled and hooded like the one they had met on the quayside. The tapster nervously waved them back but they crouched at the threshold, staring into the tavern like a huddle of ghosts peering into the land of the living. Their leader, the Fisher of Men, came from amongst them, walked soundlessly towards the coroner and Athelstan and, without invitation, sat down on the stool between them. He pulled back his hood revealing a face as sombre as any death mask – alabaster white, thick-lipped and snub-nosed, with black button eyes. Red, greasy hair fell to his shoulders. He pointed a lanky finger at Cranston.

'You are Sir John Cranston, coroner of the city.' The finger moved. 'And you are Athelstan, his *secretarius* or clerk, parish priest of St Erconwald's in Southwark. Sir John, Lady Maude went shopping today. Brother Athelstan, your sanctuary man is safe. He is helping your parishioners prepare the stage for their mystery play.'

Athelstan smiled at the Fisher of Men's implicit boast at how much he knew.

'But we are not here to exchange gossip,' the Fisher of Men continued. Again the finger pointed. 'Three days ago the ship so inappropriately called *God's Bright Light* dropped anchor opposite Queen's hithe. The captain's corpse was taken ashore. His soul has gone to God's judgement . . .' The voice trailed away.

'And what else do you know?' Cranston asked.

The man spread his hands and indicated with a nod of his head the group in the doorway.

'Sir John, of your mercy I have my brethren to feed.'

Cranston pushed a silver coin across the table. The Fisher of Men plucked it up.

'You do me great honour, Sir John. The ship was berthed and that night the crew and their doxies went ashore. I know because I had one of them. Fresh and clean she was. Black curly hair, merry eyes, active and vigorous as a puppy in my bed.'

Athelstan fought to control his face at the image of this strange figure making love to a young whore.

'Very good,' Sir John interrupted hastily. 'And?'

'Three men were left on board, one in the bows, one at the stern, the mate in the middle. Or rather, he kept to the cabin.'

'And?' Cranston insisted.

'Oh, a whore, a male whore' – the Fisher of Men grimaced – 'came down about midnight to the quayside. However, she, or he, depending on your viewpoint, was driven off by a stream of curses from the ship.' The Fisher of Men played with his lank hair. 'The sailor on board sounded drunk, but the signals and passwords continued to be perfect!'

'And nothing happened?' Athelstan asked.

'Oh yes, about two hours after midnight a small craft approached the ship.'

'From the river bank?'

'Oh no, from the admiral's cog, the *Holy Trinity*. Two men were in it.'

'And then what?'

'The small boat was there for just over an hour, but then it returned.' The Fisher of Men smiled. 'And, before you ask, Sir John, the password and the signals still continued.'

'Did anything else happen?' Cranston asked.

'A sailor returned just before dawn and the confusion began.'

'But the watch?' Athelstan intervened. 'What happened to the watch?'

The Fisher of Men licked his lips, reminding Athelstan of a frog which could see something savoury. 'If the river has them,' the fellow replied, 'it will caress and kiss them and put them ashore.' His face became solemn. 'I and my brethren have already looked, but we have found nothing. We did not see them go in. Perhaps we shall not see them come out.'

'But if you find them you will tell us?'

The man looked down at the silver coin in his hand. Cranston pushed another piece towards him. The Fisher of Men picked it up, got to his feet and gave them a solemn bow.

'You are my friends,' he declared. 'And the Fisher of Men never forgets. In the name of my brethren, I thank you.'

He slipped out of the alehouse and the gargoyles, chattering and clattering, followed him down the alleyway.

'Let's see Crawley.' Cranston drained his tankard. 'Our dear admiral has been lying through his teeth and I think we should know the reason why. But first, Mistress Roffel. Come on, Brother, sharpen your wits and open your ears. Let's see what our good widow has to say for herself.'

They left the quayside. The clouds were beginning to break up as the daylight died. The streets were busy with apprentices and traders packing away the stalls. The huge dung-carts were out, trying to clear the swollen sewers. Athelstan saw one of the dung-collectors cheerfully pick up the bloated corpse of a cat and throw it with a thud into the cart. Beggars whined for alms. Mangy dogs strutted, stiff-legged, tails up, fighting and snarling over the piles of refuse. At the corner of an alleyway, Cranston stopped and peered over his shoulder.

'Our friends are still with us.'

Athelstan turned quickly and glimpsed the two monk-like figures a good thirty paces behind him.

'Do you recognise them, Sir John?'

'They are not monks,' Cranston replied. 'They are clerks, royal officials from either the chancery or the exchequer. If they are from the latter then God help us!'

Athelstan caught Cranston's arm. 'Why, Sir John?'

'The exchequer,' Cranston replied, 'has a group of very secret, sharp-witted officials called scrutineers. They deal with many matters – debts owing to the crown, royal prerogatives, but they also handle foreign matters, particularly the financing of spies and clandestine missions abroad.'

'Shouldn't we confront them?' Athelstan asked.

Sir John smiled bleakly. 'If we walk back, they'll retreat. They'll choose the moment and the place to approach us.'

Athelstan stared up as they approached a large town house, his attention caught by the tilers working there. He stopped and stared.

'Come on, Athelstan!' Cranston shouted.

Athelstan watched the men working, smiled and hurried on. Sir John paid a link boy a penny to lead them to Mistress Roffel's house, a narrow, three-storeyed building pushed between a haberdashery shop and an ironmonger's. The windows were all shuttered up, the wooden slats covered with black drapes as a sign of mourning. Athelstan lifted the iron knocker, crafted in the shape of a ship's anchor, and brought it heavily down.

CHAPTER 7

Emma Roffel and her maid Tabitha entertained Sir John and Brother Athelstan in the downstairs parlour. The chamber was nondescript. Fresh rushes covered the floor but the room was devoid of any wall hangings and the table and chairs were old and rather battered. Emma Roffel followed Cranston's gaze.

'Not the house of a successful sea voyager, eh, Sir John?' She laughed bitterly. 'But Captain Roffel was tight-fisted with his monies. And you've met his creature, Bernicia, with her pretty face and tight bum?'

Athelstan stared at this hard-faced woman, who was so cold and distant about her husband's death. Athelstan admired her honesty. He remembered a maxim he had heard – 'the opposite of love is not hate but indifference'.

'Was it always like that?' he asked.

Tears welled in the woman's eyes.

'Mistress, I did not mean to upset you.'

Emma Roffel looked over his head, fighting to keep her face impassive.

'You do not.' Her eyes took on a haunted, distant look as her mind conjured up visions, ghosts from the

123

past. 'Roffel was a priest, you know. A curate in the parish of St Olave's in Leith just outside Edinburgh. My father owned a fishing smack and Roffel was interested in the sea. Sometimes he would go fishing with my father.'

'Did you ever accompany him?'

Emma smiled bleakly. 'Of course not. I fear the sea. It's taken too many good men.'

'What happened?' Athelstan persisted. Like all priests, he was fascinated by those of his brethren who left their calling for the love of a woman.

Emma sighed. 'William couldn't keep his hands to himself. Rumours abounded about his relationships with certain widows in the town. Eventually the archdeacon intervened, but by then William and I had met and fallen deeply in love.' She wiped her eyes with the cuff of her sleeve. 'The archdeacon was furious and my father threatened violence, so we fled across the border. At first to Hull, then south to London.' She licked her lips. 'In the beginning, I thought we were in paradise. William soon proved to be a fine seaman – competent, effective, a firm disciplinarian.' She laughed sourly. 'But then he met Henry Ospring. A friendship formed in hell. Ospring gave him money and hired a small ship and William turned to piracy. Sir Henry also introduced him to the fleshpots of the city. I was pregnant when I first found out about his—' She pulled a face. 'When I found out that he had a passion for fondling the bottoms of young boys.' She rocked herself quietly in her chair. 'I lost my baby. I also lost William and William lost me. We began the descent into our own private hells. We became strangers. William pursued his career. He had the devil's own luck – second mate, first mate and finally captain.'

'You hated him?' Cranston asked.

Her eyes darted at him. 'Hate, Sir John? Hate? I felt cold, empty, like watching someone in a dream. He left me alone and I reciprocated.'

'Before that last voyage,' Athelstan said, 'did he speak of anything unusual that was about to happen?'

'Not a word!'

'You know he was murdered?' Athelstan continued.

'Yes, I think he was, Brother. If you want to accuse me, then do so, but remember I was here at home. I really couldn't have cared if he lived or died.' She shrugged. 'It was only a matter of time before someone took a knife to him.' Her eyes narrowed. 'You are sure he was murdered?'

'Poisoned, Mistress.'

She leaned forward in surprise. 'But how? He always boasted that he ate and drank what his crew did.'

'What about the usquebaugh?' Cranston asked. 'And the flask he always filled at the Crossed Keys tavern?'

Emma Roffel pulled a face in surprise. She turned and whispered to Tabitha, who scurried off quiet as a mouse. Emma sat staring into the fire until her maid returned, carrying a pewter flask. Emma took it and thrust it at Cranston.

'This is the famous flask, Sir John. When they brought my husband's body ashore, they brought his possessions with him.'

She unstoppered the flask and sniffed its contents, then poured a little liquid from it into a goblet she took from a small table behind her. Smiling she offered the goblet in turn to Cranston and Athelstan. They shook their heads.

'You should drink usquebaugh,' she said. 'It warms the heart and fortifies the body against old age. Ah well.' And, before either could stop her, she poured the contents down her throat. She coughed, winced and smiled. 'If this flask was poisoned then I will soon join my husband.'

'You seem most confident, Mistress.'

Emma Roffel grinned, put down the goblet and re-stopped the flask. She winked at Athelstan. Her good humour made her face look younger. Years earlier, Athelstan reflected, Emma Roffel had been beautiful enough for a priest to break his vows because of her.

'That was reckless,' he murmured.

She shook her head. 'I apologise. I tease you. I sipped from the flask when it was first returned.' She pulled a face. 'I admit that *that* was stupid – risking a husband and wife poisoned by the same drink.'

'So, you think the murder was committed on board the *God's Bright Light?*' Cranston asked.

'Of course,' Emma replied. 'He was hated by the crew.'

'And by his admiral?'

Emma shrugged. 'Crawley considered my husband a pirate. He once threatened to hang him because of his depredations at sea.'

'Mistress Roffel,' Athelstan asked, 'do you know what could have happened on board your late husband's ship the night it docked to cause the disappearance of the mate and two sailors?'

She shook her head.

'As Father Stephen will testify, on that particular evening I was with my husband's corpse in St Mary Magdalene church. However, if you ask me to guess, I would say all three men, somehow or other, abandoned ship.'

'You met Bracklebury, the first mate?'

'Yes, he brought my husband's corpse to shore as well as a bag containing his few pathetic belongings, including the flask.' She watched the priest's dark eyes carefully. 'Do you want to look at these?'

Athelstan nodded.

'But don't put yourself out,' he added anxiously. 'Perhaps, if your maid Tabitha would be good enough to take me upstairs?'

The mousey, grey-haired woman smiled at her mistress who agreed. Athelstan, leaving the coroner jovially accepting Mistress Roffel's offer of wine, followed Tabitha upstairs. The rest of the house proved equally dismal, dark and rather dank. The furniture and hangings were tawdry – clean and sweet-smelling but battered and dingy. He passed the main bedchamber, where the door was ajar, and glimpsed a four-poster bed with clothing slung across the coffer at its foot. Tabitha took him into a small, dusty chamber with coffers stacked along the walls. The maid stood for a while looking around.

'How long have you served your mistress?' Athelstan asked quietly.

The maid looked at him, crinkling up her eyes. 'Oh, ever since the miscarriage sixteen or seventeen years ago.'

'And she is good to you?'

Tabitha's face became hard. 'Mistress Roffel is as

harsh as her husband ever was. They richly deserved each other. She intends to return to Leith. I will be pleased to see the back of her!'

Athelstan flinched at the venom in the woman's voice. He watched, then helped, as she pulled a pair of leather, sea-stained panniers from behind a chest.

'I slung it there after removing the flask. Shall we take it downstairs?'

Athelstan put it over his shoulder and they returned to the parlour. Cranston, now on his second cup of claret, was describing to a bored but polite Mistress Roffel his own exploits at sea many years before.

'You found what you wanted, Brother?' she asked, stopping Cranston in mid-sentence.

Athelstan put the leather bag on the floor, undid the buckles and emptied the contents out. They were not much: a pair of knee-high, woollen stockings; a needle and some thread; a quill; an inkhorn; some unused scraps of parchment; a shirt; two rings, scratched and rather battered; a St Christopher medal; a small compass; and a calfskin-bound book of hours. Athelstan picked the book up, undid the catch and leafed through the yellowing pages.

'His only legacy from his priesthood days,' Emma explained. 'Wherever he went, he always took that with him.'

'Yet,' Athelstan observed, 'he was not a man of prayer and neither are you. Father Stephen at St Mary Magdalene regarded you as strangers.'

Mistress Roffel was about to reply when Cranston burped and emitted a loud snore. Athelstan looked at his fat friend, who slouched in the chair, nodding, his eyes closed.

'Is Sir John well?' Emma asked.

'Oh, yes,' Athelstan replied sourly. 'He'll sleep like a babe and wake shouting for refreshment.'

The friar turned over the pages of the book, noticing how the blank pages at the end carried strange entries which could perhaps be accounts – sums of money, sometimes followed by the note 'in S.L.'.

'What are these?' Athelstan asked.

'God knows, Brother. My husband was a secretive man. I am still visiting the goldsmiths along Cheapside to discover where he banked his monies.'

Athelstan leafed over the pages and stopped to look at one fresh drawing; a squiggly line running across one page, small crosses carefully drawn alongside. The drawing looked fresh: the friar showed it to Mistress Roffel but she replied it made no sense to her. Athelstan sighed and placed the book back among the other possessions.

'Your maid tells me that you are leaving the city,' he said.

'My maid knows too much for her own good,' Emma retorted. 'But, yes, once these matters are finished, I intend to collect my possessions, whatever monies my husband has left me, and return to Scotland.'

'You hate London so much?'

They all turned, surprised to see Cranston awake, blinking and smacking his lips.

'Do you hate London, mistress?' the coroner repeated.

'It holds bitter memories: it's best if I forget the past.'

'And you know nothing to resolve these mysteries?' Cranston asked.

She shook her head.

'And you, Sir John, do you know who murdered my husband and desecrated his corpse?'

Cranston lumbered to his feet, shaking his head.

'No, mistress,' he breathed. 'However, if I do find out, believe me, you'll be the first to know.'

They made their farewells and left the house. Both jumped as the Fisher of Men, with two of his gargoyles trailing behind him, slunk out of the shadows.

'Satan's futtocks!' Cranston swore. 'What the bloody hell are you doing, creeping up on good Christians like that?'

'Sir John, you gave me and mine some money, so me and mine will earn it!'

'What have you found?'

'We saw the light gleaming.' The Fisher of Men turned and patted one of his creatures.

'Yes, I know about the lights!' Cranston growled. 'The ships pass signals between each other.'

'Oh, no, not those. Something else. A lamp winked from the ship *God's Bright Light* every hour until just before dawn and someone on the quayside answered it with a lamp.'

'Do you know who it was?'

'No, it was someone in the shadows. When we find out, Sir John, we'll let you know.' The Fisher of Men stepped back and disappeared as silently as he had arrived.

Athelstan, aware of the drizzle beginning to fall, pulled his cowl well over his head. 'Bernicia said that,' he remarked.

'Said what?' Cranston asked testily.

'That there was someone in the shadows of the warehouses watching the ship.'

'Satan's balls! I have had enough of this!' Cranston grumbled. 'I'm hungry, I'm cold and wet!'

He stamped down the alleyway, Athelstan hurrying behind him. The coroner sped, direct as an arrow, past the door of his own house, across a deserted Cheapside and into the Holy Lamb of God. He stopped abruptly, Athelstan almost colliding with him. Cranston glared angrily at the two men dressed in brown robes who sat at his favourite table.

'Who the sod are you?' Cranston snapped.

The men smiled in unison and waved them over to the waiting stools.

'Sir John, Brother Athelstan, please be our guests. We have already ordered blackjacks of ale.'

Cranston and Athelstan sat down as the landlord's wife placed tankards before them.

'Your good health, Sir John.' The brown-robed men raised their tankards in a toast to the coroner.

Athelstan gazed at the strange pair. They looked like peas out of the same pod – merry-faced, balding, dressed the same, they seemed to do everything in unison. They would have passed as two merry monks from one of the city monasteries, with their soft skin and easy smiles, but for their eyes, hard and watchful. The friar shivered. These men were dangerous. They followed the coroner of London around the streets and did not give a damn. Now they sat waiting for him in his favourite tavern as if they knew his every movement.

'Your names?' Cranston growled.

'Oh, you can call me Peter,' the taller of the two replied. He smiled at his companion. 'And that is Paul.

131

Yes, call us Peter and Paul, the holders of the keys. What a nice touch!'

'I could call you a lot of things,' Cranston said grimly.

'But you wouldn't, Sir John,' the one who had been given the name Paul replied. 'We are like you; we may not be Children of the Light but we are their servants.' He turned and smiled cheerily at Athelstan. 'You have been busy, haven't you, Brother?'

Cranston swung his cloak back, touching the long stabbing dirk sheathed in his belt. Peter watched the movement, grinned and held his soft, white hands up in a gesture of peace.

'Sir John,' he lisped. 'You are in no danger. We only wish to help.'

'What with?' Cranston snapped. 'My marriage, my boys, my treatise, my bowels?'

'*God's Bright Light!*' Peter snapped back, the good humour draining from his face.

Athelstan spoke up, leaning across the table. 'We appreciate your help, but who are you?'

'We are the scrutineers. Do we work for the king's council?' Peter smiled and shook his head. 'For the king himself?' Again the shake of the head. 'Brother Athelstan, we work for the crown. Princes and councillors come and go. We do not serve individuals, or noble families or a certain blood line but the crown itself.' He leaned his elbows on the table, steepling his fingers, and gazed quickly around the warm, cheery tavern. 'The life blood of the crown,' he continued, 'is its money. We scrutinise what should be the crown's, its taxes, rights, prerogatives, levies and dues.'

'So, you are treasury officials?'

Again the smile. 'Oh and much more! We are particularly interested in the crown's rights in France and, Sir John, you know what has happened there? The present king's grandfather conquered and held the greater part of northern France. However, those of the same blood, but of a more feckless nature, are fast losing this patrimony. What does the crown hold now?'

Cranston shrugged. 'Parts of Gascony around Bordeaux.'

'And in Normandy?'

'Calais and the area around it.'

Peter nodded. 'We have men working out of Calais to recover the lost lands.'

'You mean spies?' Athelstan asked.

'Yes, yes, you could call them that. Now their task is to weaken the French.' Peter shrugged and smiled at his companion. 'To keep them busy. You know – arranging the occasional accident to their ships, stirring up discontent, collecting information.'

'And how does that concern us?' Athelstan asked.

'Well, my dear friar, it really doesn't, except that you are investigating Captain Roffel's death and the disappearance of the watch from the *God's Bright Light*. Yes? Now that doesn't really concern us. What does concern us are the movements of Roffel's ship during his last voyage. You see, two of our brethren sailing on a fishing smack from Dieppe to Calais never arrived. Their ship disappeared.'

'And you think Roffel sank it?'

'Possibly. Roffel was a bastard, a pirate, a robber sailing under the king's colours. We know of his little business ventures. However, the killing of two of our agents is a different matter. Murder and piracy are

133

serious crimes. More importantly, we want to discover just how did Roffel know where to intercept that fishing smack?'

'He could have just been lucky,' Cranston interrupted.

'We don't believe in luck!' the scrutineer snapped. 'Some traitor must have paid Roffel to intercept that ship and kill our messengers.' Peter leaned across the table. 'In other words, Sir John, we are talking about treason.'

'In our investigations we discovered nothing like that,' Cranston said.

The scrutineers smiled in unison.

'Oh, but you might,' Paul purred, like a sleek cat. 'You might very well, Sir John, and, if you do, we want to know.'

'How can we inform you?' Athelstan asked.

The two scrutineers drained their tankards together, putting them back on the table in a single movement.

'You know the great statue of Our Lady and the infant Jesus in St Paul's?' the taller of the two scrutineers asked.

Athelstan nodded.

'And before it stands a great iron-bound chest where the faithful place their petitions. Well,' Peter got to his feet, indicating Paul to do the same, 'if you wish to speak to us, put a petition in the chest – *Saints Peter and Paul, intercede for us*. Within the day you'll hear from us. Good night, Sir John, Brother Athelstan.'

The two scrutineers slipped out of the tavern. Sir John whistled softly under his breath, drained his tankard and roared for another.

'And a bowl of onion soup!' he shouted. 'Brother?'

'Just ale for me, Sir John.'

'Well, well, well!' Cranston said. 'What do you make of that, eh, Brother? Piracy, murder, sailors who disappear and now treason.'

'I cannot see the connection,' Athelstan replied. 'Why should Roffel put his neck on the block when he was doing so well out of piracy?'

Cranston clicked his fingers and told a tapster to clear the table.

'Out with your parchment and pen, monk!'

Athelstan groaned but did what Sir John asked, taking a roll of parchment and smoothing it out on the table.

Leif, the one-legged beggar, had been watching them from a far corner; he now hopped across, his tall, ungainly frame balancing precariously on a makeshift crutch.

'What's the matter, Sir John? Brother Athelstan? Why are you writing here?' Leif shouted. 'Sir John, Lady Maude said you should come home. She has baked two great pies and some pastries. The poppets are asleep and Lady Maude wants to see you. Have you had a good day, Sir John?'

'Bugger off, you idle sod!' Cranston shouted. 'Bugger off and leave me alone!'

Leif touched his forelock and grinned.

'A man gets terribly thirsty, Sir John, carrying messages. Now I have to go back and tell Lady Maude where you are, what you are doing and what you've just said.'

Cranston narrowed his eyes and tossed the beggar a halfpenny.

'What you haven't seen you can't tell, can you, Leif?'

'That is true, Sir John, but lying is also thirsty work.'

Another halfpenny was tossed over.

'Drink your ale!' Cranston ordered. 'You lazy, sly bugger! Keep your mouth shut and you can join me for dinner. If you don't, you will be dinner!'

Leif grinned at Athelstan and hopped away, crowing with delight. Sir John sipped from his tankard, put it down, clapped his hands and stared at his patient clerk.

'Right, you idle friar, what do we know?' He stuck up one podgy thumb. 'Item: on the 27th September, Captain William Roffel and his good ship the *God's Bright Light* sailed from the Thames to scour the Narrow Seas. Roffel was highly unpopular, ruthless but a good captain. Young Ashby, now hiding in your church, sailed with him. He gave the captain a sealed package from Ospring.'

Sir John watched Athelstan's pen race across the parchment, admiring the clear, precise letters. The friar wrote in a code known only to him, a mixture of abbreviations and signs that would take a cipher clerk months to work out.

'Item:' Cranston continued, 'Roffel takes a few ships, including one near the French coast. This may or may not be what those two pretties who have just left were talking about. Item: was Roffel a traitor? Did he take the ship deliberately? Did he know there were Englishmen aboard? Was he paid to kill them? Certainly he was very happy afterwards, actually smiling and singing. Item: Roffel begins to sicken. Item: the ship puts in at Dover and Ashby leaves. What else, monk?'

'Friar, Sir John, friar!'

'Whatever you say, friar!'

'Item:' Athelstan spoke as he wrote, 'Captain Roffel's illness worsens. He gets violent stomach pains which, we now believe, were due to arsenic. But how and why he was poisoned remains a mystery.' Athelstan paused and looked up at Cranston.

'Yes, yes, you're right,' the coroner continued. 'We thought the poison might have been in the flask but Roffel, the cunning bastard, took that with him everywhere. He filled it himself and drank from it in the alehouse and suffered no ill effects. Moreover, as we saw for ourselves, his wife did the same. So the flask seems untainted.' Cranston took another gulp from his tankard. 'Item: my dear friar, the *God's Bright Light* returns to dock. Roffel's body is taken ashore along with his personal possessions, which didn't amount to much. They included a book of hours, probably Roffel's secret ledger of ill-gotten gains. There's a bad atmosphere on board the ship but the crew relax. In the afternoon the whores come aboard. At dusk, they and most of the crew leave. Only the first mate and two others are left as a night watch. Item: the real mystery begins. According to what we know, both the password and the signal light are passed to the watch of the *God's Bright Light* from the admiral's ship, the *Holy Trinity*, and on to the next ship in line, the *Saint Margaret*: one on the hour, the other on the half-hour. According to what we are told, the last signal was passed at half-past five. Just before dawn a sailor returns to find that the mate and the watch have disappeared without trace; there is no sign of violence or any disturbance. The *God's Bright Light* is like a

ghost ship. Everything, aboard is in order. Item:—'
Cranston scratched his head. 'What else, Brother?'

'According to Crawley no one approached the ship,
but the Fisher of Men has now told us that signals
were passed to the ship from someone on the quayside.
By whom and to whom, however, is a mystery.'

'We also know,' Cranston added, 'that the strange
creature Bernicia came down to the quayside at
around midnight. He, or she, distinctly remembers the
first mate being very much alive and was conscious of
someone lurking in the shadows. Item:' Cranston
continued, wiping his mouth, 'contrary to what we
were told, a boat did approach the ship, not from the
shore, but from Crawley's vessel. We also know the
good admiral deeply resented Roffel and had a grudge
against him. What else, Brother?'

'Well,' Athelstan replied, scratching his head, 'the
next morning, the captain's business partner and
backer, Sir Henry Ospring, who had arrived in London
to have words with Roffel, is killed by his own
daughter in his chamber at the Abbot of Hyde inn.
Meanwhile,' Athelstan concluded, 'Roffel's poisoned
corpse is plucked from its coffin and left sprawling in
the sanctuary chair of St Mary Magdalene.'

'Hell's tits!' Cranston leaned his elbows on the table.
'We have discovered a few lies, Brother, but not a
shred of evidence of who's the main mover behind all
this.'

'It might be Crawley,' Athelstan replied. 'He had
both the motive and the opportunity to approach the
ship. Or what about Ospring? Where was our good
merchant the night these strange events occurred?'
The friar sighed. 'We understand all the officers were

ashore, roistering and enjoying themselves, yet they could be lying. One or more might have stayed on board or returned later.' Athelstan flung his quill down. 'Yet, there again, no one saw any boat approach the ship from the quayside. If one did, it would have been challenged and how could three fit, strong sailors have been so quietly killed? Bernicia could be lying, she may have had a hand in this business. Finally, Mistress Roffel, though she disliked her husband, was, according to Father Stephen, praying over her husband's corpse at St Mary Magdalene church.' Athelstan wearily rubbed his eyes. 'As you say, hell's teeth, Sir John. I can't see any of the women boarding a ship at night, despatching the crew and leaving without being seen.'

Cranston drained his tankard. 'And this brings us no nearer to the mystery of who murdered Captain Roffel, how and why.' He ran his finger around the rim of the tankard. 'Have you thought that those two lovebirds in your church, Aveline and Nicholas Ashby, might be involved in this?'

Athelstan laughed. 'In God's name, Sir John, anybody and everybody could have been.' He looked down at what he had written. 'We have a number of mysteries to solve. How was Roffel poisoned? What went on during that last voyage? And what happened the first night the *God's Bright Light* rode at anchor opposite Queen's hithe? So far we have no clue, not a shred of evidence or a loose thread, except one. Our beloved admiral, Sir Jacob Crawley, he needs to be questioned again.'

'Sir John, I have finished my ale,' Leif shouted from the far corner of the taproom.

Sir John looked over his shoulder to where the beggar, crouched on a stool, sat waving across at him.

'I'd better go, Brother. Lady Maude awaits. Do you wish to join me?'

Athelstan shook his head. He rolled his parchment up and put that and his writing implements back in the leather bag.

'No, Sir John, I'd best go back.' His face brightened. 'Benedicta returns soon and I have a few questions to ask Master Ashby. I am also worried about Marston hanging around the church. We still have that problem to solve, Sir John.'

Cranston got to his feet, turning his beaver-skin hat in his hands. 'Aye,' he muttered, 'and Shawditch will be hammering on my door about that bloody footpad. You'll be safe going back, Brother?'

Athelstan stood up. 'Who,' he asked with great solemnity, 'would dare touch the secretarius of the coroner of the city of London?'

Sir John grinned and moved away.

'And don't forget, Sir John,' Athelstan called out, ignoring the surprised looks from the other customers, 'you promised to play the role of Satan in our play!'

'Don't worry!' Cranston bawled back, 'even the Lord Beelzebub will seethe with envy when he sees me dressed in all my regalia!'

Cranston swept out, Leif hopping and chattering like a squirrel behind him.

Athelstan sighed, collected his horse from the stables and rode through the silent, darkened Cheapside. He let his old horse find its own way as he half-dozed, his mind flitting back over the events of the day. All around him were the sounds of the night – shouts and songs from the taverns, a child crying from a high window, dogs barking. Cats slunk in and out of the shadows as they patrolled the sewers, ever vigilant for the mice and rats that foraged there. Athelstan crossed himself and softly intoned into the darkness *'Veni Sancte Spiritus* – Come, Holy Spirit, and send out from heaven the beam of your light.'

He reached London Bridge, showed the warrant Cranston had given him and the night watch let him by. Half-way across he stopped; peering through the huddled buildings he glimpsed the Thames. The night mist shifted, revealing the fighting ships riding at anchor.

'Oh, Lord!' Athelstan prayed. 'Solve these mysteries, these terrible murders, these secrets of the seas!'

He recalled all the people he had met that day: Emma Roffel, the Fisher of Men, the poor hapless murdered maid, the scrutineers, enigmatic and dangerous.

'We are,' he muttered to himself, 'like sharp, unsheathed knives; every time we turn, we cut.'

He nudged Philomel forward, rode off the bridge and into the maze of Southwark's alleyways.

CHAPTER 8

As Athelstan arrived at St Erconwald's, others involved in the mystery surrounding the *God's Bright Light* began to act. The man sitting in a corner of a tavern at Queen's hithe stared out through the open window, watching the mist thickening over the river. He tried to curb the murderous fury seething hotly through his veins, pounding the blood in his head and heart. He touched the dagger in his belt.

'So far,' he muttered. 'So bloody far and yet so near!'

He took a deep breath, closed his eyes and leaned back. He remembered Roffel walking the deck, the wind billowing the great sail, the ship cutting the waves like a knife through cream, bearing down on that fishing smack. Its crew never stood a chance! Roffel himself led the boarding party, closing his ears to the screams for mercy, particularly those from the English. And then, later, in the captain's cabin...

The man opened his eyes and leaned forward. Everything was set to go well, and then Roffel had sickened so mysteriously and died. Now all was lost. The man looked down at the piece of parchment that had been slipped into his hand while he had been drinking in Vintry. He read it again.

'The bloody bitch!' he swore.

He tossed the parchment into the fire, rose and walked out of the tavern.

In another part of the city Bernicia was getting herself ready for the evening. She sat in front of the polished metal disc that served her as a mirror and smiled at her reflection.

'He, she,' Bernicia muttered to herself.

She would drop all pretence, after all her secret was safe with Cranston. Bernicia saw herself as a woman; she thought like one, felt like one. Bernicia looked down at the cheap rings on her fingers. She was glad Roffel was dead! No more hacked limbs, no more bloody tributes, No more cruelty! Bernicia was determined to start life afresh. She finished her toilette, grabbed her fur-lined cape and hood, doused the candles and slipped into the shadowy street, locking the door behind her. She did not have to travel far and soon arrived at a small alehouse on the corner of Pigsnout Alley – a shoddy, dingy drinking-hole where men sat on rickety stools and battered beer barrels served as tables. Bernicia approached the prosperous-looking landlord, dressed in leather jerkin, brown woollen hose and a spotless white apron. She could tell by his face that he recognised her, but the ritual was always the same.

'Mistress, what will you have?'

'A cup of wine.'

'Red or white?'

'I would like both.'

'In particular, what?'

Bernicia remembered the password for the week. 'They say that the juice of Bastogne is fresh.'

144

The man waved her through the small scullery, across a cobbled courtyard into what looked like an outhouse. It served as a small store for tables and sacks of grain. Sheaves of yellow hay and straw thickly carpeted the floor. The landlord pushed a small handcart aside, cleared the straw with his boot and revealed a trapdoor. He tugged it open – it made hardly any sound. Bernicia smiled as she saw the light flow out, heard the chatter of gentle conversation, the thrumming of a viol and muted laughter. Clawing at her sarcanet skirt she went gingerly down the steps. The chamber beneath was vast, a great underground storeroom, its walls and pillars scrubbed clean and painted white. Sconces had been placed neatly around the room to provide light as well as some heat. Standing in the shadows at the foot of the stairs, Bernicia looked with kohl-darkened eyes at the scene. She recognised some of the customers; they were creatures like herself, living a secret life amongst those – clerks, merchants, even the occasional noble-man – whose lusts they served. Each table, with its two chairs, was carefully positioned to afford the greatest intimacy and privacy, the customers could enjoy themselves, yet carefully watch who left and entered, whether by the steps or through the secret passageways at the far end of the room. The air was sweet; the candles and braziers were scented and their fragrance mingled with the cloying perfumes with which some of the customers washed their bodies. Nevertheless, Bernicia could sense the undercurrent of excitement, even danger. Everyone was watchful, on guard against a traitor, an informant. If the officers of the crown raided such a place, the offenders would either be sent to the scaffold or, worse, to the stake at Smithfield.

A pageboy, dressed in very tight hose and an open-necked linen shirt, tiptoed up, hips swaying.

'A table, mistress?'

Bernicia smiled and kissed the boy on both cheeks.

'Of course.'

The pageboy minced away, leading Bernicia to a table wedged between two pillars. He placed a small, hooded candle there and, at Bernicia's request, brought a jug of chilled white wine and two cups.

'Captain Roffel will not be coming?' the pageboy asked.

'I doubt it,' Bernicia sneered. 'Not unless he can climb out of his coffin.'

The boy made a girlish moue with his mouth and walked away. Bernicia poured herself a cup of wine and sat waiting. Perhaps tonight she would be fortunate enough to find a new patron, someone who would appreciate a courtesan's skills. Bernicia jumped as a cowled and hooded figure appeared beside her.

'Bernicia, so lovely to see you here.'

The man, not waiting for an invitation, sat down on the chair opposite. Like many other customers he refused to pull his hood back but Bernicia caught the gleam of his eyes in a hard, sunburnt face. She looked at the stranger's hands, weather-beaten but clean, the nails sharply cut. Bernicia smiled to herself. A sailor, she thought, perhaps a captain like Roffel? Bernicia moved her chair and leaned closer.

'You wish some wine?'

The stranger put a silver piece down on the table. Bernicia's eyes widened and she hastened to fill the unexpected guest's cup.

'Who are you?' she asked.

'We had a common acquaintance,' the stranger replied.

'Who?'

'Captain William Roffel, one-time master of the *God's Bright Light*. The bastard now lies mouldering in his grave in the cemetery of St Mary Magdalene. You were his doxy?'

'I was his friend,' Bernicia corrected peevishly.

'Well, I want you to be my friend,' the man said. 'Take this silver piece as a surety of my friendship.'

The silver coin disappeared. Bernicia did not object as the stranger's hand slipped beneath the table and began to fondle her leg.

'How did you know Captain Roffel?'

Bernicia looked round and saw the pageboy standing there.

'Go away!' Bernicia pouted. 'Go and get some more white wine and a plate of doucettes for my friend.'

Bernicia waited until the pageboy had swaggered out of earshot.

'Well? Who are you?'

'I once served with Roffel on the *God's Bright Light*.'

Bernicia hid her face behind her fingers and giggled.

'What's so amusing?'

'Are you one of the watch?'

The stranger laughed softly. 'Perhaps. A man who's supposed to be dead poses no danger to anyone, particularly if he has a fortune in silver.'

Bernicia licked carmine-painted lips, leaned forward and touched the man gently on the cheek.

'Did you like Roffel?' the whore simpered.

'He was a bastard,' the stranger replied, 'who received his just deserts. As I have mine. Did you know any of his crew?'

Bernicia shook her head. 'Captain Roffel always kept me well away from what he termed his calling. However,' she added petulantly, 'some of his men knew of my existence.' Bernicia snuggled a little closer. 'I think I've seen you before. Aren't you Bracklebury the first mate?'

The sailor laughed. 'What does it matter? I think you'll see more of me, whoever I am!'

'How much more?' Bernicia teased.

The pageboy brought a fresh jug of wine and the evening wore on. Eventually Bernicia and her newfound patron left.

'Come,' Bernicia whispered as they hurried along the alleyways. 'Be my guest tonight.'

They reached Bernicia's house and the young whore led her guest into the solar where Athelstan and Cranston had sat. The fire was built up, candles lit and wine served. The sailor took off his cloak and hood and sat basking in the warmth whilst Bernicia studied him discreetly, noting the good, high-heeled boots, leather jacket and white cambric shirt open at the neck. She touched her own belt where the silver piece was hidden and smiled secretively.

'How much did Roffel tell you?' the sailor asked abruptly.

Bernicia just laughed. The man leaned forward, his eyes hard.

'About his last voyage and the silver?'

Bernicia blinked and looked coyly at the sailor.

'I don't betray secrets,' the whore whispered. 'Roffel is dead. He and his silver can go to hell. Come on! I will not discuss it. Some more wine?'

Bernicia rose, took the sailor's wine cup and went across to the small table to fill it. Bernicia was smiling, but turned in alarm at the sound of a footfall. The sailor was striding across the room, his dagger drawn. Bernicia screamed and ran to the door. The sailor caught the whore by the hair – and cursed as the wig came off. Bernicia reached the latch, sobbing and moaning; the whore tried to raise it, but her head was yanked back and the knife gouged her soft throat from ear to ear.

Athelstan, refreshed after a good night's sleep, had a larger than usual congregation at morning Mass. Ashby, who had been fast asleep on Athelstan's return the night before, again helped Crim to serve. Shaved and washed, he looked more presentable. He had kept himself busy the previous day, helping the parishioners move the great cart into one of the transepts and, from the sanctuary steps, issuing directions about the erection of the great canvas backdrop.

Athelstan smiled to himself as he pronounced the final words of the Mass, *Ite, Missa est* – Go, you are dismissed. He bowed, kissed the altar and quickly looked around at the group huddled inside the rood screen. Aveline was there, her face half-hidden behind a veil. She sat on a stool in the corner of the sanctuary, her eyes never leaving her beloved. Watkin the dung-collector crouched, glaring at Pike the ditcher.

Athelstan groaned – their animosity had spread to their respective spouses, who also sat glaring narrow-eyed at each other. Huddle the painter leaned back on his heels, dreamily staring up at his ceiling. Mugwort, the demented hunch-backed bell clerk, fidgeted furiously, impatient to run down the nave and ring the bell as a sign Mass was over. Ursula the pig-woman was also there, her great pet sow sprawled out beside her. Athelstan tightened his lips – the animal had snored vigorously during his short sermon. Next to Ursula was Pernell the Fleming; she had tried to dye her hair and now it hung like black and orange flax, looking all the more hideous against the white paint on her face.

Athelstan hid his disappointment. He had been distracted during Mass by the thought that Benedicta might come. He missed the widow with her smooth, olive skin, lovely eyes and jet-black hair. He often told her what he and Cranston were involved in, seeking her advice. Benedicta had a shrewd mind, acerbic wit and a sardonic sense of humour which proved to be an asset in placating the different factions amongst the parish council.

Athelstan sighed and swept into the sacristy. Crim helped him to divest whilst the parishioners sped like arrows across to the great cart and carried on with their usual debate about who should be doing what, when, where and how. Athelstan returned to help Crim clear the altar, of book, bell and cruets, noticing how the Lady Aveline and Master Ashby were deep in conversation. He offered them breakfast but they politely refused, Ashby pointing to the pannier of provisions Lady Aveline had brought with her.

Athelstan saw his parishioners were locked in verbal battle so he slipped out of the church and walked across to check on Philomel. Then he went into the priest's house.

He stared around in astonishment. The kitchen had been swept, fresh rushes laid and the fire built up. A bowl of steaming oat porridge, a horn spoon beside it, together with a trancher of bread, butter and cheese and a mug of ale, stood on the table. Athelstan heard a sound from the buttery and grinned as Benedicta came out.

'Lady, I thought you hadn't returned.'

Athelstan grasped the widow's warm hands and kissed her gently on the cheek. Benedicta blushed and stepped back, though her eyes danced with merriment.

'I thought I'd surprise you, Father. Well, do you like it?' She gestured around the kitchen, her face mock-serious. 'The fire was ash, the rushes hadn't been changed, the table hadn't been washed and I don't think you have bean eating properly.'

'I've been with Jack Cranston,' Athelstan muttered.

However, before he could describe what had happened, Benedicta gently ushered him across the kitchen, telling him to eat before the sweetened oatmeal lost its warmth. Athelstan did, trying to hide his real pleasure at seeing his friend again. Bonaventure, who had been out hunting and courting the previous evening, slid through the open window to mew plaintively for his pitcher of milk. He lapped this greedily and stretched out before the roaring fire as Benedicta described her visit and journey. She then patiently sat and listened as Athelstan described the mysteries surrounding the *God's Bright Light*, the death of William Roffel and the murder of Sir Henry Ospring.

'A puzzle,' Benedicta commented. 'I met the lady Aveline last night. She was with Ashby. I also told that paid thug, Marston, to leave the church. Aveline's no murderer,' she continued, 'but how can you prove that the slaying of her stepfather was in self-defence? As for the other business – as Sir John would say, "hell's teeth, plot and counter-plot".' She leaned her arms on the table. 'But there's worse to come,' she added darkly.

Athelstan put his spoon down and looked at her.

'What?'

Benedicta hid her smile. 'You know the row between Watkin and Pike the ditcher?'

Athelstan nodded wearily.

'Well, Watkin's spouse is now saying that the wife of God the Father is also superior to the wife of God the Holy Ghost.'

Athelstan hid his face in his hands.

'Never,' he swore, 'never again will I allow a mystery play in this parish!' He looked up at a knock on the door. 'Come in!' he called.

Aveline entered and smiled shyly at Benedicta. Athelstan got to his feet.

'My lady, what is it?'

'Father, last night I went through Sir Henry's papers and—'

Athelstan ushered her to a seat.

'—I found this.'

She handed across a piece of parchment, greasy and thumb-marked. Athelstan smoothed it out on the table top. There were marks on it – two lines running parallel with crosses around them. Athelstan stared at it.

'My lady, what's so special about this?'

'I don't know, Father. In itself it might mean little, but I found it concealed in my stepfather's strong box. The coffer had a false bottom. When I lifted that up, I found the drawing there.'

Athelstan stared at the parchment.

'Why,' he asked, 'should Sir Henry hide such an apparently innocuous scrap unless it was really something very precious or dangerous?' He drummed his fingers on the table top. 'I have seen this before,' he said. 'At the back of Captain Roffel's book of hours. The same drawings, the same cross marks.'

'May I have a look?' Benedicta asked.

Athelstan passed his parchment to her. Benedicta stared at it for a long time, then she looked up and smiled at Aveline.

'My husband, God rest him, was a sea captain. Athelstan, have you considered that these lines are from a map? This top one is the coast of France or, more precisely, a stretch of coast going down from Calais – she pointed to one of the crosses – to the port of Dieppe. This bottom line is the coast of England. The crosses between the lines could be ships.'

Athelstan curbed his excitement. 'For the first time,' he whispered, 'this is beginning to make sense.' He stared at Aveline. 'My lady, your stepfather was a landowner and a merchant. And what else?'

Aveline pulled a face. 'He was a commissioner of array, responsible for raising troops in the shire should the French invade.'

'What else did he do?'

'He loaned money to the exchequer.'

'Oh, come on, Aveline, what else?'

The young woman licked her lips nervously. 'At night visitors called at our manor house. Men, cowled and hooded, who came and went silently as shadows. I think they were spies. Sometimes my stepfather used to help them cross to France, not through Calais but different ports, those held by the French.'

'How do you know this?'

'My stepfather always met them at night. Sometimes I would come downstairs and go by his chamber. The men would be seated there. Always with their backs to the doors. Letters would be exchanged. Sometimes I heard the chink of coins.' She shook her head. 'I know so little. My stepfather always kept such business to himself. He had powerful friends at court and they returned his work with favours.'

Athelstan sat with his head in his hands staring into the fire.

'Was Ashby ever there?'

'Never.'

'But who would know all this besides your stepfather?'

Aveline smiled. 'Marston might. Sometimes he took these people down to the coast.'

'May I keep this map?' Athelstan asked.

Aveline nodded and opened her mouth to speak.

The friar held a hand up. 'Before you say anything, Lady Aveline, I have not forgotten you or Master Ashby.'

Aveline smiled, got to her feet and left.

Athelstan continued to gaze into the fire.

154

'What do you think, Brother?' Benedicta asked.

'My view is that Sir Henry Ospring was a very powerful nobleman with far too many fingers in far too many pies. Now we know that Roffel stopped and sank a fishing smack sailing between Dieppe and Calais. We also know that young Ashby gave Roffel a sealed package. Now, I suspect, that package contained a copy of this map as well as instructions about where and when to intercept the fishing smack. However, in the natural order of things there's nothing wrong with that. Ospring could have heard some gossip about precious cargo.' He tapped the crudely drawn map. 'Nevertheless, in this case the vessel was carrying important despatches as well as English spies.' Athelstan got to his feet and went to warm his fingers at the fire. 'My first urge is to challenge Marston, to discover if he knows anything but that may alarm people. Benedicta.' He looked over his shoulder and smiled. 'Will you do me a favour?'

'Whatever you ask, Father.'

'Forget the disputes between Pike and Watkin. I want you to take a short message and place it in the iron-bound coffer before the statue of Our Lady and Child in St Paul's cathedral.' His smile widened at the look of puzzlement on Benedicta's face.

'Just a simple message. Write "Saints Peter and Paul, intercede for us". Sign it, "Brother Athelstan". Don't worry,' he added drily, 'the blessed apostles won't intervene but two gentlemen from the exchequer will be very pleased to renew their acquaintance with me.'

He went across and took his cloak from a peg on the wall.

'But now I must see to some building work.'

Leaving a bemused Benedicta, Athelstan went round the house to saddle the protesting Philomel. A few minutes later he was making his way through Southwark's narrow alleyways. He glimpsed Marston and the other bully-boys standing at the door of a tavern, their vantage point from which to see who entered and left the church. Athelstan sketched a blessing in their direction and smiled to himself. If his suspicions proved correct, he'd give Marston something to worry about apart from poor Ashby.

The day was cold but bright; a heavy hoar frost had frozen the puddles and ruts. Philomel, whom Athelstan considered to be the most cunning horse on earth, deftly made his way around these and past the stalls and booths. At last Athelstan reached a place where builders were erecting a three-storey house, commissioned by some merchant who wished to be free of the tolls, levies and taxes imposed on houses across the river. Athelstan watched swearing and cursing men, their breath heavy on the frosty morning air, carry bricks up makeshift ladders. Carpenters sawed wood and apprentices jumped around like monkeys. Athelstan loved to watch the builders at work and, when they shouted out greetings, he waved his hand in acknowledgement. He paid particular attention to the tiler busy on the roof, admiring his skill and confidence. Then, turning his horse, he made his way back in the direction of London Bridge. As he passed his church, Crim the altar boy came flying out.

'Father! Father!'

Athelstan reined Philomel in. Anxious lest Marston and his thugs might have attempted some mischief, he looked towards the church, but all seemed quiet.

'Crim, what is it?'

'Father,' the boy stuttered. 'It's Lord Horsecruncher!'

'You mean Sir John Cranston, coroner of the city?'

'Aye, Father, old fat arse!'

'Crim!'

'Sorry, Father, but he sent a messenger across. You know, Father, the one with a tight bum who walks like a duck, his face pulled down as if he had smelt something rotten.'

'And what did this messenger say?' asked Athelstan patiently.

'Well, Sir John wishes to see you urgently in Cheapside. The lady Benedicta has left already,' Crim continued breathlessly. 'She said she would call in and tell Sir John you are already on your way.'

Athelstan tossed the lad a coin and continued his journey. For the first time in weeks he made Philomel trot and scarcely bothered to acknowledge the greetings and salutations shouted out to him. Clattering on to the bridge, he looked neither to left nor right as he wondered why Sir John so impatiently demanded his presence. As a courtesy, he called at the coroner's house in Cheapside, but a tight-lipped Lady Maude told him that 'the bird has already flown'.

'Gone to his chamber in the Guildhall, or so he says,' she announced darkly. 'And you know where that is, Father?'

Athelstan tactfully smiled back. Once the door was closed, he led a snorting, snickering Philomel, still protesting at his recent rough usage, across the busy marketplace. He gave the reins to an ostler and went in to the Holy Lamb of God's taproom. Sir John was already sitting there, two great empty wine cups before him as well as a few crumbs of a meat pie.

'Good morrow, Sir John.'

Cranston burped gently.

'In fine fettle as usual, I see,' Athelstan continued, joining him.

'There's been another bloody murder,' Cranston announced. 'Do you remember Bernicia, Roffel's little tart? Well, he or she is dead! Throat slashed from ear to ear and the house ransacked.' Cranston slapped the table top with his hand. 'God knows whether to call him him or her. Anyway, Bernicia's dead.'

'Bernicia lived in the shadows,' Athelstan replied.

'I couldn't give a toss where the creature lived,' Cranston snapped. 'God rest the poor bastard! But, listen to this, Brother.' He eased his bulk on the chair. 'There's not many places in London where people like Bernicia can go! Four or five drinking-holes in all and all within walking distance of each other.' Cranston stopped and paused to roar for another drink. 'Usually, I leave such places alone. I have a pity for the poor people who use them. However, this morning I went as soon as I had seen Bernicia's corpse. After the expected protests, the silver-tongued landlord produced a page-boy who swore to a number of facts. First, Bernicia had been there the previous evening. Secondly, the whore had met and left with someone.'

'And?' Athelstan asked.

'According to the boy, this stranger might have been Bracklebury. Anyway, he was a sailor who knew Roffel and the ship *God's Bright Light*.'

Athelstan leaned back and whistled through his teeth.

'Strange,' he whispered. 'Mistaken logic, Sir John. I

always considered all the watch were either dead or had fled.'

'If it was someone from the watch,' Cranston continued, 'we have to draw another picture – and one so simple it's a wonder we never thought of it before. The first mate killed his two companions and then jumped ship. Why, or with what, we don't know.'

'I think we do,' Athelstan replied.

He produced the crudely drawn map that Aveline had given him that morning and tersely told Cranston of his own conclusions.

Cranston sipped from the cup the landlord had placed before him. 'So Ospring gave instructions to Roffel to stop and sink that fishing smack. But why? Are you saying that Ospring and Roffel were traitors?'

'It all depends,' Athelstan answered, 'on what the ship carried. To find that out I have sent Benedicta with a petition to St Paul's. Only our friends the scrutineers can tell us that.'

'There are others we need to question,' Cranston added. 'That's why I have invited everyone involved in this business – Sir Jacob Crawley, the other officers, not to mention Mistress Roffel – to meet us in the Guildhall just after midday. I also told the ship's clerk, Coffrey, to bring the log book.' Cranston smacked his lips and stretched. 'So, Father, we have some time to waste. What more can we do?'

Athelstan gazed despairingly at the empty wine cups.

'There is one further thing, Sir John, the footpad who is house-breaking. I think we can set a trap.'

Cranston slammed his wine cup down.

'No, don't ask me how!' Athelstan smiled. 'I know

you, Sir John – you have a generous heart but a wagging tongue. What I want is for one of your powerful merchant friends to go on a journey for two or three days, to take his family with him and to make sure it's publicly announced.'

Cranston stared up at the rafters. 'There's no one,' he said. 'Oh yes, my dear physician Theobald de Troyes. He could go to some property he owns in Suffolk. Perhaps I can persuade him?'

'Do so now,' Athelstan urged, hoping to put as much distance as possible between Cranston and a cup of wine. 'But tell him not to leave for two or three days.'

'And if he doesn't agree?' Cranston asked.

Athelstan shrugged. 'Then we'll have to find someone else.'

Mumbling and protesting, Cranston lumbered out of the tavern. Athelstan sighed, sat back, closed his eyes and wondered if Benedicta had delivered the message.

'Father, do you wish something to eat or drink?'

Athelstan sat forward and stared into the anxious face of the landlord's wife.

'No, thank you.' He smiled. 'I think Sir John has done gallantly for both of us.'

The friar felt self-conscious sitting there by himself so he walked back into Cheapside and into the church of St Mary Le Bow. For a while he knelt before the altar and said a few prayers, then he admired the beautiful stained-glass window in the nave. Athelstan could never stop admiring the brilliant colours and skills of the artist. Portraying the risen, glorified Christ, harrowing hell and freeing souls who had waited for his coming, he had expertly caught the rapture on the faces of the saints and the anger on the black-visaged demons, who stood glaring from behind their wall of fire. Cranston had promised that, as soon as the good weather allowed, he would purchase a similar window for St Erconwald's.

The church bell began to toll on the hour so Athelstan walked slowly back to the tavern. He had hoped to find Sir John. Instead, the two scrutineers sat smiling in unison, almost as if they had been sitting there since the previous evening.

'We received your request, Brother Athelstan.'

'I wish all my prayers were answered so swiftly,' the friar replied.

'And where is that excellent coroner?'

'Involved in other business.'

'And what, my dear priest, do you have to tell us?'

Athelstan again repeated the conclusions he had drawn after his conversation with Lady Aveline and showed both scrutineers the crudely drawn map. The smiles on their faces faded.

'Very clever,' Peter, the taller one, replied. 'Very clever indeed. So, Brother, you think that Sir Henry told Roffel about the ship and our pirate captain sank it?'

'In a word, yes. What puzzled Sir John and me is why?'

'Well, that's simple enough,' the scrutineer replied. 'Sir Henry may not have been a traitor, but he was certainly a thief and a murderer. You see, Brother, we thought the ship had been sunk because of our agents and the despatches they carried. Now, I confess, it was sunk because of the belt of silver one of our agents wore.' The scrutineer waved Athelstan closer. 'Let me explain. You know the treasury is empty. We therefore take loans at a high rate of interest from men like Sir Henry. We thought he could be trusted. He often landed agents in France. A week before Roffel sailed, we sent one of our agents, a young clerk, to Sir Henry, who provided him with warrants and papers and also gave him a large leather belt with a veritable fortune stitched in the secret pockets within it. Our agent and a companion were to go to Calais and then, on an appointed day, sail from there to Dieppe. That bastard Ospring—' The scrutineer paused to draw in his breath. 'I am sorry,' he muttered. 'I am losing my temper.'

'You can't do that,' the other one replied.

'No, no, I shouldn't, but it's apparent that Sir Henry Ospring lent the treasury that silver and saw to the despatch of the agent. He then informed his piratical friend Roffel when the man would sail from our garrison in Calais to Dieppe.'

'Clever, subtle trickery,' Paul the scrutineer interrupted. 'Sir Henry lends his money at a high interest. The treasury is forced to repay it whilst Sir Henry steals back the original amount.'

'Roffel and Ospring deserved to die,' his companion declared. 'Thieves, murderers, Ospring particularly. He met our young agent and, even as he gave him the silver, was planning his death. Believe me, friar, whoever killed Sir Henry Ospring deserves a pardon.' He caught the smile on Athelstan's face. 'Does that amuse you, Brother?'

'No, sir, it does not. But many a true word is spoken in jest. Sir John and I may return to you on that matter.'

'What is important,' Peter remarked, 'is to discover if Roffel had any accomplices and to get that silver back.'

The two scrutineers got to their feet.

'We entrust everything to your capable hands, Brother Athelstan,' the taller one announced. 'When the game is over and the full truth is known, come back to us.'

CHAPTER 9

Sir John and Brother Athelstan sat at the head of a dusty table in a shabby room on the top floor of the Guildhall. Both stared at their truculent-faced guests. Emma Roffel, pale and anxious, looked eager to be away; Tabitha her maid crouched next to her like some frightened lap dog. At the far end of the room, Sir Jacob Crawley refused to meet their eyes but drummed his fingers on the table top, lost in his own thoughts. The men from the *God's Bright Light* – Philip Cabe, Dido Coffrey, Vincent Minter and the master-at-arms Tostig Peverill – looked ill at ease. They had protested at being so peremptorily summoned, only to be roared into silence by Cranston who, to Athelstan's despair, was now taking generous swigs from his wineskin. The coroner pushed the stopper back and beamed falsely around.

'Everything we've been told is a pack of lies,' he began sweetly. 'Except that Captain William Roffel, God assoil him, was a pirate and a thief as well as a murderer.'

Emma Roffel made to protest but she closed her mouth and sat smiling wanly to herself.

'I object to this,' Cabe said. 'Roffel can go to hell and

probably has, but that's no reason to insult us, Sir John.'

Cranston clicked his fingers at Coffrey, the ship's clerk.

'You brought the log book?'

'Sir John,' the man whined, 'you looked at that when you first visited us.'

'Well, I want to look at it again. I also have questions to ask all of you.'

Coffrey pushed the calfskin-bound book down towards him. Cranston, half-watching the admiral from beneath bushy eyebrows, opened the book and leafed through the water-stained parchment. The entries were innocuous enough – they gave the ship's daily position, recorded the booty taken and noted the occasional alarum or occurrence on board. Cranston closed the book, keeping his podgy finger as a marker, and stared at Sir Jacob.

'Captain Roffel was under your command?'

'In theory, yes,' the admiral replied. 'But his orders were quite explicit. He was to sail the Narrow Seas, attack enemy shipping and give assistance to any English ship in need of it. But he was free to seek out and take any prizes he could.'

Cranston smiled. 'In which case, why is there no mention here of a fishing smack, ostensibly French, taken outside Calais? The vessel was destroyed and its crew killed. I believe it was sailing to Dieppe.'

'Roffel took many ships,' Coffrey whined.

'Yes,' Cranston said. 'But aren't you supposed to enter them in the log? Why miss this one out?'

'It was only a fishing smack,' Cabe said. 'Nothing

more than a floating log with a ragged sail.'

Cranston, bristling with rage, glared down the table at him.

'You are a bloody liar!' he roared. 'There were men aboard that ship and they weren't French. Or, at least, not all of them.'

'These are treasonable matters,' Athelstan pointed out softly. 'If we do not get the truth, we can only draw the conclusion that you were accomplices in Roffel's nefarious activities.'

Emma Roffel made to rise.

'This is none of my business,' she declared, clutching at the hem of her cloak. 'Sir John, I beg you, I have been through enough.'

'My lady,' Athelstan answered tactfully, 'this concerns you very much. Don't you want to know who murdered your husband?' He smiled and Emma Roffel sat down.

'It's true,' Tostig Peverill spoke up, 'that we took a fishing smack outside Calais.' He blinked and rubbed his eyes. 'Calais is in English hands but we thought it was a French ship – sometimes they do hop between the coastal towns.' He pointed to the log book. 'On reflection, however, it was obvious that Roffel was waiting for it. You see, we were fighting a head wind, a blustery north-westerly, and we should have run before it. Roffel, however, insisted we kept into the headland, keeping the coast of France just over the horizon. On the day we took that fishing smack we let bigger craft sail by. When that one appeared, Roffel ran it down.' Peverill looked around at his companions. 'Come on,' he coaxed. 'We all thought it was suspicious. Although it was only a fishing smack, once we were alongside, Roffel ordered my archers to loose as if it was some bloody war cog. He then led the boarding party himself.'

'How many crew did it have?' Athelstan asked.

'No more than six or seven,' Peverill replied. 'By the time we reached the deck they were all either wounded or dead. Roffel was like a raging bull and headed straight for the cabin.' The master-at-arms paused.

'Then what?' Cranston asked.

'None of the rest of us went on board that ship,' Cabe interrupted. 'Only Peverill, the captain and fifteen archers.'

'But something happened?' Athelstan insisted. 'Master Peverill?'

Peverill closed his eyes before continuing. 'As I said, the crew were either wounded or dead. I thought they were Frenchmen – but as I turned one over he cursed me in English. Then I heard Roffel talking to someone in the cabin. I am sure the other voice was English. There was a scream and Roffel came out, grinning from ear to ear, carrying a bundle of papers, possibly the ship's log and manifesto. We took a tun of wine we found below. Roffel ordered the smack to be burnt. He tossed the papers he'd taken into the fire and we sailed on.'

'Is that all?' Athelstan asked.

Peverill spread his hands. 'What more should there be, Father? Oh, I confess, looking back, there was something suspicious going on, but Roffel was a cunning, ruthless bastard, a law unto himself.'

'The crew were French,' Athelstan mused, 'but Englishmen was on board. So it must have been from our garrison at Calais.'

'Yes, yes,' Coffrey conceded, looking sheepishly around, 'Roffel was not a man to care about such niceties.'

'And how—?' Athelstan broke off as Cranston leaned back in his chair and gave a loud snore. Athelstan gazed in bewilderment at his fat friend, then blushed as he heard a snigger further down the table.

'The fellow's drunk!' Cabe whispered.

'Sir John is not drunk!' Athelstan snapped. 'But tired, exhausted after his labours. So, I ask my question of you, Master Cabe, and I'll ask it more bluntly, do you know if more was taken from that vessel than a tun of wine and some papers?'

Cabe shook his head.

'You are sure?'

Cabe raised his right hand. 'I will take my oath upon it. As Peverill said, the whole business was suspicious. Roffel seemed as pleased as a pig in shit though the devil knows why.'

'Who here,' Athelstan asked, 'would have access to Roffel's cabin? Or, to put it more bluntly, who had the opportunity to put arsenic into the flask he carried?'

'Only Bracklebury,' Cabe replied. 'The captain was very jealous of his flask. When he wasn't carrying it he hid it away.' He smiled thinly. 'Perhaps we should ask Bracklebury?'

'Oh, I will.'

Cranston opened his eyes, smacking his lips.

'Bracklebury is now a hunted man, Master Cabe.' The coroner smiled at the astonishment on their faces. 'Oh, I forgot to tell you, last night Roffel's whore

169

Bernicia was brutally murdered in her house – or should I say his house? Anyway, the place was ransacked as if the murderer was looking for something. We believe that earlier in the evening Bernicia met a sailor, perhaps Hubert Bracklebury, at a secret drinking-place and that they left together.'

'Bracklebury's still alive?' Emma Roffel whispered.

At the end of the table Crawley stirred. 'But, Sir John, I thought he was either dead or had fled. Why jump ship and hide in London?'

'Perhaps you could help us there, Sir Jacob,' Cranston suggested, his face devoid of any compassion for his one-time friend.

'What do you mean?' Crawley stuttered.

'You claimed to have stayed aboard your own flagship, 'the *Holy Trinity*, the night Bracklebury disappeared.'

Crawley abruptly got to his feet. 'Sir John, Brother Athelstan, a word in private?'

Athelstan looked at Cranston, who shrugged.

'Perhaps outside,' Cranston murmured.

He and Athelstan rose and went out into the draughty corridor outside the room. Sir Jacob joined them, closing the door firmly behind him.

'I know what you are going to say,' Crawley stammered. 'But, Sir John, you must believe me. I have an honest tongue, but I refuse to be interrogated in front of my men.' He shuffled his feet. 'For God's sake, I have my honour. Perhaps you and Brother Athelstan will join me aboard ship for supper tonight?'

'If you serve good food,' Cranston replied, 'we'll come for that, as well as the truth. Now, come, I still have questions to ask the rest.'

They went back into the chamber where their forced guests sat in sullen silence. Athelstan could understand Emma Roffel's isolation but he sensed also that the seamen had a great deal to hide.

'We know,' Athelstan began, as Sir Jacob and Cranston took their seats, 'that something mysterious happened aboard the *God's Bright Light*. Peverill's story about the crew being frightened of ghosts may be accurate – Bracklebury wanted them off the ship for his own purposes. Using a lantern, he certainly sent signals to someone hiding on the quayside. And who could that have been?'

'This is monstrous!' Cabe blustered. 'Bracklebury was first mate! He ordered us off the ship and we went. Ask my companions. We spent the night roistering together. I'll be honest, we toasted Roffel's death. But none of us went back to that quayside.'

'Yes, yes, yes,' Cranston said testily. 'But the mystery remains, Master Cabe. I think Bracklebury stayed on board to look for something.'

'Such as what?' Vincent Minter, the ship's surgeon, who had sat tight-lipped throughout, now asserted himself. 'Such as what, Sir John? You apparently know something we don't, so why not tell us what it is, instead of trying to trap us?'

Cranston's white moustache and beard seemed to take on a life of their own. Athelstan placed his quill down and tapped the coroner gently on the wrist.

'Let me tell them,' he said. His glance swept around the table. 'We know, from another source, that Captain Roffel stole a great deal of silver from that fishing smack. This treasure had been sent by the exchequer to the king's agents in Calais, as bribes or as payment for spies working in French-held towns. Roffel knew it was being sent. That's why he attacked the vessel and killed its crew, including two of the crown's good servants.'

Athelstan studied his listeners' faces closely. He sensed that he was edging slowly towards the truth.

'Roffel was happy with his crime,' Athelstan continued. 'He took that silver aboard the *God's Bright Light* and hid it. We think that Bracklebury, after Roffel's death, was looking for it.' Athelstan picked up his quill and tapped it against the parchment. 'Now, I thought, given all these facts – and they are facts – that Bracklebury may have seized the silver and fled. But this seems not to be the case. Apparently Bracklebury found nothing and fled the ship, perhaps after killing his two shipmates. I think that he believed he had been tricked and his suspicion fell on the whore Bernicia, hence the murder and the ransacking of Bernicia's house.' Athelstan spread his hands and smiled. 'That may only be conjecture, but I am certain Roffel stole that silver.' He shrugged. 'After that come the questions. Who killed Roffel? Where is the silver now? Why did Bracklebury flee? Why did he kill Bernicia?' He stared down the table at Emma Roffel. 'Mistress Roffel, now you see why you were summoned here.'

The woman gazed disdainfully around at her late husband's shipmates. 'Brother Athelstan, I cannot help you. These matters are beyond my ken. My husband was secretive, if not sinister, in his dealings. For all I know he might well have wealth hidden all over the city.'

'Tell me.' Cranston leaned forward. 'Bracklebury brought your husband's corpse and his possessions to the house. Is that correct?'

She nodded.

'Did Bracklebury say anything to you?'

'No, he was rather silent, secretive and treated me with little respect. If Tabitha hadn't intervened, he would have left both my husband's corpse and his bag of possessions out in the street.' She lowered her head. 'Indeed, I saw him spit in the direction of the body.' She glowered at Cranston. 'Perhaps it was Bracklebury who broke into St Mary Magdalene church?'

Cranston leaned back in his chair. 'Muddy waters,' he murmured. 'And the more we stir, the more dirt rises to the surface.' He wagged a finger. 'But let me assure you of this. Bracklebury is hiding in the city. Somehow he believes he has been cheated.' He let his words hang like a noose in the air. 'I think,' he added softly, 'that Bracklebury may well kill again. Mistress Roffel, gentlemen, we are finished with you. Sir Jacob, Brother Athelstan and I will be your guests tonight.'

The coroner took another ostentatious swig from his wineskin to show his disdain for the seamen, all of whom he believed to be liars. He put the stopper back, not even bothering to look at Crawley, and never stirred until the door closed behind his reluctant guests.

'Well, what do you think, Brother?'

'A muddle of lies.' Athelstan got to his feet. 'We should accept Sir Jacob Crawley's invitation. Oh, Sir John, you've seen to the other business?'

'Yes.' Cranston tapped his belly. 'Tomorrow Theobald

de Troyes is taking a short journey into the country. He will leave his mansion in the care of his steward, servants and maids.'

'Good!' Athelstan bit his lip in annoyance. 'These lies and mysteries are beginning to vex me, Sir John. I suggest we go down to the harbour now. That mis-named ship the *God's Bright Light* holds the key to this mystery.'

'What do you suggest, Brother? That we go aboard and search Roffel's cabin?'

'Aye, and, if necessary, take it to pieces!'

'You mean the silver?'

'Yes, Sir John, I mean the silver.'

'But we know,' Cranston objected, 'that the cabin wasn't disturbed on the morning Bracklebury and the other two sailors were found to be missing.'

'No, Sir John, we were *told* that. Now we must act on the principle that everything we have been told is possibly a lie.'

They left the Guildhall. The skies had clouded over and a cold drizzle was beginning to fall. They walked down Bread Street, keeping a wary eye out for the water dripping from broken guttering as well as for patches of slippery mud underfoot. It was an uncomfortable journey across Trinity, through Vintry and along to the quayside. Surprisingly, they found the place a hive of activity. Boats, full of archers and men-at-arms, were going backwards and forwards to the ships anchored in mid-stream. From the *Holy Trinity*, Crawley's flagship, a trumpet could be heard. Cranston seized a captain of archers who stood yelling at his men as they clambered, hooded and cowled, down to the waiting barges.

'What's the matter, man? Why all the excitement?'

The officer turned. Athelstan glimpsed cropped hair, grey eyes and a hard-bitten, rain-soaked face. The man looked Cranston up and down.

'What business is it of yours, sir?'

'I am Jack Cranston, coroner of the city!'

The man forced a respectful smile. 'Then, Sir John, you will soon hear the news. French galleys have appeared in the mouth of the Thames. They have already taken one ship and burnt a village on Thanet.'

Cranston whistled through his teeth and stared out at the fighting cogs. Despite the rain, he could see that all the ships were preparing their armaments.

'Are the French a serious danger?' Athelstan asked.

Cranston did not reply. He stared out across the river. He remembered the low-slung, wolf-like enemy galleys. They could sneak into a small harbour or up a river – manned by the best French sailors and carrying mercenaries, they had brought terrible damage to the coastal towns of Rye and Winchelsea. Their crews had plundered and burned, and killed every inhabitant they could lay their hands on.

'How many galleys?' Cranston asked the captain.

'God knows, Sir John. Well over a dozen, under the command of Eustace the Monk.'

Athelstan closed his eyes and muttered a prayer. 'Oh Lord, Sir John,' he whispered, 'as if we didn't have enough trouble!'

Cranston nodded. Eustace the Monk, a French pirate captain, had been a Benedictine until he had fled his monastery and gone to sea. He had proved to be the great scourge of English shipping. Legend had it that English free companies in France had burnt his parents' farmhouse, killing all of Eustace's family. Now Eustace was sworn to wreak vengeance against the 'tail-wearing Goddamns'. Excommunicated by the Church, publicly condemned as a pirate, Eustace was secretly encouraged and supported by the French crown.

Athelstan peered through the drizzle. Although the ships were arming, there seemed little sign of them getting ready for sea.

'What will happen, Sir John?'

'Well—' Cranston paused to thank the captain of archers and walked to the quayside steps, watching another barge pull in. 'Our good admiral has two choices. He can sail down-river and fight, but he will be at a disadvantage – he won't be able to manoeuvre and the galleys may well slip by, land their soldiers along the East Watergate, or even here, wreak terrible damage and then escape.'

'Couldn't the Thames be blocked?' Athelstan asked.

Cranston grinned and shook his head. 'The danger is that our dear Eustace may wreak his damage and still fight his way past the blockade.'

'And what's the admiral's second choice?'

'To turn his ships into fighting castles and wait to see what happens. Crawley's a sensible commander, I think that's what he'll do. Then if Eustace penetrates further up the Thames he'll find our flotilla ready to receive him.'

Cranston took Athelstan by the arm and they went down the slippery steps to the water, shouldering their way past the archers.

'But we can't wait, Brother! The *God's Bright Light*

must be searched and I am not going to stand on idle ceremony.'

He almost tumbled into a waiting barge, manned by four oarsmen who teased Sir John about his weight. The coroner returned their good-natured abuse and ordered them to take him and Athelstan across to the *God's Bright Light*, telling the archers 'to piss off and wait for the next bloody barge!'

The barge pulled away, the oarsmen impervious to the driving rain; they fairly skimmed across the black, choppy waters of the Thames, swinging round with a bump against the side of *God's Bright Light*. Athelstan climbed the rope ladder first, trying to shut his ears against Cranston's roars of encouragement. He made his way slowly up until a pair of strong arms helped him over the side. Athelstan leaned against the rail, gasping his thanks to a sailor who grinned from ear to ear. Cranston landed beside him, as heavy as a great beer barrel, muttering curses and damning every sailor under the sun. Athelstan stared about. The ship had been cleaned and cleared since their last visit and was now thronged with sailors and archers scurrying about under the commands of their officers. Hooded braziers had been lit and two small catapults rigged on deck. A youngish, sandy-haired man came out of the cabin in the stern castle and walked towards them. He was dressed casually, in black hose pushed into sea boots and a bottle-green cloak covering a leather jacket. He challenged Sir John.

'Who are you? What are you doing here?'

'Sir John Cranston, city coroner, and Brother Athelstan. And who, sir, are you?'

'David Southchurch, recently appointed captain of

the *God's Bright Light.*' The young man stroked his moustache and beard. 'Sir John, I am a busy man. You have heard the news?'

'Aye, Master Southchurch, and you must have heard mine.'

The captain shrugged. 'Sir John, I wish to be helpful, but that is not my business. Roffel has gone, as have his first mate and two other sailors.'

'All we want' – Athelstan spoke quietly, feeling slightly sick as the deck heaved under him – 'is permission to search Roffel's, or rather your, cabin, Master Southchurch. It is important that we do that before the ship sails again.'

The young captain smiled. 'Of course,' he agreed immediately. 'You will find the cabin still empty – my belongings are not even aboard yet. Sir John, Brother Athelstan, be my guests.' He waved his hand and ushered them into the cabin, closing the door behind them.

The small chamber was swept and clean. Athelstan gazed despairingly about. Above them, they could hear the patter of feet and spate of officers' orders as the ship prepared itself for battle. Now and again the cabin lurched slightly as the choppy Thames caught and rocked the cog as it strained on its anchor. Athelstan slumped down on the small cot bed, clutching his stomach. Cranston grinned at him, took a generous swig from his wineskin, burped and sat down beside him.

'Not much one can hide in here,' he murmured. 'Come on, Brother, use your sea legs!'

Athelstan sighed, got up and moved around the cabin.

'If I were captain,' he whispered, half to himself, 'and I wanted to hide something bulky like a belt, what would I do?'

He looked around the small cabin, realising how insubstantial it was. There was nothing beneath the deck planking but the cavern of the hold – this wasn't a house, where secret tunnels could be dug. Nor were there thick walls within which cupboards might be concealed behind the wainscoting. 'I'm sorry,' he said. 'Sir John, we have wasted a journey. Bonaventure could not even hide a mouse in here. The cot's nothing, the table and stools are so simple. There is no real wall, ceiling or floor.'

A loud snore answered him. He turned around, almost tripping as the ship lurched again.

'Oh, sweet Lord, no!' he moaned. 'Oh, Sir John, not now!'

But Cranston lay flat on the cot, legs and arms spread out, head back, mouth open, snoring like one of his own poppets.

Athelstan sat on a stool and gazed around the cabin. He became used to the motion of the ship and found his eyes growing heavy. He just wished to get away from all this. He should go back to St Erconwald's and to his parishioners – to Watkin's petty ambitions, Pike's bold-faced teasing, Pernell the Fleming's desperate attempts to dye her hair and the sardonic amusement, as well as something else, he'd glimpsed in Benedicta's lovely eyes. He wondered how Ashby was faring with Aveline. He felt more comfortable about her now – by the time Cranston finished this business, Sir Henry Ospring would not be held in high regard by the king. He began to think about the mystery play and to work out where the congregation would sit . . .

His eyes closed and he began to doze. He started awake as someone on the deck above him dropped something with a crash. The cabin was growing dark. He wondered whether Sir John had a flint so that he could light the lantern that hung from one of the thick wooden posts that supported the deck above. He got up and opened the front of the lantern then stared at the thick, bronze or copper hook from which it hung. The hook was carried on a plate which in turn was screwed to the post. Athelstan felt a flicker of excitement. Why such a heavy hook to carry a lantern which felt much lighter than those that good citizens hung outside their doors at night? The plate was at least nine inches across. Athelstan took the lantern down and tugged at the hook. Nothing happened. He tried twisting the hook clockwise, but it held fast. Then he tried to turn it in the opposite direction and this time he felt it give and the base plate move a little. He turned the hook further, as though unscrewing it, and the plate began to loosen and eventually come free, revealing a recess in the post behind it. Athelstan pushed his hand inside. His fingers touched soft shavings of wood, then a cold, hard object. He got two fingers around it and pulled it out. A silver coin rolled in the palm of his hand.

He heard a boat pull alongside and hastily replaced the hook in the post and went across to rouse Cranston.

'Sir John!' he hissed. 'For God's sake, wake up, Sir John!'

The coroner opened his eyes and smacked his lips.

'A cup of claret,' he breathed. 'A beef and onion pie and I'll see the poppets immediately.'

'Oh, for God's sake, Sir John!' Athelstan shook him. 'We are on board ship!'

Cranston rubbed his face and struggled to his feet.

'What the bloody hell?' His voice trailed off as Athelstan held the silver piece in front of his eyes.

'You ferret of a friar! You little ferret of a friar!' Cranston chortled and, grabbing Athelstan by the shoulders, kissed him on both cheeks.

Athelstan, not knowing whether to rub his shoulders where they ached or wipe his face, pointed to the lantern. Cranston lumbered across, his face still heavy with sleep.

'In there? That's a daft place!'

'No, Sir John, behind the hook plate is a small recess. Whatever Roffel took from that fishing boat he hid there, but now it's gone.'

'So!' Cranston breathed. 'It all fits together.'

Athelstan hid the silver coin at the rap on the door. Southchurch entered.

'I told Sir Jacob you were here,' he said, 'and he sent a messenger. Despite the present alarums, he still wishes you to be his guests aboard the *Holy Trinity*.'

Cranston looked down at himself. 'I would like to change but' – he grinned – 'I suppose I'm handsome whatever I wear.' He ran a finger along the stubble on Athelstan's chin. 'Which is more than I can say for you, my little friar. Come on, I'm starved and Crawley can be a good host.'

As a thick mist blanketed the river, the frenetic activity of the afternoon began to die. News of the French galleys had reached the city and church bells were already ringing the alarm. Many taverns were closed. Even the whores moved east of Southwark

Bridge, confident that if any galleys penetrated the Thames this would prove a natural barrier to the invaders. A group of traders went down to Westminster to protest to the king's council about this further sign of a fall in English fortunes. The more selfish began to hide belongings and place precious objects in strong-boxes. Darkness fell; the quaysides were deserted except for the Fisher of Men and his gargoyles, who began to peer out of the shadowy alleyways and filthy runnels which ran down to the Thames. The Fisher of Men's strange eyes gleamed at the prospect of profit. If there was a battle on the river, corpses could be plucked from the water, purses cut and fees demanded from the city authorities. He and his group of cowled figures crept by the Steelyard towards Queen's hithe. They stood on the quayside staring out at the ships. The Fisher of Men turned.

'Well! Well!' he whispered hoarsely. 'We must be ready. Stay along the river bank, watch the water.' He chuckled. 'Like the good book says, the deep shall yield up its riches.' His face became serious. 'Oh, yes, my beauties. Father Thames has many secrets.'

He hid his flicker of annoyance as he made out the lights of the *God's Bright Light*. The Fisher of Men felt cheated. Three sailors had disappeared from that cog. The Fisher of Men had heard about the murder of Bernicia and the search for Bracklebury, but what had happened to the other two members of the watch? Why wouldn't the river give up this secret to him?

CHAPTER 10

Sir Jacob Crawley greeted Cranston and Athelstan warmly. The friar was embarrassed by Sir John's slight unsteadiness, but Sir Jacob chose to ignore it as he welcomed them into his cabin. A small trestle table had been set up, covered with white linen cloths and laid with silver goblets, cutlery and the very best pewter dishes. Lanterns had been lit and candlesticks, carefully fixed on to the table, bathed the cabin in a soft warm glow. Like its slightly smaller sister ships, the *Holy Trinity* was ready for war. Athelstan had seen these preparations as he and Cranston had come aboard. The *Holy Trinity*'s deck was cluttered with buckets of seawater against fire, while archers were bringing up bundles of arrows and placing them into small, iron-hooped barrels around the mast. As the admiral closed the cabin door behind him, Athelstan sensed he was entering a different world. Crawley ushered them to their chairs. They were served dishes that had been bought from cookshops and bakeries in Vintry. The food was not of the best, but still hot and spicy – venison pies, beef pastries, hot broth, quince tarts and different wines by the jugful. At first the conversation was a mere exchange of pleasantries, broken now and again by a knock on the

183

door as an officer came to ask for advice or receive instructions.

'Do you think Eustace the Monk will bring his galleys this far up the Thames?' Athelstan asked.

Crawley nodded. 'Within the hour, that mist on the river will be boiling thick and afford him the best protection.' The admiral drank from his goblet and sat back. 'It's to be expected. For weeks we have been raiding towns along the Normandy coast and Eustace is insolent enough to try something daring. That he is here at all is danger enough.' Crawley leaned closer. 'Why, Brother, do you wish to go ashore? Please feel free.'

'No.' Cranston burped, smacked his lips and peered at a piece of velvet damask hanging on one wall of the cabin. 'Sir Jacob, Brother Athelstan has fought in the king's armies in France.' Cranston did not elaborate on Athelstan's brief military career, when his younger brother had been killed. 'And old Jack Cranston is not frightened of any pirate.' The coroner's fat fingers drummed on the table top. 'Moreover, Sir Jacob, we have business to attend to.' He turned and winked quickly at Athelstan as a sign that they should tell Sir Jacob nothing about their discovery on board the *God's Bright Light*.

The admiral spread his hands. 'Sir John, ask your questions. This time I will tell you the truth.'

'Good, you disliked Roffel?'

'No, Sir John, I hated him with every fibre of my being as a pirate, as a killer and a degenerate. In my eyes Roffel received his just deserts.'

'Were you involved in his death?'

'By the sacrament, no!'

'Did you know about his attack on the fishing smack between Calais and Dieppe?'

'No, Sir John, I did not. Once at sea, my captains are free to act as they wish. Their task is quite simple – to seek out and destroy as many of the enemy as possible. No questions are asked and, if they are, they rarely receive an honest answer.'

'And on the day the *God's Bright Light* came to anchor?'

Crawley shrugged. 'I went aboard. I saw Roffel's stinking corpse. I had a few words with Bracklebury and came back here.'

'You sensed nothing wrong?' Athelstan asked.

'Yes, there was a feeling of unease. Bracklebury refused to meet my eye and seemed to resent my presence on board.'

Cranston cleared his throat and took one deep gulp from his goblet. Athelstan watched him warily. Sir John was already deep in his cups, his red face was now fiery, his whiskers bristling.

'Sir Jacob,' Cranston boomed, 'there are two matters about which you have lied.' He held a hand up as Crawley flinched at the insult. 'Yes, sir, I say lie because I am your friend, not because I am a coroner. You told us you did not go back to the *God's Bright Light* that night. We now know you did approach the ship, sometime after midnight, and spent some time there.'

Crawley chewed the corner of his lip. He played with a piece of crust on his trancher. 'I am admiral of this flotilla. Roffel's death disturbed me and Bracklebury's suspicious conduct only deepened my mistrust. I saw the crew leave and I was concerned that just Bracklebury and two others stayed on board.' He twisted his shoulders. 'At first I accepted that. The passwords were carried, the signal lamps shown, the ships seemed quiet. But while I was on deck, I noticed light from the quayside signalling the *God's Bright Light*.' Crawley paused. 'You said there were two matters?'

'Aye!' Cranston snapped. 'The whore Bernicia came down to the quayside and hailed the *God's Bright Light*. Bracklebury drove her off with a stream of curses. Surely you heard their altercation?'

'Yes, yes, I did,' Crawley answered wearily. 'I heard that and I also saw a lantern blinking through the mist from the quayside. I became suspicious, so I went across. On board I found everything in order. The two sailors were on watch. Bracklebury was in the cabin, he was eating ship's biscuit and drinking quite heavily, but he wasn't drunk. I asked him about the signal, but he just smiled. He said it was from a whore he had befriended and this often happened when he stayed aboard on watch. He was polite in rather an offensive way, smirking as if treasuring some secret.'

'How was the cabin?' Athelstan asked. 'Did you notice anything untoward?'

'No. I went back on deck. I talked to the other two sailors.' Crawley shrugged. 'You know how seamen are, Sir John? They were awake and on watch but they'd made themselves comfortable. One was playing a game of dice against himself. The other joked about the different ways he would take the first whore he met ashore.'

'So there was nothing wrong?' Athelstan asked.

'Yes there was, but I can't put my finger on it. Something untoward. Something out of the ordinary. I went below deck. All was dark and silent, but I could see nothing wrong so I returned.' The admiral sipped his wine. 'The rest you know.' He smiled apologetically. 'When daylight came and the sailor returned and found Bracklebury and the watch missing, I became frightened. Something was dreadfully wrong and I did not want to take the blame so I lied.'

Athelstan sat back, cradling the cup between his hands. He remembered the entries at the back of Roffel's book of hours.

'Tell me, Sir Jacob, do the letters S L mean anything to you?'

The admiral shook his head. 'No, I have told you the truth. I committed no crime.'

'Oh, but you did,' Athelstan replied. Even Cranston looked at him in astonishment.

Sir Jacob's face paled. 'What do you mean?' he spluttered.

'Well, a sort of crime,' Athelstan continued. 'You broke into St Mary Magdalene church. You plucked Roffel's corpse from its coffin, cut its throat and left the proclamation ASSASSIN pinned to its chest.'

Athelstan watched the admiral carefully. He had reached this conclusion only as Crawley had given vent to his feelings about Roffel.

'You have no proof of that,' Crawley said.

'Oh, come, Sir Jacob, let's examine it logically. First, if any of the crew of *God's Bright Light* had wished to abuse their dead captain's remains, they would have done so on the return journey. But once Roffel's corpse was removed from the ship they were only too pleased to see the back of it. Secondly, whoever perpetrated the crime was strong and fit. Now where would we find such a person?' Athelstan looked Crawley straight in the eye. 'Emma Roffel hated her husband, but she lacked the skill and strength to scale a church wall, force a window, pluck a man's corpse out of a coffin and place it in a sanctuary chair. And, in any case, why should she? Thirdly, you, Sir Jacob, had the motive. You are the only one who holds against Roffel a specific crime – the murder of a kinsman.' Athelstan smiled and relaxed. 'You are, undoubtedly, innocent of Roffel's murder. But you felt cheated. So you carried out your own trial then passed sentence.'

'It could have been Bracklebury,' Cranston smacked his lips and gazed blearily at the friar.

Athelstan frowned at him. 'Sir John, Master Bracklebury has spent most of his time hiding from everyone. Why should he risk all on such a crime? I am right am I not, Sir Jacob?'

The admiral picked up his cup and glared defiantly at Athelstan.

'Yes, Brother, you are. I was glad Roffel died. He was a murderer. On the day his corpse was taken ashore, I sent a member of my crew to find out where the body had been taken. He returned saying it now lay before the high altar in St Mary Magdalene church, but that Roffel's widow was with it.' Crawley slammed the cup down. 'So I decided to wait.' He wiped his mouth on the back of his hand. 'What I did was wrong but Roffel deserved it!'

'Tush! Tush!' Cranston placed his hand over that of

his former comrade. 'Sir Jacob, you have told the truth?'

'Jack, I have. I swear that!'

Any further conversation was cut short by a bump alongside and the sound of raised voices. Men ran along the deck outside, then the cabin door was thrown open and an officer rushed in.

'Sir Jacob, my apologies.'

'What is it, man?'

'You had best come on deck, sir.'

Sir Jacob, with Cranston and Athelstan in tow, followed him out. Darkness had fallen and the admiral's words had proved prophetic: the river mist now boiled and swirled like steam from a cauldron, obscuring the bows of the ship. The river itself was hidden, almost as if a heavy cloud had descended, cutting the ship off and shrouding it under a thick wall of silence and mystery. Athelstan peered through the gloom. Now and again he could see lights from the other ships. Then he heard the sound that had caused the alarm.

'What the bloody hell is it?' Cranston slurred.

Athelstan made his way cautiously to the ship's side.

'Bells, Sir John. Church bells sounding the alarm.'

'There's something else as well,' the officer who had interrupted their meal shouted from the other side of the ship. 'Sir Jacob, a boatman's here. He calls himself Moleskin!'

Athelstan crossed the slippery surface of the deck and peered over the side. He could just make out Moleskin's cheery face in the light from the lamp the boatman held up.

'Moleskin, what are you doing?' Athelstan cried.

'Father, I knew you were here. I went across to the city side and they told me you were aboard the *Holy Trinity*.'

'For God's sake, man!' Sir Jacob, who had joined Athelstan, shouted down. 'What is so urgent? Have you not heard the news, man?'

'I belong to Brother Athelstan's parish,' Moleskin retorted. 'He looks after me. Came out to see my old mother he did.'

'Sweet Lord!' Crawley whispered. 'The fellow's mad!'

'What do you want, Moleskin?' Athelstan asked.

'Oh, nothing really, Father. I was just worried. You see, those clever bastards on board think the French galleys are coming up-river against them. Well, I've seen them near the far bank, on the Southwark side. I couldn't care what happens to the other buggers but I was worried about you and Lord Horsecruncher!'

'Piss off!' Cranston yelled.

'And a very good evening to you, Sir John,' Moleskin replied.

'You had best go,' Athelstan shouted down.

'Don't you worry, Brother, no bloody Frenchmen will catch me! I was working this river when they were little tadpoles!'

Moleskin's voice echoed out of the depths of the mist. Athelstan peered down, the mist shifted for a few seconds but Moleskin and his boat had gone. Cranston leaned drunkenly against the side of the ship and looked at Crawley. Sir Jacob peered into the mist, rubbing his fingers through his small pointed beard. 'What do you know of Moleskin, Father?' the admiral asked.

'One of the best boatmen on the Thames,' Athelstan replied. 'Shrewd, honest and sober. He knows the Thames like the back of his hand.'

'Oh, sweet Lord!' Cranston muttered. The cold night air was beginning to clear the wine fumes from his brain. 'Farting Frenchmen!' he said viciously.

'What's the matter?' Athelstan asked.

Sir Jacob began shouting orders, instructing his officers to send a message to the ships along the line.

Athelstan grasped Cranston's arm. 'Sir John, what is happening?'

Cranston pulled him into a corner.

'Look, Brother, the Frenchman is a cunning sailor. He's probably come up the Thames, shadowing its north bank, passing Westminster, coming within sight of the Temple, Whitefriars, even Fleet Street. He did that to cause consternation, put everyone on their guard. Now, we expect an enemy coming up-river behind us, from the west. What the clever bastard Eustace has done is taken his galleys across river to the Southwark side. He'll turn just before London Bridge and come sliding down from the opposite direction Sir Jacob's expecting.'

'And?' Athelstan asked.

'Oh, for God's sake, Brother! It's the element of surprise!' Cranston's whiskers bristled at the prospect of action. 'Can't you see? It's like me expecting a knifeman to come from my left but he rushes from my right. What will happen is this. Eustace has turned his galleys round. He'll come sliding back, do as much damage as he can here, using the element of surprise, and then press on to the river mouth. He'll make fools of the city, not to mention the king's admiral. But not,' Cranston bellowed into the mist-shrouded darkness, 'of Sir John Cranston!' He clapped Athelstan on the shoulder. 'Thanks to you, most favoured of friars and to that cheeky bugger, Moleskin, we'll be well prepared!'

Athelstan stared around as the ship was prepared for action. Sailors now thronged the decks. The charcoal braziers glowed red under their metal hoods. Archers strung their bows and boys ran around filling quivers. Crawley went into his cabin and came out with a war belt, mailed hauberk and a conical steel helmet with a nose guard. Other officers followed suit. A drum beat began to roll, but Crawley quickly silenced it. Small catapults were wheeled out from beneath their tarpaulin covers. One last message was despatched via the ship's boat to the other cogs, confirming the change in plan and warning their captains to expect an attack from the east after the French galleys turned at London Bridge. Crawley shouted up to the look-outs.

'A silver piece for the first man who sights the enemy!'

'Thick as soup!' a voice shouted back. 'No sign of anything, Sir Jacob!'

Athelstan felt the fear and apprehension. Long poles and grappling hooks were brought up from below. Swords and daggers were eased in and out of scabbards. One man came up, begging Athelstan to shrive him. Athelstan crouched and heard the man's whispered, hurried confession. He was no more than eighteen or nineteen summers old. 'In a few minutes,' he whispered as they crouched in a corner of the deck between the ship's side and the stern castle, 'I might be killing people.'

'God will be your judge, my son,' Athelstan responded. 'All I can say is, do what you think right in whatever the moment presents to you.'

Other men, too, wanted him to hear their confessions. In the end Athelstan pronounced a general absolution. Cranston meanwhile had been walking impatiently up and down, peering into the mist.

'Sir John,' Crawley called out, 'you can go below or, if you wish, we can put you ashore!'

'Sod off!' Cranston roared. 'Never will it be said that Jack Cranston scuttled away!'

'But what about Brother Athelstan?'

Cranston stared at the friar. 'Brother, you must go ashore.'

Athelstan shook his head. 'I am here. That means God intended me to be here. Anyway, Sir John, someone's got to protect your back.'

Cranston walked closer. 'Sod off, you little friar!'

'Sir John,' Athelstan replied evenly, 'what if something happened to you? Your face is as red as a beacon, so large a target. What could I say to Lady Maude or the poppets?'

Cranston looked over his shoulder at Crawley. 'We stay,' he bawled. 'Sir Jacob, a sword belt, dagger and shield. Oh yes, and a helmet.'

'If you have one big enough,' Athelstan said under his breath.

Sir John busily armed himself, his curses and black good humour easing the tension around him. Once finished, he looked a veritable fighting barrel, made all the more ridiculous by the too-small helmet on his head.

The chatter and laughter died as a look-out on the forecastle shouted. 'I see something! No, it's gone! It's gone!'

Now all the ship's company were turning, gazing up-river. Athelstan walked to the side. What was it he heard? A creak?

'God in heaven!' Cranston shouted as fire-arrows hissed through the mist. One hit the deck, another hit an archer in the shoulder, sending him whirling like a doll, screaming with pain.

'Blazing bollocks!' Cranston shouted. 'The bastards are here!'

More fire-arrows fell, followed by a ball of blazing pitch which crashed to the deck but was quickly doused in water. Athelstan felt his stomach lurch; his mouth went dry. He peered into the mist. Long shapes appeared, low-slung with ornate poops resembling snarling wolves' heads. Athelstan stepped back in fear. There were three or four, no, five galleys, oars up, racing towards the *Holy Trinity* like loping greyhounds for the kill. The speed and silence of their approach was unnerving.

'Why don't you fire?' Athelstan shouted at Crawley.

The admiral stood, hand raised. A galley smashed into the larboard side of the *Holy Trinity*. Another, its oars drawn inboard in one sweeping movement, swung under its stern. A third came to a foaming stop under its bows. A grappling hook snaked out and caught a bulwark.

'For St George!' Crawley shouted, and brought his hand down.

The long bows sang their song, a low musical thrum, as goosequill-flighted arrows swooped into the darkness. The night air was shattered by screams and yells.

'Again! Loose!'

A Frenchman, his dark face bearded, the only man yet to reach the deck of the *Holy Trinity*, stared at Athelstan in stupefaction. An arrow caught him straight between the eyes. He fell back.

'Again!' Crawley shouted. 'Loose!'

Athelstan felt himself pulled back by Cranston and stared at the archers. They were hand-picked master bowmen; they fired one arrow whilst keeping another between their teeth. Athelstan guessed each one must be shooting at least three a minute. They worked in a silent, cold way. Now and again a French arbalester replied and an archer fell screaming to the deck. He was pulled away and another took his place. Other, more enterprising archers were climbing the rigging. Athelstan hurried to those who had been wounded. The first, a youth of about sixteen, was already coughing up blood, his eyes glazing over. Athelstan sketched the sign of the cross over his face and trusted that Christ would understand. Now Crawley was bringing up fire archers, exposing them to danger as they leant over the side of the ship to shoot down into the galleys. The French replied with their crossbows. One archer disappeared screaming over the side, half his face ripped away. Athelstan stood with Crawley and a small knot of officers at the foot of the mast and listened to the din of battle. He realised how fortunate they had been – without Moleskin's warning the entire ship's company would have been unprepared and looking in the opposite direction when Eustace the Monk's freebooters struck.

'To starboard!' someone shouted.

Crawley turned. A galley had come in on the shore side to complete the encirclement of the *Holy Trinity*. Athelstan glimpsed the top of its mast, where a monk's hood fluttered as its pennant. Now the danger was acute. Archers hurried over, but the grappling lines snaked up and caught the ship's rigging and bulwarks. In a mad rush, armed Frenchmen, wearing the livery of a monk's hood over their chain mail, gained a footing. They pushed back the lightly armed archers, so skilled with their long bows and yet unprotected against these mailed men-at-arms.

'Now!' Cranston shouted and, not even waiting for Crawley's orders, the fat coroner led the ship's company of men-at-arms against the invaders. Athelstan would have moved too but Crawley pushed him back. Cranston hit the Frenchmen like a charging bull.

The friar watched, petrified. Cranston swung his great sword like a scythe. Athelstan smelt fire. He turned and saw smoke billowing from the galley at the other side of the ship. The fire-arrows had at last begun to take effect. Crawley, his face blackened with smoke, left the fight on the deck to run over and scream at his men.

'Push it away! Push it away!'

The galley, flames licking it from bow to stern, was pushed out into the mist. The screams of the men on board were terrible. Athelstan saw at least three, their clothes aflame, throw themselves into the icy Thames. Now free on one side, more archers rushed to help

Cranston. Athelstan retreated towards the shelter of the stern castle. As he did so, a Frenchman broke free of the mêlée and darted towards him. Athelstan moved sideways to dodge. The ship lurched. The deck underfoot was slippery, the seawater edged with a bloody froth. Athelstan crashed to the deck, jarring his arm. The Frenchman lifted his sword to strike but he must have realised Athelstan was a priest, for he smiled, stepped back and disappeared into the throng. The friar, nursing his bruised arm, limped towards the cabin. Behind him, he could hear Cranston's roar. The friar closed his eyes and prayed that Christ would protect the fat coroner. Then he heard the bray of a trumpet, once, twice, three times, and immediately the fighting began to slacken. The arrows ceased to fall, shouted orders faltered. Athelstan, resting against the cabin, glanced along the ship, experiencing that eerie silence which always falls as a battle ends. Even the wounded and dying ceased their screaming.

'Are you all right, Brother?'

Cranston came swaggering across the deck. The coroner was splashed with blood, his sword still wet and sticky. He appeared unhurt except for a few scratches on his hand and a small flesh wound just beneath his elbow. Cranston grasped Athelstan by the shoulder and pushed his face close, his ice-blue eyes full of concern.

'Athelstan, you are all right?'

'Christ be thanked, yes I am!'

'Good!' Cranston grinned. 'The farting Frenchmen have gone!' The coroner turned, legs spread, big belly and chest stuck out, and raised his sword in the air. 'We beat the bastards, lads!'

Cheering broke out and Athelstan could hear it being taken up on the cogs further down the line. He walked to the ship's side. A number of French galleys were on fire and now lay low in the water, the roaring flames turning them to floating cinders. Of Eustace the Monk's own galley and the rest of his small pirate fleet there was no sign.

'What will happen now, Sir John?' Athelstan asked.

'The buggers will race for the sea,' the coroner replied. 'They have to be out before dawn, when this mist lifts.'

Cranston threw his sword on the deck, his attention caught by the cries of a group of men under the mast. Cranston and Athelstan crossed to where Sir Jacob Crawley lay, a surgeon crouched over him tending a wound in his shoulder. The admiral winced with pain as he grabbed Cranston's hand.

'We did it, Jack.' The admiral's face, white as a sheet, broke into a thin smile. 'We did it again, Jack, like the old days.'

Cranston looked at the surgeon.

'Is he in any danger?'

'No,' the fellow replied. 'Nothing a fresh poultice and a good bandage can't deal with.'

Crawley struggled to concentrate. He peered at Athelstan.

'I know,' he whispered. 'I remember. Everything was so tidy, so very, very tidy!' Then he fell into a swoon.

Athelstan and Cranston drew away. The ship became a hive of activity and the friar winced as the archers, using their misericorde daggers, cut the throats of the enemy wounded and unceremoniously tossed their corpses into the river. Boats were lowered and messages sent to the other ships about what was to be done with the English wounded, the dead of both sides and the enemy prisoners.

Athelstan, nursing his arm, sat in the cabin and listened as Cranston, between generous slurps from his wineskin, gave a graphic description of the fight. Crawley, now being sent ashore to the hospital at St Bartholomew's, had won a remarkable victory. Four galleys had been sunk and a number of prisoners taken. Most of these, perhaps the luckiest, were already on their way to the flagship to be hanged.

The news had by now reached the city. Through the fog came the sound of bells and sailors reported that, despite the darkness and the mist, crowds were beginning to gather along the quayside.

'Sir John,' Athelstan murmured. 'We should go ashore. We have done all we can here.'

Cranston, who was preparing for a third description of his masterly prowess, rubbed his eyes and smiled.

'You are right.'

The coroner walked to the cabin door and watched as a French prisoner, a noose tied around his neck, was pushed over the side to die a slow, choking death.

'You are right, Brother, we should go. No charging knights, no silken-caparisoned destriers, just a bloody mess and violent death.'

They crossed the deck to the shouts and acclamations of the sailors and archers. Athelstan glimpsed the dangling corpses.

'Sir John, can't that be stopped?'

'Rules of war,' Cranston replied. 'Rules of war.

Eustace the Monk is a pirate. Pirates are hanged out of hand.'

Crawley's lieutenant had the ship's boat ready for them. Cranston and Athelstan gingerly climbed down the rope ladder, the shouts and praises of the crew still ringing in their ears.

'Where to, Sir John?' the oarsman asked.

Cranston glanced at Athelstan. 'You are welcome to stay at Cheapside.'

Athelstan shook his head. He kept his eyes down. He did not wish to see the terrible executions being carried out on the flagship, the corpses now hanging like rats from the ship's sides.

'No, Sir John, I thank you. Ask the oarsman to take me to Southwark.' He smiled and patted Sir John on the arm. 'You are a hero, Sir John. A brave, courageous heart. Lady Maude will be proud.' Athelstan grinned. 'And I shall tell the two poppets how their father is a veritable Hector!'

The Fisher of Men crouched on the quayside. He saw the boat carrying Athelstan to Southwark leave the *Holy Trinity*. He made out the outline of the flagship and saw the grisly burdens twitching at the ends of their ropes. He smiled at the gargoyles grouped around him.

'Harvest time, my sweets!' He turned his head, ears straining into the darkness. 'There's living men as well as dead in the river. As they come ashore, say that you are here to help. If they reply in French, kill them! If they are English, help them. But don't forget to look for the corpses.'

One of the gargoyles tugged at his sleeve and

pointed to the river, where a corpse in white shirt and dark hose bobbed, face down, towards them.

'Yes, yes.' The Fisher of Men smiled. 'Harvest time at last!'

CHAPTER 11

Athelstan slept late next morning. He woke at dawn, aching from head to toe, though his arm felt better. The mist still boiled outside. He couldn't even glimpse the church from his upper chamber window.

'God forgive me!' Athelstan muttered. 'But I feel terrible!' He went downstairs, built up the fire, drank a little wine and returned to bed. This time he slept for hours and was only awakened by Watkin pounding on the door an hour before noon. Athelstan, pulling his thin blanket around him, hurried down. He unlocked the door and smiled at the look of astonishment on the dung-collector's face.

'Father, you have been asleep?'

Athelstan took him into the kitchen. Behind Watkin other parishioners were gathering on the church steps. Even Marston was there, looking apprehensively towards the priest's house. Athelstan slumped down at the table.

'Father, what's wrong? You are always up. Shaved, bathed, Mass said, church clean?' Watkin hid his love for this gentle priest behind his usual bluster.

Athelstan smiled thinly. 'Watkin, I was on the river last night with Sir John.'

'You were there, Father?'

'I was, God help me, on the *Holy Trinity* when the French attacked.'

Watkin strode to the door and threw it open.

'Father's a hero!' he bellowed at the other parishioners. 'He and Fat Arse, I mean, he and Sir John Cranston, fought the bloody French on the river last night!'

Athelstan hid his face in his hands.

'Our priest's a real hero!' Watkin brayed. 'So, it's true what Moleskin told us. Crim, go down to the river and give Moleskin my apologies for calling him a lying fart!'

'Father needs me here,' Crim complained.

'Piss off, you cheeky little sprog!' Watkin slammed the door behind the boy and waddled towards Athelstan. 'Father, you look pale and shaken.'

'Actually, Watkin, I feel much better. By the way, I was not a hero, just a very frightened priest.'

'Modest as always, modest as always!' Watkin patronisingly tapped Athelstan on the shoulder. 'We'll get Huddle to do a painting and put it up in the church, depicting Brother Athelstan's role in the great sea battle. All of Southwark will know about it.' He breathed noisily through hairy nostrils. 'They are hunting Frenchmen along the mud flats. The gallows are full and they're putting pirates' heads on London Bridge!'

Athelstan crossed his arms over his stomach. 'God have mercy on them!' he whispered.

The door opened. Athelstan's parishioners thronged in, necks craning for a glimpse of their hero priest.

'Go away! Go away!' Watkin grandly ordered.

'Brother Athelstan needs comfort and solace. I, as leader of your parish council, will give you the news later.' He slammed the door. 'Piss off!' he roared as the door opened again.

Benedicta stepped into the room. Watkin fell back, his hands dangling at his sides, his head hanging – like a naughty boy.

'Mistress Benedicta!' He shuffled his great, muddy boots. 'I didn't mean you.'

The widow smiled, glanced at Athelstan's pale and unshaven face then took a key off the hook near the door.

'Watkin, open the church and continue your work, getting the stage ready for the play. Tell them Brother Athelstan will be across soon. Go on!'

The dung-collector slipped by her. Once he was outside, he grandly announced that he was in charge of the church, that he would keep Father Athelstan's secrets and that they were to do what he told them. Pike the ditcher immediately objected. Athelstan smiled as the usual row broke out, their voices fading in the distance. Benedicta came and crouched before him.

'You don't look so bad for a hero,' she whispered.

'I'm not a hero, Benedicta. I was frightened. All I did was slip on the deck. A Frenchman was going to kill me but then he smiled and turned away.' Athelstan stared at the dying flames of the fire. 'I hope he got away. I hope he returns to his loved ones. I shall remember him at Mass.'

'And Sir John?'

Athelstan shook his head. 'That man is a mountain of legends. He belches like a pig and drinks as if there's no tomorrow but he's got the heart of a lion.'

Athelstan quickly described Cranston's exploits to Benedicta.

'Oh, Lord!' Benedicta said when he had finished. 'Sir John will be full of himself.'

'He deserves to be,' Athelstan replied. 'And remind me to remind him, Benedicta, that Moleskin must be rewarded. If it hadn't been for him the French would have taken us unawares.'

'What will you do now, Father?'

'I am going to go upstairs. I am going to wash, shave, change and then say Mass. Oh, by the way, where's Bonaventure?'

'He's with Ashby,' Benedicta replied. 'Lady Aveline has brought her swain all the comforts of life, including a pitcher of cold milk. Bonaventure can't believe his luck.'

'Cranston's right,' Athelstan muttered, 'that cat's a bloody little mercenary!' He stared into Benedicta's face. 'You shouldn't be here,' he said. 'People will talk.'

'About you?' Benedicta smiled.

'I couldn't give a damn!' Athelstan replied. 'It's you I'm thinking about.'

Benedicta laughed, turned and went to crouch by the fire. She sprinkled some kindling, put a fresh log on and grinned over her shoulder at him.

'They can say what they like, but they'll believe nothing ill about you, Father. As Pike the ditcher so aptly put it, you could put Brother Athelstan in a room full of whores and he wouldn't know what to do!'

Athelstan blushed and went upstairs. Benedicta, still laughing to herself, went into the buttery to prepare some breakfast.

An hour later Athelstan, shaved and much more refreshed, went into the church, where he celebrated Mass. His parishioners, drawn in by the rumours of their priest's heroic exploits, thronged into the sanctuary. Athelstan, however, had vowed to say nothing. He was about to raise his hand to dismiss them when he glimpsed the hurt on Watkin's face. He lowered his hand and smiled.

'I am sorry I overslept,' he said. 'I was at the battle on the river last night. I wasn't a hero, though.'

'Nonsense!' Tab the tinker shouted.

'But Sir John was,' Athelstan continued.

'Good old Fat Arse!' someone shouted.

'Well done, Horsecruncher!' Crim piped up.

Athelstan glowered at them.

'You are in God's house. Sir John is a very brave man and so is Moleskin. He may well get a letter from the mayor, not to mention a suitable reward.'

Athelstan glanced over to where Ashby sat on the ledge of the sanctuary. The young man was shaved and wearing clean robes and he was surrounded by bolsters and blankets. Athelstan glimpsed a book, a bowl of fruit and a large jug which Bonaventure, crouching in the corner, watched attentively. Aveline was also there, kneeling piously, her hands in her lap, head down.

'I also thank you,' Athelstan continued, trying to keep the humour out of his voice, 'for looking after Brother Ashby, whose troubles may soon disappear. Now' – he peered through the rood screen, towards the makeshift stage and raised his hand – 'Mass is over, we have got work to do.'

The friar went into the sacristy and took off his

vestments. He helped Crim and Ashby clear the candlesticks and cloths from the altar, hung a new sanctuary lamp above the tabernacle and went to join Ashby and Aveline. As usual, they sat in the corner of the sanctuary whispering together. Athelstan pulled across the stool Crim used when serving Mass.

'Lady Aveline,' Athelstan began, 'I have some very sad news about your stepfather.'

The friar then tersely described the conclusions he had drawn about Sir Henry Ospring's nefarious activities. Ashby gasped. Aveline's face went paler than usual, tears brimming in her eyes.

'What you are saying, Brother,' she whispered once Athelstan had finished, 'is that my stepfather was a traitor and a murderer.'

'The words are yours, my lady, but, God forgive me, the truth is as I have described it.'

'Will the crown seize his estates?' Ashby spoke up.

'I doubt it,' Athelstan replied. 'Sir Henry died before any allegations could be made and he is not here to defend himself against them.' He shrugged. 'The crown will undoubtedly, through the exchequer, demand the return of its silver.' Athelstan smiled thinly as he remembered the hard scrutineers, Peter and Paul. 'I strongly recommend, Lady Aveline, that either you or your stepfather's executors double the amount and dismiss it as a gift.' Athelstan stared at the young man. 'You, however, were his squire. Questions may well be asked of you.'

'I will go on oath,' Ashby said, 'and I have witnesses, that I was not involved in Sir Henry's business affairs.' He pulled a face. 'Certainly not those involving the men who visited him at the dead of night.' He chewed his lip and grinned. 'I doubt if Marston could claim the same.'

Athelstan nodded. 'Nevertheless, as Sir John keeps saying, every cloud has a silver lining. God forgive me, Lady Aveline, but I don't think anyone, and certainly not the king, will weep for your stepfather. Consequently, Sir John and I believe a pardon will be freely issued to both of you for the death of Sir Henry.' He stilled their excited clamour with an upraised hand. 'Nevertheless, Master Ashby, you are still a felon and a wanted man.' Athelstan picked a piece of candle grease from the back of his hand. 'But, don't worry,' he murmured. 'Before the day is much older I shall give Marston something to think about.'

'Is there anything more we can do?' Ashby asked.

'Did you know Bracklebury?'

Ashby shook his head. 'A dark, violent man, Father. A good knife man. He was like his captain, he feared neither God nor man. Why do you ask?'

'We have established,' Athelstan replied, 'that Roffel took the silver and hid it on board the *God's Bright Light*. To cut a long story short, Bracklebury may have dismissed the crew, keeping two back so he could search the ship.' Athelstan paused, choosing to ignore the unanswered questions that still nagged at his brain. 'God knows what happened then. Perhaps Bracklebury killed the two members of the watch and escaped ashore. The only problem is that the *God's Bright Light* kept passing signals and no one saw any boat leave the ship.'

'Bracklebury could have jumped overboard,' Lady Aveline suggested, 'and swum to the quayside.'

'No, no, that's impossible,' Ashby replied.

Athelstan stared at him. 'Why's that?'

'Father, can you swim?'

Athelstan recalled golden days from his boyhood, he and his brother Francis leaping into a river, naked as the day they were born.

'Well, Father, can you?'

'Yes,' Athelstan replied, a little embarrassed. 'Like a fish. My parents owned a farm where a river ran through some pasture land. Why?'

'You see, Father, men like Bracklebury probably grew up in the slums of London or Bristol. Many people think every sailor can swim, but that's not true. They board ship as boys. If they survive through to manhood, they fear the sea, Father, much more than we do. They have seen its power.' Ashby shrugged. 'To put it bluntly, Bracklebury, like many of his kind, couldn't swim.'

'How do you know that?' Athelstan asked. 'Is that a guess or a fact?'

'Oh, it's a fact, Father. Bracklebury told me himself. I suspect the same applies to Cabe, Coffrey and even poor old Roffel himself. You ask most sailors, if they have to abandon ship they always take something to cling on to.'

Athelstan stared down the nave where his parishioners, busy as bees, thronged around the makeshift stage.

'God help us!' he whispered. 'So, how the hell did bloody Bracklebury, to quote the famous Cranston, leave that bloody ship?'

'Suppose he had an accomplice?' Ashby said. 'Someone who brought a small boat alongside?'

'Without anyone seeing it?' Athelstan asked.

'What if it came from the Southwark side?'

Athelstan nodded and got to his feet. 'Aye, and what if pigs fly? Would you trust Cabe?'

'About as far as I can spit. Of the same ilk as Bracklebury! The two were as thick as thieves and the same goes for the other officers. They were hard men, Father. They all have murky pasts which they prefer kept hidden.'

Athelstan thanked him, told them both to be careful and walked into the nave of the church. He stood for a while admiring the cart now being transformed into a stage. Posts had been set up around it and fixed to them was the great piece of canvas that would serve as backdrop and wings. It was sagging woefully. Huddle was putting the finishing touches to his painting of the yawning mouth of Hell, blissfully ignoring the comments and advice from the rest of the parish council. Athelstan smiled and slipped by. He was half-way across to Philomel's stable when he guiltily remembered that he had left the old warhorse at the Holy Lamb of God.

'Oh, he'll be all right,' he comforted himself. The landlord, he knew, was a warm-hearted man and, as long as Philomel was warm and dry and had plenty of food within inches of his greying muzzle, he wouldn't care where he was.

Athelstan went back to the house, which Benedicta and Cecily the courtesan had cleaned and swept. He took some bread and cheese from the buttery and sat at his table, moodily reflecting on the battle of the night before.

'What,' he asked the fire, 'did Crawley mean by his remark "everything was so tidy"?'

211

The friar shook his head and popped another piece of cheese into his mouth. What had Bracklebury done to the other two crew members? How did he get off the ship? And, if he had the silver, why did he murder Bernicia? He was interrupted by a knock on the door. Bladdersniff the ward bailiff swaggered in, his fleshy face quivering with self-importance.

'I bring a message, Father, from Sir John Cranston. One of the Guildhall servants brought it to me.' The bailiff pursed prim lips. 'Sir John Cranston, coroner of the city, is desirous of meeting you at the Holy Lamb of God.' Bladdersniff coughed. 'He also mentioned something about a doctor's house.'

Athelstan groaned. Bladdersniff looked at him suspiciously.

'What does that mean, Father?'

'Nothing, Master Bladdersniff,' Athelstan replied. He waited until the bailiff had left. 'Nothing,' he muttered to himself, 'except another night away from my parish!'

The friar sighed, went upstairs, took off his sandals, put on woollen hose under his gown and pulled on an old, battered pair of boots. He then banked up the fire, fastened the windows, collected his cloak and staff and walked down to the area in front of the church. Crim and others were playing with counters on the porch steps.

'Crim! Come here!'

The young boy scuttled down, yelling at his friends that it was his turn next.

'Crim, tell Benedicta I may not be back this evening.'

'Is it the French pirates again, Father?'

'No, it isn't. However, tell your father to lock the church, though he is to let Lady Aveline in.'

'They are in love, aren't they, Father? I saw them kissing! That's a sin in church isn't it, Father?'

Athelstan smiled at the thin, dirty face. 'No, it is not,' he said solemnly. 'But it is a sin, Crim, to spy in church.'

'I wasn't spying, Father. I was just hiding from my sister behind a pillar.'

Athelstan tousled the boy's head and put a farthing in his hand. 'Buy some marchpane from Merrylegs' shop. Give some to your sister and your friends – even though,' Athelstan added darkly, 'they are moving your counters!'

Crim turned around and ran back screaming.

'Don't forget to give your father my message, Crim!' Athelstan called out after him.

He walked out into the alleyway. Marston and two of his bully-boys were sitting just inside the doorway of the Piebald tavern. Marston saw him, hawked and spat. Athelstan, swinging his great staff, a gift from Cranston, walked across and confronted him.

'You'd best leave, Marston,' he said.

'I can stand where I bloody well like, Father!' He smirked. 'This isn't your church.'

'No, it isn't,' Athelstan replied. 'I am just concerned for your welfare.'

'Why?' Marston asked, the grin fading from his face.

'Well,' Athelstan whispered, grasping his staff and leaning forward, 'we know now that Sir Henry Ospring was not what he claimed to be. Some people allege he was a thief. Others that he was a traitor. Gossips even whisper that there were others involved in his crimes and that these should hang.'

Marston's face paled.

'What are you saying, Father?'

Athelstan shrugged. 'Just gossip. Perhaps it's best if you went back to Kent, claimed what was yours and put as much distance between yourself and the eagle eye of Sir John Cranston as possible.'

Athelstan walked on. Half-way down the alleyway he stopped at Basil the blacksmith's. Basil, together with his swarthy elder son, was working in a great open shed at the side of his cottage. A pug-nosed apprentice, his face covered in smuts, blew with the bellows, making the forge fire flare with life. Basil was hammering away, his huge body hidden behind a bull's-hide apron, his hairy legs sheathed in leather against the sparks of the fire. He turned and saw Athelstan.

'Good morrow, Father. What can I do for you?'

'We need you at the church, Basil,' Athelstan replied, 'to fix some iron clasps to hold up the canvas around the stage for our mystery play.'

Basil wiped the sweat from his brow with the back of his wrist. 'I told that big-headed bastard Watkin that poles as long as that needed iron clasps!' He pointed at Athelstan with his hammer. 'What you did on the river, Father, was heroic, so I'll do it free. I'll put iron clasps on your poles.' He lowered his voice as Athelstan turned away. 'I'll even hammer one into that daft bugger Watkin's head!'

Athelstan, grinning, walked on. The grey day was beginning to die, but the shabby stalls and makeshift markets were still doing a brisk trade and the alehouses were full of roisterers celebrating the river victory of the previous evening. Slipping quietly by, Athelstan made his way towards London Bridge, where at the gatehouse he was brutally reminded of the battle. Some of the French pirates had been decapitated and their heads impaled on poles that were being erected on the gatehouse. Robert Burdon, the diminutive gatekeeper, was dancing around supervising this grisly event. 'Put that one there!' he bawled at one of his assistants. 'No, you idiot, turn it round so he's looking at our ships!' He glimpsed Athelstan. 'Busy day! Busy day, Father! They say a hundred Frenchmen died. A hundred, Father, but how many heads do I have? No more than a baker's dozen. Terrible, isn't it? Bloody city officials! Heads should be where heads should be! A warning to the rest!'

Athelstan closed his eyes, sketched a blessing in the air and hurried on. He reached the other side, now relieved to be away from Southwark, and pushed his way through the throng. When he reached the Holy Lamb of God in Cheapside he found the tavern crowded. Cranston, resplendent in his best jacket of mulberry, white cambric shirt and multi-coloured hose, was sitting at his favourite table. He was holding court, giving a graphic description of the river battle.

'And you fought Eustace the Monk?' Leif the beggar, acting as Cranston's straight man, called out.

'Oh yes – a giant of a man,' Cranston replied, 'six foot six inches tall, eyes like burning coals and a face as dark as Satan! We met sword against sword.'

'Then what?' Leif asked breathlessly.

'The tide of battle swept us apart.' Cranston, on his fourth cup of claret and keeping a wary eye on the door lest Lady Maude should appear, saw Athelstan standing on a stool at the back of the crowd. 'And, credit where credit is due,' he boomed. 'My secretarius and clerk, Brother Athelstan, a man of prodigious valour!'

All heads turned. Athelstan went puce-red.

'Down he went,' Cranston continued, 'fighting like a fury. A Frenchman runs up and lifts his sword—'

'Then what?' Leif asked again.

'The man staggers back unable to give the death blow.'

'A miracle!' Leif exclaimed.

'Aye.' Sir John's voice dropped to a dramatic whisper. 'God's angel came down and caught his arm just like he caught David's when he was about to kill that bastard Judas Iscariot!'

Athelstan bit his lip to hide his laughter; Cranston, as usual, was mixing up his biblical texts.

'A toast!' Leif shouted. 'Surely, Sir John, a toast to Brother Athelstan?'

Cranston readily agreed and offered a coin. The beggar grabbed it and thrust it into the tapster's hand.

'You heard my lord coroner. We celebrate his victory.'

Cranston, catching Athelstan's warning look, now clapped his hands.

'But enough for today. Enough is enough! Go on, have your drink. Leave me alone!' Cranston drew himself up. 'City business, city business awaits!'

The crowd reluctantly dispersed and Athelstan slid into the seat beside Sir John.

'A great victory, Sir John.'

Cranston looked at him slyly. 'Aye, Brother. Only five galleys reached the open sea. We gave Eustace the

Monk a smack across his arse he won't forget in a hurry!'

'But now we have to capture a felon,' Athelstan reminded him.

'Aye,' Cranston muttered. 'Our glorious physician Theobald has left and the news is bruited abroad.' He narrowed his eyes. 'You think the felon will strike tonight, Brother?'

Athelstan nodded. 'I do, Sir John. It's been some time since the last murderous crime and the city is fairly distracted by the fight on the river. How is Crawley?'

'Drinking himself stupid at St Bartholomew's.'

'And the Lady Maude and the two poppets?'

'Proud as peacocks! Proud as peacocks!' Cranston dug his face into the cup of brimming claret. 'Strange,' he muttered, smacking his lips.

'What is, Sir John?'

'Well, our under-sheriff's reported, as we expected, that no boats were hired to go to the *God's Bright Light* but that mad bugger the Fisher of Men sent me a message.'

'What did he want?'

'To see me, but he'll have to wait.'

Athelstan thanked the tapster who placed a tankard of ale in front of him.

'Sir John, are you sure no other boat approached the *God's Bright Light* the night Bracklebury disappeared?'

Cranston nodded. 'First, before you ask, Brother, I have already arranged for the city to reward Moleskin. But, to answer your real question, no boat went there.'

'So, how did Bracklebury leave?' Athelstan asked.

'Don't forget he was laden down with the silver.'

'He probably swam.'

'He couldn't. Ashby told me that.'

Cranston's face became serious. 'Tasty tits!' he muttered, 'I hadn't thought of that. What I have done is issue a proclamation throughout the city that Bracklebury is to be taken, if possible, alive.'

They sat for a while discussing plans and possibilities as the day began to die. Cranston demanded and got a pie and a dish of vegetables which he shared with Athelstan.

After that they left, crossing a dark, cold, empty Cheapside and walking through a maze of streets to Theobald de Troyes' house. A steward let them in, his face full of surprise.

'Sir John, Master Theobald has gone!'

'I know,' Cranston replied. 'And, while the cat's away, the mice will play, eh?'

The steward looked puzzled.

'Where is everyone?' Cranston continued.

The steward pointed down the passageway to the kitchen. 'We are having our evening meal.'

Cranston's podgy nose twitched at the savoury smells.

'What is it, man?'

'Capon, Sir John, marinated in a white wine infused with herbs.'

'I'll have two plates of that,' Cranston said immediately. 'With a couple of loaves. Bring them to the garret. Now, no one here is to leave this house, you included! And no one is to come upstairs until I say. Be a good fellow and piss off and do what I have told you!'

The steward scurried away. Athelstan and Cranston

made their way through the opulently furnished house to the bleak garret at the top. The steward, now in total awe of Sir John, came up with the food. Cranston ordered him to bring candles and the thickest woollen blankets he could find. The steward obeyed. Cranston and Athelstan settled down.

At first the coroner insisted on recounting every blow of the river battle, with anecdotal references to his days of glory when he served with Prince Edward against Philip of France. At last, his belly full of capon and after generous swigs from his wineskin, Cranston began to doze. For a while Athelstan just sat in the darkness, remembering his own days in France and his brother Francis who had died there. He shook his head to clear it of the still-painful memories and thought instead about his parish. He prayed that Basil the blacksmith and Watkin the dung-collector would not come to blows. His eyes grew heavy and he, too, slept for a while. Then he found himself being vigorously shaken awake by Cranston, his fat face pushed close to his, a finger to his lips. Athelstan felt cold and cramped, his arm a little sore. He strained his ears. He heard occasional sounds from the house below, then the cry of the watch.

'Twelve o'clock midnight! Cold and hard, but all's well!'

'That will be Trumpington!' Cranston whispered.

Athelstan was on the point of dozing off again when he heard a movement, a mere slither on the tiles above. Cranston gripped his arm and hissed, 'Blow out the candles! Don't move!'

Athelstan stared up through the rafters at the tiles. Was it only a cat? he wondered. Then his stomach lurched as one of the tiles was removed. Another was prised loose, then another, so within minutes a square was opened, revealing the starlit sky. Athelstan saw the evening star and idly wondered why it was there before a dark shape leaned down and a bag was lowered. Cranston heard a clink, a rope slithered through the gap and a dark shape flitted down as quietly as any hunting cat. Cranston waited. The man crouched in the garret, his boots covered in soft woollen rags. He was moving towards the door when Cranston sprang with an agility which took even Athelstan by surprise.

The man crashed to the floor under the full weight of Cranston's massive body, the wind knocked out of him.

'I arrest you!' Cranston roared, leaning over the man and grasping him by the neck. 'I, Jack Cranston, coroner, have got you!'

The man tried to wriggle free, but Cranston ripped his hood off and grabbed him by the hair.

'You are trapped, my little beauty!' he boomed. He banged the man's head on the floorboards. 'That's for me!' He banged it again. 'That's for Brother Athelstan!' And again. 'And that's for that poor maid you killed, you heartless bastard!'

Cranston then dragged the man to his feet. He deftly plucked the dagger from the robber's sheath, pushed him through the garret door and dragged him down the stairs into the passage on the floor below. Athelstan lit a candle and followed. He held the flame up against the felon's bruised, dazed face.

'I've never seen him before.'

'No, you won't have done,' Cranston said. 'But you are right, Brother. I bet this bastard's a tiler!'

The sounds of doors opening and shouts below showed that the rest of the household had been roused. Cranston went to the top of the stairs and bellowed for silence.

'Shut up!' he roared, clutching the footpad in one hand. He shook the man as a cat would a rat. 'We've still got business haven't we?'

The man could only groan in reply. Cranston marched down the stairs, dragging his prisoner with him. Athelstan followed behind, pleading with Sir John to be careful.

'I'll be bloody careful!' the coroner roared.

The servants had gathered, their faces pallid in the candlelight. Cranston shook the man again, put a finger to his lips for silence and waited by the front door. He must have waited five minutes before Athelstan heard the crunch of a boot and the voice of beadle Trumpington.

'Well past midnight. Cold and hard, but all's well!'

Cranston flung open the door, dragging the felon with him.

'Oh no, it's not, my lad! The time is bloody ripe to say just how unwell things really are!'

CHAPTER 12

Sir John Cranston stretched his long, stockinged feet in front of the roaring fire. He beamed at his lady, the adoring Maude, who sat beside him, hands in her lap, her girlish face wreathed in a beatific smile, her corn-coloured hair tied in braids. She had been summoned from her bed by her husband's triumphant return home. Cranston sipped from his favourite wine goblet and stretched his great legs until the muscles cracked. He wagged a finger at the astonished under-sheriff, Shawditch, who had also been summoned. Athelstan could only stare into the fire and quietly pray that he wouldn't laugh.

'You see,' Cranston explained for the third time, 'my secretarius and I had the same line of thought.' He pointed a finger at Shawditch. 'Always remember, Shawditch, Cranston's famous axiom "if a problem exists then a solution to it must also exist".' Cranston winked at Lady Maude. 'And we knew the problem. A merchant's house – empty except for the servants, who live on the ground floor – is entered without any visible sign of force and looted. The housebreaker disappears.' Cranston drummed his fingers on his fat knee. 'Now that problem would tax any law officer. However, when Athelstan and I visited the last house, where the poor girl was killed, we noticed that the straw beneath the garret's roof was rather damp. Well' – Cranston leaned over and squeezed Athelstan's hand – 'in the normal course of events, the average law officer would have thought, "Ah, I know how the felon got in – through the tiles. He removed some, climbed down, robbed the house, went out through the roof and replaced the tiles behind him. Easy enough for a professional tiler." The trouble with that theory, though, is that another tiler could easily detect what had been done.' He glared at Shawditch. 'Is that clear?'

The man nodded vigorously.

'So we asked Trumpington if a tiler had been summoned, and when he said yes we accepted his story.' Cranston leaned over for Lady Maude to fill his goblet. 'And if the beadle had had the roof examined by a tiler, who had found no signs of disturbance, then this could not be how the thief entered the house. But' – he waved an airy hand – 'this is where our logic comes in. Brother Athelstan and I considered the following possibility: what if Trumpington, the beadle, was involved in the housebreaking and the tiler used to check the roofs was also involved?' Cranston slurped from the goblet. 'A subtle little piece of trickery that might have deceived us had we not noticed those damp rushes.' Cranston licked his lips. 'Isn't that right, Brother?'

'Sir John,' Athelstan said, 'your logic is impeccable. Trumpington and the tiler were working hand in glove. The beadle would find out which houses were empty and how they were organised. Then, while he was patrolling the streets, bawling out all was well, his accomplice was busy robbing the house.'

224

'Have they confessed?' Shawditch asked.

'Oh yes, and some of the plunder has been found in their houses,' Cranston replied. 'They are now in Newgate awaiting trial. For the murder of that girl, both will hang.'

He got to his feet and warmed his great backside before the fire. 'Master Shawditch,' he said magnanimously, 'you may have credit for the arrest.'

'Sir John, I thank you.'

'Nonsense!' Cranston replied. 'Now be off with you. Make sure that all the stolen property is returned to its owners.'

Once the under-sheriff had left, Cranston was about to continue with his tales of triumph, even threatening to go back to his great victory on the river. But Athelstan yawned and stretched.

'Sir John, I thank you for your hospitality, but the hour is late and tomorrow we have other business.'

'I know, I know,' Cranston replied testily. 'That bloody Fisher of Men is still sending messages to me. He probably wants to be paid for the corpses he's plucked out of the river.'

Lady Maude got to her feet and pointed to a corner of the parlour.

'Brother Athelstan, I have made up a comfortable bed for you.'

Athelstan thanked her, rose and stretched.

'Now, come on, Sir John.' Lady Maude seized her husband by the elbow. 'Come. The poppets will be up early and you know they always cry for Daddy.'

Sir John, mollified, headed towards the door and the stairs to the bedchamber. He turned and waggled a finger at Athelstan.

'You sleep well, Brother, and don't worry about Gog and Magog. They are both locked in the kitchen. They won't get out and eat you!'

Athelstan breathed a sigh of relief – Cranston's new acquisitions, two great Irish wolfhounds, were harmless enough but so boisterous in their greetings they could knock the wind from the unwary visitor.

Sir John and his wife left. Athelstan snuffed out the candles and knelt by his bed to say his prayers, but his mind kept going back to Crawley lying on the deck and to the words he had uttered just before he swooned.

The door opened behind him.

'Brother?'

'Yes, Sir John?' Athelstan replied without turning.

'You know I am a terrible teller of tales?'

Athelstan smiled. 'You are a great man, Sir John.'

'No, Brother, it is you who deserve the credit. On behalf of that little murdered girl, I thank you. You saw old Jack do justice.'

The door closed. Athelstan finished his prayers, crossed himself and climbed into bed. He had intended to lie awake and think, but his head had hardly touched the bolster before he was fast asleep.

His awakening the next morning, however, was far from peaceful. He woke to find one of the great wolfhounds lying on top of him. The poppets, who viewed Athelstan as a favourite uncle, were staggering about with pieces of bread smeared with honey. They were screaming with laughter as they tried to force the bread between his lips. Athelstan climbed sleepily from the bed in a whirl of hurling limbs, soft little bodies and pieces of honey-coated bread. The other wolfhound, Magog, also appeared and made his contribution to the growing clamour. If Athelstan didn't want the bread and honey, the dogs certainly did. They began to butt the baby boys in their fat little stomachs.

Lady Maude arrived and her few quiet words had their desired effect. The wolfhounds disappeared beneath the table. The two poppets would have joined them, but their mother grabbed them both and dragged them off for their morning wash. Boscombe, Cranston's small, fat steward, a model of courtly courtesy, appeared with soap, towel and razor.

Athelstan washed and shaved before the fire then joined Sir John, dressed now in more sober attire, to breakfast in the kitchen. Leif the beggar also arrived. Athelstan was always astonished at the skinny beggar's appetite – it was as if he was constantly on the verge of death through starvation. Leif had brought a companion, Picknose – so named because of a disgusting personal habit. The two were listening in rapt admiration as Sir John, using knives and pieces of bread, described Eustace the Monk's attack along the Thames. Athelstan ignored them all, ate a hasty breakfast and went outside. The morning, despite the clear skies, was bitterly cold. Athelstan crossed to St Mary Le Bow, where the friendly priest allowed him to celebrate Mass in a chantry chapel.

Cranston was waiting when Athelstan left the church. He handed the friar his cloak and staff.

'I have just visited that old nag of yours,' he said.

'Philomel is not an old nag, Sir John. He's a bit like yourself, a stout warhorse who may have seen better days.'

Cranston roared with laughter as they made their way down Bread Street across Old Fish Street and Trinity towards the quayside. The city was beginning to stir, carts crashed along, pulled by great dray horses with hogged manes, the steam from their sweaty flanks raising clouds in the cold morning air. Pedlars pushed their barrows; sleepy-eyed apprentices, not alert enough for mischief, laid out stalls and extinguished the lamps hanging outside their masters' houses. Night pots were being emptied from upper windows and a burly-faced trader, covered in someone's night soil, was fairly dancing with rage. The dung-carts were out scraping the muck from the sewers and picking up the detritus from the previous day, which included dead cats and a dog, its back broken by a cartwheel. A group of Benedictine monks escorted a coffin down towards one of the churches. A chanteur entertained the early morning crowds with a story of being spirited away to a fabulous fairy city under a mountain outside Dublin. Some drunken roisterers, halters around their necks, their hose pulled down about their ankles, were being led up to the Tun to spend the morning in disgrace in the huge cage there. At the entrance to Vintry two poles stuck in the ground bore the heads of executed French pirates, their features unrecognisable under the muck and refuse that had been thrown at them.

Cranston and Athelstan reached the quayside, which was thronged with merchant ships; the sky was almost blacked out by a forest of masts, spars and cranes. They passed the *Aleppo*, the *George*, the *Christopher* and the *Black Cock*, their holds open to receive bundles of English wool, iron, salt, meat and cloths from Midland towns. Athelstan looked between the ships and glimpsed the war cogs riding at anchor. Cranston led him down to the alehouse where they had last met the Fisher of Men. He quietly asked the tapster to fetch the fellow, ordered two blackjacks of ale, sat in the same corner of the tavern as before and waited. The Fisher of Men soon appeared. His narrow, skeletal face glowed with pleasure at the profits he had harvested by plundering the dead and taking corpses from the river. His gargoyles thronged in the doorway waiting. The Fisher of Men refused Cranston's offer of refreshment but clapped his hands and gave Cranston and Athelstan a mocking bow.

'My Lord, your Holiness! At last you grace us with your presence!'

'Bugger off!' Cranston snapped. 'You are wasting time!'

'Would I waste the time of the mighty Cranston? No, come with me, my lord coroner, I'll show you a great mystery.'

Cranston shrugged. He and Athelstan followed the sinister figure and his motley gang out into the alleyway and through a maze of urine-smelling runnels until they stopped before a large, shabby warehouse.

'Oh Lord!' Cranston breathed. 'Mermaid's paps! He is going to show us his wares!'

The Fisher of Men produced a key, unlocked the door and led them into the darkness. Athelstan immediately gagged at the fishy, stale-water smell mingled with the sickly-sweet stench of corruption. The gargoyles thronged around him.

'Lights!' the Fisher of Men shouted. 'Let there be light, for the darkness cannot comprehend the light.'

Athelstan put his hand out to steady himself and felt something cold, wet and spongy beneath him. He peered down and bit back his cry as he saw it was the grey, puffed face of a corpse. He rubbed his hand on his robe and waited as torches and candles were lit.

'Oh, for the love of God!' Cranston breathed. 'Brother, look around you!'

The warehouse was built like a great barn. Everywhere, in makeshift boxes which the Fisher of Men must have filched from different places, were the corpses of those hauled from the Thames – forty or fifty at least. Athelstan glimpsed a thin-faced young woman, an archer with a bloody wound in his chest, an old woman who lay on a sopping yellow rag, even a small lapdog that must have fallen from someone's arms.

'Come this way! Come this way!'

The Fisher of Men led them to the far end of the barn, where an arrow box was propped against the wall. There was a man's body in it. Athelstan, thinking he was going to be sick, looked away. Cranston, though, studied the corpse carefully. It was that of a tall, well-built man with black hair and thin features; the eyeless face bore the marks of fish bites and the flesh was puffy and white like old wool after it has been dipped in dirty water. The man's boots were gone – they, along with other possessions, were the perquisites of the Fisher of Men. The thin linen shirt was open and Cranston saw a purple-red bruise on the chest and marks on the neck. The Fisher of Men fairly danced beside the body.

'See, see, see who it is!'

'I see a corpse,' Cranston replied drily. 'Probably a sailor's.'

'Correct! Correct! But which sailor?'

Cranston glowered at the man. 'One of those killed in the battle?'

'Oh no! Oh no! This is Bracklebury!'

Athelstan opened his eyes in amazement. Cranston peered closer.

'It fits your description, my lord coroner, though there was nothing on him to identify him by.'

Cranston swore under his breath. 'By a fairy's futtock, so it is! Black-haired, a scar under his left eye, past his thirtieth summer, but—'

'He's been in the water for at least, oh, five or six days,' the Fisher of Men said.

Athelstan shook his head. 'But Bracklebury was alive two days ago! He murdered Bernicia!'

The gargoyles standing behind them tittered with laughter.

'Impossible!' the Fisher of Men shouted, stretching out his hand towards Cranston. 'How can a man be drowned and be walking about murdering people?'

Athelstan forgot his disdain and walked closer. 'Is there any wound?' he asked.

'None,' the Fisher of Men replied. 'Not a scratch. Only these.' He pointed to the purple bruise on the man's chest and the slight lacerations on either side of the throat. 'Something was tied around his neck.'

Cranston stepped back, shaking his head.

'It can't be,' he muttered. 'Bracklebury's alive.'

'I claim my reward,' the Fisher of Men said.

'Sir John, let's get out of here,' Athelstan murmured.

They walked back to the alleyway, the Fisher of Men and the gargoyles clustered around them.

'Look!' Cranston bellowed, 'I need proof.' He stamped his feet and stared around. 'I need proof! Proof that this is Bracklebury.' He pointed a finger at the Fisher of Men. 'You've got spies all over the city. Bring these people to meet me at the alehouse. He rapped out a list of people he wished to see – the ship's officers as well as Emma Roffel. 'I want them at the tavern within the hour. I don't give a rat's arse what they are doing!'

The Fisher of Men seemed delighted by the prospect of wielding so much power. It was not often that he was able to order about the ordinary inhabitants of the city in which he lurked. He and the gargoyles swept down the alleyway, Cranston still roaring at them that they were to bring everyone to the tavern. He took Athelstan back there. Cranston slumped on to a stool. He pushed his great back into the corner of the wall and roared for refreshment until all the slatterns in the place were hopping like fleas on a frisky dog.

'It can't be Bracklebury,' he breathed. 'Yet it must be Bracklebury.'

Athelstan thanked the landlord and pushed the platter of food he had brought and a goblet of claret towards Cranston.

'If the corpse isn't Bracklebury's,' he said, 'then he is still our principal suspect. But if it is, then, to quote a famous coroner I know, Hell's teeth!'

'Or mermaid's tits!' Cranston smiled.

'Aye and those too, Sir John.' Athelstan sipped from his tankard of ale. 'If it is Bracklebury, then who is the murderer of Bernicia? And, more importantly, who killed Bracklebury? Why and how?'

Cranston rubbed his face. 'You know, I have this awful nightmare, Brother, that we have been concentrating on Bracklebury and forgetting the other two sailors. We don't even know their names. What if they are the villains of the piece?'

Athelstan's mind teemed with the possibilities.

'The war cogs will sail soon,' Cranston said. 'The officers on board the *God's Bright Light* will go with them. Everything will remain a mystery.'

'Do you have the silver, Sir John?'

Athelstan whirled around and Cranston looked up at the two scrutineers who had come to stand silently beside them, the false smiles on their plump faces belied by the hardness of their eyes.

'The exchequer wants its silver back,' Peter said.

'And soon!' the other added.

Uninvited, they pulled stools over but shook their heads when Cranston offered them refreshment.

'No, Sir John, we have not come for meat and drink. We are here for the king's silver. Any progress?'

Cranston described what they had discovered on board the *God's Bright Light*.

'So you found the hiding place but not the money,' Paul summed up.

Cranston nodded.

'We have the tally men out,' Peter said. 'You see, the silver was freshly minted.' He smiled sourly. 'When you buy spies and traitors, they always bite the silver first.'

'But how could it have been freshly minted?' Cranston asked. 'Sir Henry sent it to the exchequer!'

'The silver bullion he sent was melted down and coins struck from it at the royal mint in the Tower.'

'And you have searched for these coins?' Athelstan asked.

'Yes, we have.'

'And you've found no trace?'

'I didn't say that. A goldsmith just off Candlewick Street was visited by one of our tally men. Some of the coins are already in circulation.'

'How much was your spy carrying when Roffel attacked the ship?'

'A hundred groats,' Peter replied.

'A hundred groats in freshly minted coins on the open market!' Cranston exclaimed.

Athelstan held up his hand. 'And, of course, you have questioned this goldsmith?'

'Oh, of course! We even threatened him with a short sojourn in the Tower's deepest dungeon.'

'And what did he tell you?'

'Very little. But he described a man – a strong, well-built sailor dressed in a battered leather jacket, hair tied in a knot at the back of his head. Or so he thinks.'

'And his features?'

'He had his cowl and hood pulled full across his face. The goldsmith did not think it was suspicious. The man claimed the silver was payment for booty handed over to the crown. Of course, any further questions were silenced by the goldsmith's greed.'

'And how much was exchanged?'

'Ten groats. What concerns us is that it's easy to chase money in London but what happens if this fellow goes to Norwich, Lincoln, Ipswich or Gloucester?'

Cranston put his finger to his lips as the officers of the *God's Bright Light*, led by Cabe, entered the tavern. Most of them looked tired and rather angry at being dragged away for yet another interrogation. One of the scrutineers looked over his shoulder; he tapped his companion on the arm and they both got to their feet.

'We'll be back, Sir John.' They pulled up their hoods and slipped soundlessly out of the alehouse. Cabe, Coffrey, Minter and Peverill now stood over Cranston, thumbs pushed into broad, leather belts, their salt-stained jackets pulled back to display daggers and short swords. Athelstan fleetingly wondered what would happen if all four of these men were taken to that goldsmith? But that would prove little and might only alert suspicions. The goldsmith would be frightened of implicating himself. Moreover, the mysterious sailor who had brought the silver might be an innocent third party only used by the thief and murderer for that particular transaction. Athelstan blinked as Cabe leaned over and whispered to Cranston. The coroner just glared back.

'I appreciate you coming,' Sir John declared falsely. 'My excuse for asking you is that I thought you might want to meet an old friend.'

'What the bloody hell do you mean?' Peverill asked.

Cabe stepped back. 'You are not saying Roffel's climbed out of his grave?' Cranston shook his head, grinned and sipped from his wine cup.

'No, but Bracklebury might have.'

'Bracklebury!' Coffrey exclaimed. 'Have you caught him?'

'In a manner of speaking, yes.'

'What do you mean?' Cabe snarled. 'What is this, Sir John? To be summoned by some benighted sloven from our duties on the quayside.'

Cranston gazed beyond him at the door where Emma Roffel now stood with the ubiquitous Tabitha in tow. Behind her was the thin-faced, red-haired Fisher of Men.

Emma swept grandly towards the coroner.

'You'd best not be wasting my time, Sir John!' She flicked a look of contempt at her dead husband's officers. 'What is it now?'

'You'll see! You'll see!' the Fisher of Men called from the door. 'A mummer's play is about to begin. The cast is waiting.'

'Come on, Sir John,' Athelstan whispered. Cranston realised that the ship's officers and Emma Roffel were in danger of walking off in protest, so he lumbered to his feet.

'This is no petty matter,' he said. 'All of you had best follow me.'

They followed the Fisher of Men, surrounded by his gargoyles, back to the warehouse. He opened the door and ushered them in. While others lit candles and torches, he led them past the grisly, decaying corpses laid out on the floor or on the makeshift tables.

Athelstan watched the others. Emma Roffel, pale at the sights she glimpsed, was supporting Tabitha. The maid clutched her mistress's arm, her eyes half-closed, her face turned inwards so she did not have to look at the pale faces and open, staring eyes. Even the sailors, used to battle and sudden death, lost their arrogance. Coffrey became distinctly nervous and, on one occasion, turned away to gag at the offensive stench. At last they reached the arrow chest. The Fisher of Men held up a torch, giving the corpse's face an eerie light of its own.

'Oh, sweet Lord!' Minter the ship's surgeon crouched down.

Coffrey turned away. Peverill gazed in astonishment. Cabe, who seemingly couldn't believe his eyes, walked closer and stared at the dead man's face.

'Is it Bracklebury?' Sir John asked.

'God rest him!' Minter whispered. 'Of course it is!'

'Do you all recognise him?'

'We do!' they chorused.

'Mistress Roffel, is this the man who brought your husband's corpse back to your house?'

'Yes,' she whispered. 'It is.'

'Then I pronounce and declare,' said Cranston formally, 'that this is the corpse of Bracklebury, first mate of the *God's Bright Light*, murdered by person or persons unknown. May God bring them swiftly to judgement!' Cranston pointed at the Fisher of Men. 'You may apply for the reward.' He turned to the ship's surgeon. 'Can you tell us how this man died?'

Minter, overcoming his distaste, pulled the water-sodden corpse from its box and laid it on the ground.

'Do you need me any more, Sir John?' Emma Roffel asked.

'No, no, of course not. I thank you for coming.'

Minter was now stripping the corpse and examining it carefully, turning it over as if it was some dead fish on the quayside.

'Well?' Cranston snapped.

'No signs of any blow to the head or stab wound. No marks of violence, except these—' He turned the grisly corpse over and indicated the lacerations on each side of the neck and the large purple welt on the chest.

Emma Roffel, turning to leave and still holding the tearful Tabitha, slipped on the wet floor. Athelstan caught her by the hand.

'Steady!' he whispered.

'Thank you,' she replied. 'If you could help me, Brother.'

Athelstan helped both women out into the cold, fresh air. Emma Roffel pushed Tabitha away.

'Come on, woman!' she said. 'For God's sake, it is not you laid out like a fish in a box!'

Tabitha moaned and drew closer to her mistress. Emma looked at Athelstan.

'When will this business end?' she asked. 'Can't you see, Brother, that those pirates in there are no better than my husband? They know the truth!' And, spinning on her heel, she led the sobbing Tabitha away.

Athelstan went back to where Cranston and the others were still staring down at Bracklebury's corpse.

'Why?' the coroner asked suddenly.

'Why what, Sir John?'

'Well, Bracklebury had apparently been in the water for some time. But no one knows why or what caused these bruises on his chest and neck. Yet what really puzzles me is why his corpse appears now?'

Cranston looked at Cabe, who was leaning against a wooden pillar. Still shocked, the second mate was staring down at his dead comrade.

'Master Cabe, who were the other two sailors? What were their names?'

Cabe didn't answer.

'Master Cabe, the names of the other two sailors?'

'Eh?' The second mate rubbed the side of his face.

'Clement and Alain. They were London men, or I think they were.'

Athelstan was staring at the Fisher of Men, who caught his glance.

'What is it, Brother?'

'Can you explain why Bracklebury's corpse should suddenly appear?'

'No, Father, I can't.'

Athelstan recalled the battle on the river. Images flitted through his mind – the catapults being loaded with stones, the galleys crashing against the cog to set it rocking on the swift flow of the Thames. The friar smiled down at the corpse. 'Of course!' he whispered and tapped his foot in excitement.

'Sir John!' Athelstan exclaimed. 'I think we should return to the *God's Bright Light*. Our good friend here, the Fisher of Men, might be able to help us.'

'How?' the strange creature asked.

'Do you have a swimmer?' Athelstan continued, indicating that Cranston should keep quiet. 'Someone who is not frightened of the currents of the Thames?'

The Fisher of Men grinned mirthlessly, put a finger to his lips and gave a long whistle.

'Icthus!'

One of the hooded gargoyles detached himself from the rest and ran forward.

'This is Icthus,' said the Fisher of Men. 'We call him that because it is the Greek word for fish. Where they can go, he can follow, can't you, Icthus?'

Icthus drew back his hood. Athelstan gazed at him in a mixture of shock, revulsion and compassion. Either he had been born disfigured or he was the victim of some terrible disease. He was very thin.

Although only a boy, he was completely bald. But what caught everyone's horrified attention was his face. It was the face of a fish – with scaly skin, a small, flat nose, a cod-like mouth and eyes so far apart they seemed to be on either side of his head.

'This is Icthus,' the Fisher of Men repeated. 'And his fee is one silver piece.'

Athelstan forced himself to look at the boy.

'Will you swim for us?' he asked.

The cod mouth opened. Icthus had no teeth or tongue, only dark red gums. The only sound he could make was a guttural choking noise. But he nodded vigorously in answer to Athelstan's question.

'Good,' Athelstan said. 'Now let's return to that God-forsaken ship.' He grinned at Cranston. 'And no questions, please.'

CHAPTER 13

The *God's Bright Light* was preparing for sea when Cranston and Athelstan and their two strange companions went aboard. The friar was jovially welcomed by the young captain, who listened carefully, studying the Fisher of Men and Icthus. Then he nodded.

'Whatever you want, Brother, but the Thames is a broad river.'

Athelstan stared around. All signs of the night battle had disappeared. Thankfully, even the French corpses had been removed. He walked over to the ship's side and stared out towards Queen's hithe, trying to imagine that dark night and the lamps winking back and forth. Who, he wondered, had been that watcher on the shore? Who had killed Bracklebury? Athelstan stood back. Someone with sharp eyesight could see him from the shore. But, on the night Bracklebury had disappeared a heavy sea mist had been boiling along the river. Athelstan beckoned Cranston over and, watched by a curious ship's crew, the Fisher of Men led Icthus across by his skinny arm. Athelstan went and pointed over the starboard side, near the stern.

'Dive there!' he said.

'For God's sake, Brother!' the captain breathed. 'Are

241

you sure? Any corpse would be swept away by the currents.'

Even Cranston looked doubtful.

'Will you do it, Icthus?' Athelstan asked gently. He stroked the youngster's cheek. 'You needn't if you don't want to, but you might help us discover the truth.'

The boy's strange mouth opened in a grin. He stepped out of his gown, leaving it crumpled on the deck and stood with his thin body clad only in a pair of woollen breech clouts. Ignoring the laughter of the sailors at his thin body, he climbed on to a bulwark, bared his gums at Athelstan in a brief smile and slipped into the river. A few bubbles appeared on the surface and then he was gone. Athelstan stared into the dark water, waiting for the boy to reappear, but time passed and his stomach churned with fear. He looked across at the Fisher of Men.

'Will he be safe?'

'Safe as he would be here,' the Fisher of Men replied caustically, glaring at the sniggering sailors behind him.

Cranston took out his wineskin. He offered it to the captain who shook his head so the coroner took a generous swig, belched and lumbered to the ship's side.

'Come on!' he roared down at the water. 'Where the bloody hell are you?'

The water rippled and, as if in answer to Cranston's shout, Icthus appeared. He spluttered, smiled strangely, closed his mouth, breathed through his nose, then disappeared again. He reappeared a bit quicker this time, clapping his hands as he trod water and gestured with his hands in a stabbing motion, holding one finger up.

'He wants a dagger!' the Fisher of Men cried. 'Sir John!'

Cranston took out his long stabbing dagger and tossed it to Icthus, who caught it expertly before disappearing again. This time he re-emerged with a grisly burden in his arms.

'May God be blessed!' Cranston breathed. 'If I hadn't seen it with my own eyes, I would not have believed it!'

Ropes and nets were lowered and sailors ran forward to help. They grasped the body Icthus brought to the surface and pulled both the swimmer and the water-logged corpse on board.

'It's Alain!' Peverill declared, pushing his way through. 'Hell's teeth! What's that?'

Icthus had put his robe on and now crouched by the corpse, in his hand a rope with a metal ball attached. He made signs to indicate that it had been tied around the corpse's neck. Athelstan stared at the corpse's thin face, which had turned a pale green and bore the same purple marks as Bracklebury's. The corpse was sodden with water, disfiguring both features and body. Athelstan noted the purple welts on either side of the neck and the bruise where the ball had hit against the dead man's chest.

'Well, Brother?' Cranston asked, swaying rather dangerously on his feet.

Athelstan took the heavy, metal ball, noting how the rope was laced through a small loop on top.

'Captain, the ship's armament includes these?'

The seaman nodded and pointed further down the

deck where crates of similar iron balls were stacked.

'We place them in the catapults,' he explained. 'Sometimes the rope is hardened with pitch and set alight so the ball not only causes damage but spreads fire.'

The captain stared down in disgust at the corpse. He noticed one of the eyes had been eaten through and walked away.

Minter, the ship's surgeon, now crouched by the corpse and began to examine it carefully.

'Whoever killed Bracklebury and Alain,' Athelstan explained, 'rendered them unconscious and placed those metal balls around their necks so they would sink to the bottom.'

'As far as I can see, apart from the lacerations on the neck and the blow to the chest, there is no other wound,' Minter reported.

Cranston snapped his fingers, inviting the Fisher of Men and his strange companion to join them. He placed a silver coin in Icthus's hand.

'Was there any other corpse down there?'

Icthus shook his head.

'Are you sure?' Cranston persisted.

Icthus nodded.

Cranston shuffled his feet in anger and stared up at the darkening sky.

'Hell's teeth, Brother, what are we to do?'

The friar, too, stared at the sky; his mind was a jumble of different ideas, sensations and impressions. He wanted to go back to St Erconwald's, sit before his fire and impose order on this chaos.

'Brother?' Cranston asked suspiciously. 'Are you all right?'

Athelstan smiled and turned to the captain. 'Tell me, sir, do the stars move in the heavens?'

Southchurch shrugged. 'Most people say they do, Father.'

'And you?'

'I once served in the Middle Sea. I met an Egyptian sea captain who claimed the stars didn't move but the earth was a sphere spinning in the heavens.'

Athelstan stared up at the dark clouds. He'd heard such theories before.

'Athelstan!' Cranston snapped.

The friar winked at Sir John. He stared across at the officers, watching Cabe carefully. The man still seemed deeply shocked by what he had seen that afternoon.

'We've found Bracklebury,' Athelstan said, 'and we've found Alain, but where's poor Clement's corpse?'

Athelstan dug into his own purse and gave coins to Icthus and the Fisher of Men. He thanked the captain and grasped Cranston by the elbow.

'Come on, Sir John, enough is enough. God knows I have had my fill of human wickedness.'

A bumboat took them ashore. They walked quietly back through the warren of streets to the Holy Lamb of God, where Athelstan could collect his horse.

Cranston grew increasingly infuriated at the friar's prolonged silence. Athelstan even refused refreshment, muttering he must get back to St Erconwald's.

'Brother!' Cranston roared in exasperation as Athelstan made ready to leave. 'What are you thinking about?'

Athelstan shook his head. 'I don't even know myself, Sir John.'

'Should I issue a description of Clement?' Cranston asked. The coroner hawked and spat. 'At this rate I'm going to make a bloody fool of myself. Every time I look for someone he turns out to be drowned!' He glanced at his companion. 'You still haven't told me how Bracklebury and Alain were killed!'

Athelstan stood in the stable yard waiting for Philomel to be saddled. 'Bracklebury, Alain and Clement were all drugged.' He shook his head. 'I don't know how or by whom, but when I examined Bracklebury's corpse I surmised someone had tied a weight around his neck and tossed him overboard. A vigorous man, Bracklebury must have been unconscious not to resist. However, there's no bruise to his head or wound in his body, hence my conclusion that he had been drugged.' Athelstan paused to greet Philomel. 'The same fate befell Alain and Clement. They were probably all thrown overboard from the deck near the stern castle; this, and the heavy river mist, would give the assassin every protection.'

'So, how did Bracklebury's corpse surface?' Cranston asked.

Athelstan smiled. 'For that we must thank Eustace the Monk.' He grasped the fat coroner's arm. 'Just think, Sir John, the dipping oars of the galleys, their crashing into our ships, the corpses tumbling into the river making the water eddy and swirl.' Athelstan scratched his head. 'The assassin must have worked quickly. Perhaps the rope around Bracklebury's neck wasn't so secure and worked loose, aided, perhaps, by the battle. The weight slips away, the corpse surfaces.' Athelstan shrugged. 'And the deep gave up its dead. The discovery of Alain's corpse simply proves my—'

He smiled. 'Our theory.' He patted Cranston's shoulder. 'So, forget about Clement, only God knows where his poor corpse is.'

'And the murderer?' Cranston snapped.

Athelstan seized Philomel's reins, mounted and stared down at Cranston.

'Sir John, go home, kiss the Lady Maude, play with the poppets. Rest and think.' He urged Philomel forward, leaving an even more infuriated Cranston glaring speechlessly behind him.

Athelstan found St Erconwald's quiet. Marston had long disappeared and so had the parishioners who had been working on the stage. Huddle's painting of the backcloth was at last near completion and for a while the friar stood gazing in silent admiration at the great mouth of Hell, from which sprang black demons with the red faces of monkeys. Behind the canvas he found the metal pans and wooden tubs that Crim and the other boys would use to create sounds. He picked up the silver trumpet that would be blown before God spoke. He put it to his lips and blew a short blast then blushed with embarrassment as Ashby suddenly appeared from behind the rood screen.

'Father, what's the matter?'

'Nicholas, I had forgotten you were still here. Are you well?'

'Yes, Aveline has just left. She says Marston has fled.'

'And do you need anything?' Athelstan asked, hoping the young man would not draw him into conversation.

'No, Father.' Ashby leaned against the rood screen. 'I have never rested, eaten or drunk so well in my life.'

He pointed to the stage and the canvas backcloth. 'It will be a grand play, Father.'

Athelstan smiled. 'It will be, Nicholas, if my parishioners don't kill each other first!'

Ashby laughed. 'Benedicta shooed them all out when Watkin the dung-collector started a row. He claimed that God the Father should sit higher than God the Holy Ghost. You can guess at Pike's reaction to that.'

Athelstan nodded. 'And Bonaventure?'

'Oh, he's in the sanctuary.'

'Of course he is,' Athelstan said to himself. 'The little mercenary!'

He bade farewell to Ashby and walked out of the church and across to the stable, where Philomel was chomping away at a small truss of hay hung over the door of the stable. Athelstan put his battered saddle away, replenished the old horse's water and walked back to his house. Benedicta had built the fire up and had left a pie on the small plinth in the inglenook.

'I am going to reward myself,' Athelstan muttered.

He went into the buttery and took out a small jug of wine Cranston had given him at Easter. 'The best of Bordeaux,' Cranston had described it. Athelstan now unsealed the stopper, poured himself a generous cup and sipped it. He then washed his hands and face in a bowl of rose water, took his horn spoon and sat down to enjoy Benedicta's pie.

'Thank God for food!' Athelstan muttered. 'And thank God I don't have to cook it!'

Athelstan finished eating, cleaned his mouth and fingers and went upstairs. He slept for an hour on his small cot bed. He woke refreshed, went downstairs and cleared the table except for the wine cup. After this, he took out a large piece of parchment and began to write down everything he knew about the strange events on board the *God's Bright Light*. He scribbled down everything – every thought, every impression. Now and again he had to break off because of minor interruptions. Mugwort the bell clerk claimed that the bell rope was getting frayed and needed to be replaced. Ranulf the rat-catcher wanted Athelstan to say another Mass for his newly formed Guild of Rat Hunters. Crim wanted assurances that he would beat the drum during the play. Pernell the Fleming wanted to know if eating meat on a Friday was a serious sin.

Athelstan went across to the church to ensure all was well with Ashby and, finding it was, locked the church for the night. He went back to his writing. The din from the alleyways and streets around faded until the loudest sound was the hooting of the owls hunting above the long grass in the cemetery. Athelstan carried on. He kept writing and, using pieces of wood, even created tiny models of the war cogs moored off Queen's hithe. Only when he was satisfied that he had recorded all the information available to him did he attempt to draw conclusions. His vexation grew – time and again he tried to create a case, but it always fell apart like some syllogism which cannot survive the probe of logic. He took a fresh piece of parchment and wrote carefully at the top, '*Si autem*?, What if?' He then began to list his doubts and, when he had finished, rubbed his hands together. He looked at these, fingers splayed.

'You are soft, Athelstan,' he murmured. 'Soft hands.'

He went back to his writing. A thought occurred to him.

'What if there are two murderers? What if there are three? Or is there just one? A master of this dance?'

Once again he began to write, taking one central fact as if it were a divinely revealed truth and building his case around it. At last, long after midnight, he finished and threw the quill down.

'What if?' he muttered. 'What if? But how do I prove it?'

Athelstan put his head on his arms and, before he knew it, drifted into one of his nightmares. He was on a boat being rowed by a masked oarsman along a fog-bound Thames. The mist cleared and he saw, in the prow of the boat, a hooded, cowled figure. Athelstan knew this must be the murderer. The boat bumped. Athelstan shook himself awake and realised he had knocked the cup off the table. He yawned, stretched, got to his feet and, leaving the manuscripts where they were, damped down the fire and slowly climbed the stairs to his bed.

The next morning he slept later than he intended, being roused by Crim pounding on the door below.

'Come on, Father!' the lad shouted. 'It's time for Mass!'

Athelstan decided to hurry down immediately rather than wash and change first. He followed Crim out of the house and through the swirling mist to the church door. A few of his parishioners were already waiting.

'You are late, Father!' Tiptoe the tapster accused.

'And I can't ring the bell!' Mugwort declared mournfully.

'I was tired,' Athelstan answered impatiently. 'But, come!'

He opened the church door, letting Ashby slip out to relieve himself. Ursula the pig-woman stood guard to make sure that Marston or one of his thugs didn't reappear. Athelstan quickly donned his vestments, trying to ignore Bonaventure, who kept rubbing up against his leg.

'Go away, cat!' Athelstan muttered. 'You are a mercenary and a traitor.'

The cat's rubbing became even more vigorous so Crim had to put him outside. Athelstan lit the candles, celebrated Mass and, when he had finished, still distracted by the conclusions he had drawn earlier that morning, gave Crim a penny and a message for Cranston. Then he hurried back to his house, washed and shaved. He hastily ate some bread and cheese, told Mugwort he was in charge of the church until Benedicta or Watkin appeared, saddled Philomel and rode down to London Bridge.

Athelstan found his journey slow. Philomel was sluggish and London Bridge was thronged with barrows, carts and pack-horses as people fought to get across before the markets opened. Athelstan stopped off at the church of St Thomas Becket half-way across. He said a prayer and lit a candle before the statue of the Virgin to ask for her guidance and wisdom in establishing the truth. Once in the city, Athelstan had to face more delays. In Bridge Street a house had caught fire and, further along, a group of Abraham men performed one of their crazed dances to the amusement of some of the onlookers and the exasperation of others. By the time he reached Cheapside,

Athelstan was saddle-sore and bitterly cursing a journey that had taken over an hour. He found Cranston ensconced in the Holy Lamb of God. The coroner was sitting at his favourite table, watching the innkeeper and his wife and their army of scullions building fires and starting the ovens. Because the hour was early, the fat coroner was for once content just to sit back and enjoy the savoury smells beginning to come from the kitchen.

He grinned at Athelstan. 'Monk, you look angry.'

'Sir John, I'm a friar and I'm fretful.' Athelstan gingerly sat down and peered into Cranston's tankard.

'It's watered ale!' Cranston said. 'But I have ordered a minced-beef pie with onions, leeks and a dash of garlic and rosemary.' He closed his eyes. 'Just think of it, Brother, rich, savoury meat simmering under a thick, golden crust. By the way, I have sent for him.' Cranston cocked open one eye and peered across at the hour candle on its iron spigot near the door. 'So you had best tell me what you plan.'

Athelstan did, haltingly at first, but becoming more articulate as his confidence in his conclusions grew. At first Cranston roared with laughter.

'Bollocks and tits!' he scoffed.

'And the same to you, my son!' Athelstan replied.

Sir John calmed down. Once again Athelstan described his conclusions, hammering home his every point with both reason and evidence and Cranston's merriment began to fade. Athelstan paused as the landlord's wife, who always cosseted the coroner, brought a blackjack of ale and served a steaming pie on a large trancher. The sight of the pie made Athelstan hungry, so she cut a piece off for him. They both ate and drank in silence. Once Cranston was finished, Athelstan outlined his strategies. The coroner asked a spate of questions. Athelstan answered and Sir John finally nodded.

'I accept what you say, Brother! Perhaps just in time, here he comes!'

Philip Cabe had slipped through the doorway. He caught sight of Cranston and Athelstan, swaggered across and slumped down on the stool Athelstan pulled over.

'Sir John, the hour is early.'

'Master Cabe, the matter is pressing.'

Athelstan studied the seaman carefully. Cabe looked much the worse for wear – he was unshaven and his grey eyes were bleary from a heavy night's drinking.

'What are you worried about, Master Cabe?' Athelstan asked gently.

'Nothing, Father.'

'You want something to drink?'

The seaman shrugged. 'Perhaps watered ale?'

Cranston called out the order and they waited until it was served. Cabe sipped gingerly from the tankard.

'What do you want?' he asked.

'The truth,' Athelstan replied.

'I have told you that already.'

Cranston leaned over and squeezed the man's wrist.

'No, you haven't. You are a liar, a thief and a murderer! And, if you don't tell me the truth, I'll see you hang!' Cranston smiled bleakly. 'Now, be a good boy and put both hands on the table, well away from the knife tucked in your belt. Come on!'

Cabe obeyed.

Cranston smiled. 'You may touch your tankard but nothing else. Now, my secretarius will describe things as they are.'

Athelstan edged closer. 'You were second mate on the *God's Bright Light*,' he began, 'when it attacked and sank a fishing smack off the French coast, killing all its crew. But this was no chance attack. Roffel knew that there was silver on board. He found the silver and carried it back to the *God's Bright Light*. However, Roffel, in Sir John's words, was a mean bastard. He should have shared the silver with his crew, especially his officers, as well as with the crown. Instead he hid it away in some secret place. By some chance you and Bracklebury found out about it.'

Cabe stared dumbly at his tankard.

'Now Roffel fell ill and died. In fact, he was poisoned.'

'I didn't do that,' Cabe muttered.

'I do not claim you did, but Roffel's demise provided you and Bracklebury with an excellent opportunity to search the ship. You found nothing. But once the *God's Bright Light* had anchored in the Thames you and Bracklebury could search more thoroughly. You drew up your plans. The crew, apart from a small watch, would be sent ashore and Bracklebury would take the opportunity to search the ship thoroughly from poop to stern.'

Cranston sipped from his own tankard.

'Now, if both of you had stayed behind it might have created some suspicions – after all, no sailor is eager to stay on board a ship back into port after a time at sea.' Athelstan placed his tankard down. 'Now,

Bracklebury had Roffel's corpse taken ashore. The whores came on board and then you and most of the crew left. However, you didn't fully trust Bracklebury, so you insisted that he stayed in communication with you. You devised a system of signals between Bracklebury, with the lantern on board ship, and you, in some darkened recess on the quayside.

'Now, everything went according to plan until that sailor and his whore returned, just before dawn, to find the ship completely deserted. Master Cabe, I can only imagine both your fury and doubt over what had happened. You must have been mystified by his disappearance! How had this been done? Where was Bracklebury and, above all, where was the silver?'

'A fairy story!' Cabe scoffed.

'Oh no,' Athelstan persisted. 'Sir John here knows I am telling the truth. You, Master Cabe, began to believe you had been double-crossed. And you began to wonder who it was. Now, while you were hiding in the shadows, you had seen the whore Bernicia come down to Queen's hithe. Perhaps you thought she and Bracklebury had planned to steal the silver and make a fool of you?'

'How would Bracklebury know Bernicia?' Cabe muttered.

Athelstan shrugged. 'Oh, you never know, Master Cabe, in this world of lies, greed makes strange allies. Anyway, somehow or other, you became convinced Bernicia knew where the silver was. So you planned to meet her and used Bracklebury's name.'

Cabe drank from the tankard and sneered.

'But, if Bracklebury was her ally, how could I appear as him?'

'That I don't know,' Athelstan replied truthfully. 'Something had changed your mind so that you believed Bracklebury may not have double-crossed you but that Bernicia certainly had. Anyway,' Athelstan continued, 'you took Bernicia to a secret drinking-place, invited yourself back to her house, cut her throat and ransacked the place.'

'What proof do you have of this?' Cabe snapped.

Cranston leaned over, tapping the table. 'I'll be honest, not much, my bucko. But, there again, perhaps if we took you back to that secret drinking-place, who knows who might recognise you?'

Cabe's face became even paler.

'Come on,' Cranston urged gently. 'Sooner or later the truth will be out.'

'What happens—' Cabe looked up. 'What happens if I tell the truth, as I see it?'

Cranston gestured with his hand. 'Murder is murder, Master Cabe, and murderers hang. But those who turn king's evidence may seek the royal pardon and agree to leave England' – Cranston screwed up his eyes and looked towards the door of the tavern – 'for, shall we say, three years?'

Athelstan grabbed the seaman by the arm. 'For the love of God, Master Cabe, tell us the truth!'

'Can I have some wine, Father?'

Cranston ordered him a goblet of claret. Cabe sipped at it carefully.

'These are the facts,' he began tonelessly. 'Roffel was a murdering bastard. God forgive us, it wasn't the first time he attacked a ship and killed the prisoners, but this time it was special. Roffel was looking for something.' He shrugged. 'Ah, well, you know what

256

happened. Afterwards Bracklebury and I decided to confront him. Now, perhaps, Roffel meant to lock the cabin door but he didn't; anyway it was very rare for us just to walk in. On that morning, however, we did; Roffel was sitting at his table, the money belt before him, silver coins spilling out. We knew at a glance what had happened. Roffel just roared at us to get out and said he would hang us if we ever did that again.' Cabe rubbed his face. 'Well, Bracklebury and I were furious. It wasn't the first time Roffel had stolen our shares.' Cabe glanced at Athelstan. 'Whatever you think of me, Father, I am a good seaman and I am not frightened of anything that walks on earth. My whole body is one scar from head to toe. And for what? Stale wine, cheap whores, a damp bed in some seedy alehouse?' He picked up his goblet and gulped at the wine. 'Bracklebury and I laid our plans, but then Roffel fell ill and died.'

'Did you murder him?' Cranston interrupted.

Cabe raised his hand. 'Before God, I had no hand in Roffel's death!'

'Did Bracklebury?'

'God knows! Anyway,' Cabe continued, 'Roffel's death gave us the opportunity to search the cabin. We went through everything but there was no trace of a belt full of silver. The ship anchored in the Thames, Bracklebury took Roffel's corpse ashore and, for a while, we acted our parts. We allowed the sailors to have their whores on board then, as you said, Bracklebury cleared the ship. Bracklebury was a good mate but I didn't trust him fully so we agreed that, about each hour, he would flash the signal lamp towards shore and I would answer.' Cabe licked his lips. 'The rest of the officers were too drunk to remember where each of us wandered off to. I spent most of the bloody night on that quayside fearful of everything. What happened if Bracklebury didn't find the silver? What happened if Bracklebury did and decided to flee? It was then that I saw the whore Bernicia standing on the quayside, looking out to the ship. I heard Bracklebury curse her and the misbegotten creature disappeared.' Cabe slurped his wine. 'The mist shifted – sometimes it blanketed the *God's Bright Light* completely, at other times it parted. I saw the signals being flashed and the admiral's boat go across. We had expected that but Bracklebury said he would fob him off.' Cabe splayed his fingers out on the table top. 'The next morning I thought I was in a nightmare. The *God's Bright Light* was deserted. There was no sign of Bracklebury or the rest of the watch. I immediately concluded that Bracklebury had found the silver and either killed his two shipmates and fled or shared it with them and jumped ship.' He smiled thinly at Cranston. 'But it wasn't as simple as that, Sir John, was it? There was all the mystery of who kept passing the signals between the ships and neither myself nor anyone else had seen anyone leave or approach the *God's Bright Light*.' Cabe tapped the table top. 'That did intrigue me, because Bracklebury couldn't swim.' Cabe gulped at the wine and stared beseechingly at Cranston. 'You promise I won't hang?'

'I promise.'

'Well, two days ago I got a note. It was written in some scrivener's hand but it bore Bracklebury's mark, a circle with a dot in the centre. It simply said that he had jumped ship and was in hiding from the law.

The message also claimed that, somehow or other, Bernicia had seized the silver. The whore had double-crossed everyone!'

'You know Bernicia was a man?' Athelstan asked.

'Yes, I discovered that when I killed the slut.'

'So, you did murder Bernicia?'

'Oh, yes,' Cabe replied. 'I followed her to that drinking-hole.'

'You didn't wonder how Bernicia could have found the silver?'

'At first I did. But then I remembered Bernicia being on board, just after we docked, and thought perhaps she could have found it then.'

'Why did you use Bracklebury's name?'

'Well, in his note he said that he was in hiding because you, Sir John, had circulated his description along the riverside as well as in the city. Now, I was still suspicious. I thought Bracklebury could be playing some devious game.' Cabe shrugged. 'So I went to that tavern and met Bernicia. I didn't actually say I was Bracklebury but merely hinted at it.' He blew his lips out. 'Bernicia didn't seem to know the difference and that, I thought, proved the message correct – Bernicia must have the silver. So I killed her. I then ransacked the house but found nothing.' Cabe laughed softly. 'Do you know, I still thought Bracklebury was alive and that I'd fallen into some subtle trap. When his body was washed up, I just gave up.' Cabe paused and looked at Athelstan. 'You never explained how that happened?'

The friar shrugged. 'Perhaps it was the river battle or perhaps the rope worked loose!'

'When I saw his corpse,' Cabe continued flatly, 'I

didn't know anything any more.' He blew his cheeks out. 'I've told you everything.'

'Do you know who sent that message?' Cranston asked.

'No, but—'

'But what?' Cranston insisted.

'What if Bracklebury is still alive? What if that corpse is someone who just looks like him? Where is the other member of the watch, Clement? Who else knew about the silver? Who knew Bracklebury's personal mark?' Cabe leaned over the table. 'Sir John, in God's name, what did happen?'

'In God's name,' Cranston replied slowly, 'we don't really know.'

'What about me?' Cabe asked.

'When does the *God's Bright Light* sail?'

'In two days' time.'

'Be on it!' Cranston ordered. 'And I'll see to it that, before it sails, you'll get a royal pardon. That pardon will only be effective provided you are not seen in London, and I mean London, for the space of three years!'

Cabe got to his feet. He turned to walk away, stopped and looked around.

'I hope you trap the bastard!' he hissed. 'I hope you hang him high!'

Athelstan watched the sailor leave.

'Do you know what to do now, Sir John?'

'Yes, Brother, I do,' Cranston replied. 'One thing, however, does puzzle me, Brother – how did Roffel and Ospring expect to steal that silver and escape the scrutineers?'

Athelstan sighed. 'Both men would have lied,

perhaps even blamed the spy. Sir Henry was powerful enough to bribe officials.' He drained his tankard. 'Sir Jacob is still in St Bartholomew's?'

'He is and none the worse for wear.'

'Good! Then let the dance begin!'

CHAPTER 14

Tabitha Velour answered the door and her face crinkled in a smile as she waved Athelstan in.

'Good morrow, Brother, surely not more questions?'

She ushered the friar into the small parlour where Emma Roffel sat before the fire, a book of accounts in her lap. She smiled as Athelstan entered.

'Brother, why are you here? Please take a seat? She turned to Tabitha. 'Bring Brother Athelstan some ale!'

Athelstan sat down. Tabitha came back with the ale and a platter of fresh milksops which she placed on the corner of the hearth.

'Well, Brother, what can I do for you?' Emma Roffel's face seemed softer, calmer.

Athelstan smiled. 'I was on my way to see Sir Jacob Crawley at St Bartholomew's hospital and I stopped by to see if you could stitch this' – he showed a rent in the sleeve of his robe – 'as well as to ask you a few questions before this matter is ended.'

'Ended?' Emma Roffel straightened up in her chair.

Athelstan nodded. 'I am going to meet Sir John at St Bartholomew's. He will be there with bailiffs and warrants to arrest Sir Jacob Crawley for the murder of your husband and of Bracklebury and his two shipmates.'

Emma Roffel closed her eyes. 'God save us!' she muttered.

She leaned over and took the sleeve of Athelstan's gown. 'As you know, Tabitha is a good seamstress. She can stitch this.' She snapped her fingers. 'Come on, woman!'

Tabitha hurried to the small box seat under the window, opened it and took out a small casket and crouched beside Athelstan. The friar jumped at a loud knocking on the door.

'I'll see to that!' Emma Roffel declared.

Athelstan heard her go down the passageway, open the door, say a few words and close the door again.

He didn't look up as she came back into the room.

'Who was it?' Tabitha asked.

Emma didn't answer. She went into the kitchen and returned, her hands up the sleeves of her voluminous gown. She sat down and stared into the fire.

'We have a clever, clever little priest here, Tabitha!'

Athelstan looked up. Emma Roffel's face was a mask of fury, pale, tight-lipped, her dark, powerful eyes blazing.

'Mistress?' he asked.

'Leave his gown, Tabitha, and come and sit next to me!'

The maid scurried across. Athelstan clasped his arms over his stomach and hoped his fear wouldn't show. Emma leaned across. 'A cunning, conniving priest, who's not going to St Bartholomew's!' she spat out. 'Do you know who knocked on the door, Tabitha?'

Her eyes never left Athelstan's face. 'Another priest, that stupid, ancient, dribbling Father Stephen from St Mary Magdalene church.'

'Why should that alarm you, mistress?' Athelstan asked innocently.

Emma Roffel shuffled in her seat. She, too, smiled, as if enjoying this clash of minds.

'You know full well, priest, but tell me anyway!'

'Oh, yes, I will, madam. I'll tell you a story about a young Scottish girl born in a fishing village near Edinburgh. She married a defrocked priest, but a marriage she thought was made in heaven became a hatred forged in hell. You, Mistress Roffel, hated your husband. It curdled both your souls. Roffel turned to his male whore Bernicia, and you to your love, Tabitha.' Athelstan looked at Tabitha, who gazed coolly back. 'You planned to murder your husband,' he continued, 'by poisoning his flask of usquebaugh. You thought that, if this was detected, someone on board the *God's Bright Light* would surely be blamed, for your husband was hated by his crew.'

'But, Father,' Emma Roffel purred, 'William always kept the flask by him. He, not I, took it to be filled at Richard Crawley's tavern.' She hugged her arms closer. 'I am sure that, if you and that fat coroner make enquiries, you will find that my husband drank from the flask and suffered no ill effects. Indeed, as you know, I drank from it. You drank from it, too. There was no poison in it.'

'Don't mock me, madam,' Athelstan snapped. 'I shall tell you what happened. You took that flask when it was empty and put the arsenic in. Captain William filled it with usquebaugh. It would take more than one swig for the poison on the bottom to mingle and make its presence felt. As you planned, it eventually did, but only when he was at sea. Any apothecary will tell you that white arsenic is not a poison that kills immediately. It takes time to build up in the victim's body.' Athelstan shrugged. 'When the flask was brought back here, you washed and scoured it. You then found some usquebaugh and refilled it, placing it back among your husband's possessions as if it had never been disturbed.'

Emma Roffel just gazed coolly at him.

'Now, the death of your husband,' Athelstan continued, 'was reward enough for you, but when Bracklebury brought his corpse back you noticed something amiss. Perhaps Bracklebury made one last search of the corpse? Or did you study the pages at the back of your husband's book of hours and realise that "in S.L." stood for "in *secreto loco*, in a secret place". The last entry was fresh, so you knew that your husband had recently taken something precious and hidden it away.' Athelstan paused to wet his dry lips. 'It wouldn't be hard to make Bracklebury talk – his only thought was to find that silver.'

'And?' Emma Roffel asked, in mock innocence.

'You knew, God knows how, about this secret place of your husband's and so you entered into an unholy alliance with Bracklebury. You would find the silver and share it with him. You'd then act the grieving widow, maintaining your cool mistress-and-servant relations with Tabitha until you could both disappear and go to some other city in England or Scotland under new names.'

'But I never went aboard the *God's Bright Light* that night,' Emma Roffel scoffed. 'I was in the church of St Mary Magdalene, mourning for my husband.'

'Nonsense!' Athelstan replied. 'You did go aboard that day. You disguised yourself as one of the whores and Bracklebury hid you in the cabin so that you could begin your search – or rather pretend to, because you already knew where the hiding place was. Bracklebury told you about his agreement with Cabe and about the signals that had to be passed between the ships and between himself and Cabe on the quayside.'

'But how could I do all this,' Emma insisted, 'if I was in a church mourning for my husband?'

'You were not,' Athelstan retorted. 'Your maid Tabitha was. Father Stephen is old, his eyesight is failing and you, of course, are no church-goer. So you sent Tabitha to the priest's house pretending to be you. Father Stephen accepted her for what she claimed to be. It was Tabitha who was there that night.'

'But the funeral?' Tabitha interrupted. 'Both Mistress Roffel and I attended the funeral and Father Stephen was there.'

'Oh, I'm sure you did.' Athelstan smiled, noting how the maid had lost her cool appearance of severity. 'Both of you attended, cowled and hooded. But you, Tabitha, maintained the pretence of being Mistress Roffel and she acted the part of your maid. You knew that Father Stephen would soon forget, time would pass. Anyway, you planned to leave the city. And if Father Stephen should visit the house then you could sustain the pretence, even explain away any confusion.' Athelstan pushed his tankard aside; he had not drunk from it, nor would he. 'Of course, when Father Stephen came today while I was here you realised that it was no coincidence. Father Stephen was given clear sight of whoever answered that door.'

'Do continue,' Emma Roffel whispered. She sat back in the chair, tense, her chin thrust forward aggressively. 'Oh, yes, on board the *God's Bright Light?*'

Athelstan paused to collect his thoughts but kept his eyes carefully on Emma Roffel's hands hidden up the sleeve of her gown.

'On board the *God's Bright Light*,' Athelstan continued, 'you remained hidden from the other two members of the watch as well as from Sir Jacob Crawley when he visited the ship. Nevertheless, the admiral was uneasy. After he left, you carried out your plan and murdered Bracklebury and his companions.'

'Me, a frail woman?'

'Who mentioned anything about frailty?' Athelstan asked. 'You may not be young but you are vigorous, strong, a fisherman's daughter. Anyway, it's not difficult to deal with the bodies of drugged men. Only Bracklebury had access to the cabin where you were hidden. You would declare little success in your search but hold out hope. In fact, you were only waiting to kill Bracklebury and any witnesses and so deepen the mystery further.' Athelstan paused, hoping that Cranston would soon appear. 'You laced the cups from which Bracklebury and the other two men were drinking with a powerful sleeping draught. They fell into their drugged sleep, you fastened the weights around their necks and slipped their bodies over the side. I doubt if the poor souls would have regained consciousness.' Athelstan stared at the lantern over the hearth. 'Your movements would have been concealed by a heavy sea mist. The same mist, as well as the speaking trumpet, disguised your voice. You had heard Bracklebury say the password and wink the lantern and you kept matters on an even keel. However' – Athelstan tensed in the chair – 'that sailor returned, laughing and singing, with his whore. You left at about the same time, a misty, cold dawn when the sailors from the two nearest ships were drowsy and the quayside deserted.'

'And what did I do?' Emma cried. 'Fly!'

'No, Mistress Roffel, you put the silver belt round your neck, slipped over the ship's side away from the quayside, and followed the river current downstream, before swimming into shore well away from Queen's hithe and the watching eyes of the Fisher of Men. You then stripped. Tabitha was nearby with a fresh set of clothing and you returned to your house to continue the role of the withdrawn, grieving widow.' Athelstan paused, listening to the creaks and groans of the old house. 'You must have enjoyed yourself, Mistress Roffel, watching everyone run around, allegations being laid, Cabe wondering where Bracklebury was. You are a powerful woman, Mistress Roffel.'

'Not powerful enough for the swim you have credited me with!'

'Nonsense!' Athelstan replied. 'You are a fisherman's daughter. You could swim before you walked, out at sea helping your father with his nets. I felt your hand as you left the Fisher of Men's warehouse – it was rough, rather callused. You were born with the sea in your blood. You can probably swim better than any man on board those ships waiting in the Thames.

'You watched us all run around like mice in a cage. You thought you would muddy the water still further as well as take vengeance on the whore Bernicia. Tabitha wrote that note to Cabe, pretending it came from Bracklebury, pointing the finger at Bernicia. All the time you were preparing to leave. You disguised yourself as a sailor, cowled and hooded, and took some of the silver to a goldsmith. This not only deepened the mystery but provided you and Tabitha with the necessary monies to leave London.' Athelstan leaned forward accusingly. 'The only flaw in your plan was that Bracklebury's corpse was discovered.'

Tabitha clapped her hands mockingly. 'You are right, mistress. A clever, clever little priest!'

'How did you know Bracklebury's sign for the letter to Bernicia?' Athelstan asked. 'I suppose you found it among your husband's documents.' He looked around the room. 'So tidy,' he murmured. 'That's what Sir Jacob Crawley said. He meant that the galley was so tidy. All the cups and goblets cleaned! As if a good housewife had been there, as well as an assassin, hiding what she had done!'

'Clever!' Emma murmured.

'Not really,' Athelstan replied. 'More a motley collection of scraps – finding Bracklebury's corpse, feeling your callused hand, the cleaning of the galley cups, your talk about your youth, your husband's book of hours. And, of course, the sheer weight of logic.'

Emma Roffel smiled into the flames of the fire as Tabitha leaned forward to stroke her gently on the knee.

'Have you ever been to hell, Father?' she murmured.

'Sometimes,' Athelstan replied quickly without thinking.

Emma Roffel sneered. 'Funny, I have never seen you there.' She glared at the friar. 'I have been there, Father. I gave up everything for Roffel, everything for a defrocked priest who turned out to be rotten to the core. A man who used me like a dog with a bitch. He still wasn't satisfied but hired a succession of pretty bum boys. A man who caused death in my womb and created a wilderness in my heart. Yes, I killed the bastard! Bracklebury didn't take long to tell me what had happened, he was furious and eager to find that silver. I played with him as you would a fish. The rest is as you say.' She pulled her face straight. 'I went on board with the whores and hid. First in the hold, then in the cabin. I heard the password and saw the signals.' She grinned. 'That was easy. I drugged the watch and coated my body with grease – an old fisherman's trick, it cloaks the body against the cold. I waited till the tide turned then swam, like I'd never done before, for my freedom!' Her voice rose. 'Freedom from the world of men! Tabitha was waiting with a cloak and some usquebaugh and I was safe. So very, very easy!' She glared at Athelstan. 'Until you came along, you with your dark face and hooded eyes. Our lives are ruined, aren't they, Tabitha? Ruined by clever, clever priests who are not what they appear to be.' Emma sucked the air in through her mouth. 'Clever! Clever!'

She moved, her hand snaking out from the sleeve of her gown and the dagger struck straight for Athelstan but the friar moved quickly. He picked up the tankard and, flinging it at her, dodged sideways even as

Tabitha grabbed him by his cloak. He and the maid crashed to the floor, rolling on the rushes as he tried to break free. Athelstan looked up and glimpsed the hem of Emma Roffel's dress as she moved towards him.

'Oh, for God's sake!' a voice roared.

Tabitha was bodily picked up and flung to one side and the coroner grinned wickedly down at him.

'Brother, what would your parishioners say?'

Athelstan scrambled to his feet. Emma Roffel was held by a burly bailiff whilst the under-sheriff, Shawditch, was helping Tabitha to her feet.

'God knows what my parishioners would say,' Athelstan muttered. 'Sir John, you heard?'

'I did,' the coroner replied cheerily, staring at Emma Roffel. 'I also talked to Father Stephen. He quite categorically states that the person who opened the door to him today was not the person by Roffel's body that night in St Mary Magdalene church. Take them away!' he ordered Shawditch. 'Then come back and search this house from garret to cellar!'

'What are we to look for, Sir John?'

'White arsenic,' Athelstan replied, 'any powder you find hidden away and more silver, Master Shawditch, than you have ever seen in your life!'

The under-sheriff made to lead the two women away.

'Sir John!' Emma Roffel struggled and broke free from Shawditch's grip. 'On my oath, Tabitha Velour was not a party to the deaths!'

Sir John walked across to her. 'In which case,' he told her, 'she may go free. But you, Mistress Roffel, deserve to die.' He laughed sourly. 'Not for

Bracklebury, but for two sailors – good, hard-working men and loyal subjects of the king. Those poor bastards paid with their lives because of your greed and murderous malice!'

He walked back to Athelstan.

'Shawditch!' he called over his shoulder, 'take both of them to the Fleet!'

Cranston waited until the door closed behind them. The house fell silent and the coroner grinned sheepishly at the friar. 'You know, Brother, I never thought you were in any danger but then I remembered that her husband was once a priest. I wondered what would happen when another priest confronted her with her crimes.' He rubbed his thigh. 'I am getting too old to climb walls. But enough of that! Athelstan, my son, you owe me a drink!'

Three days later Athelstan wearily made his way down the Ropery, turning right at Bridge Street and on to the crowded bridge back to Southwark. He'd spent the afternoon at Blackfriars reporting to the prior what had been happening, both in the parish and in his work with Cranston. The old Dominican had heard him out, whistling softly under his breath at Athelstan's description of the mystery surrounding the *God's Bright Light*.

'You are to be congratulated, Brother Athelstan,' he concluded. 'You and Sir John. For no man or woman should be able to slay and hide from the hand of God.' He beamed across the table and wagged a bony finger at Athelstan. 'You were always sharp, Brother.' Then he sat back, fingers to his lips. 'Are you tired of your work, Brother?'

'No, Father Prior, it's God's work.'

'But God's vineyard is a wide one. Would you like to return here? You could lecture in logic, philosophy and astronomy. I know your skills would be appreciated, even in the halls of Oxford.'

Athelstan gazed in astonishment. 'You want me to leave St Erconwald's, Father Prior?'

The old man had smiled. 'It's not what I want, Athelstan,' he replied quietly. 'Like me, you have taken a vow of obedience to the Order, nevertheless, it's what you want. Now think on that.'

Athelstan had and, as he fought his way across the thronged bridge, he sensed the temptation in the prior's words. No more grubbiness, no more violent deaths. He remembered Emma Roffel, her face a white mask of fury above the stabbing knife. He paused for a while, stopping in the church of St Thomas Becket which jutted out over the bridge. He crouched just within the entrance and gazed unblinkingly at the red sanctuary light. He thought of all the violence – the murdered merchant Springall, Sir Ralph Whitton killed in the Tower, other murders in Southwark and at Blackfriars. Athelstan chewed his lip and rested his face against the cold wall. Yet there were also rewards. Pardons had been issued to Ashby and Aveline. The two love-birds had ridden off into the sunset, shouting that Athelstan would have to visit them as soon as possible. The scrutineers were delighted to get back the silver that had been found in the cellar of Roffel's house and Sir Jacob Crawley's name had been cleared. Moleskin the waterman was now a local hero and, of course, there was always old Jack Cranston. Athelstan crossed himself. He rose, genuflected towards the tabernacle and went back on to the bridge. Darkness was beginning to fall as he made his way through the alleys back to St Erconwald's. He felt hungry so he stopped at Merrylegs's bakery to buy a meat pie, his first meal of the day. A beggar on the corner of Catgut Alley, however, looked so plaintive that Athelstan groaned and handed it over to him.

Athelstan had expected to find the church deserted and was rather surprised to see an excited group of parishioners standing on the steps thronging around Watkin and Pike. The portly dung-collector had his back to the door as if guarding it.

'What's the matter?' Athelstan asked.

Watkin looked worried as he put his finger to his lips.

'Father, do you have a crucifix or holy water?'

'Yes, of course I do. Why?'

'Well, there's a demon in the church!'

'A what? Watkin, have you been drinking?'

'Father, there's a demon! Crim saw it. Standing in the entrance to the rood screen!'

'Oh, don't be stupid!' Athelstan said. 'Watkin, stand out of the way!'

'I don't think you should go in, Father!'

'Don't be stupid! Out of my way!'

Athelstan pushed by and entered the darkened nave. No lights or candles burnt and, peering through the dusk, he could make out the outlines of the stage, the entrance to the rood screen and the red tabernacle light winking in the sanctuary. Athelstan carefully walked down the church, surprised to feel the fear starting in his belly.

'Who's there?' he called.

No answer.

'In the name of God!' Athelstan shouted. 'Who is there?' He heard a sound and his anxiety deepened. A tall, dark figure appeared in the entrance to the rood screen, dressed in black from head to toe. He looked like some huge goat with demon features, huge sweeping horns, made all the more ghastly by the thick, fat tallow candle he carried.

'Go and hang thyself, priest!'

Athelstan relaxed and closed his eyes.

'Sir John, for the love of God! You've got half of my parish terrified!'

Behind the mask Sir John's laugh boomed louder than ever. The coroner swaggered down the church, every inch the terrible demon.

'Do you like my costume, Brother? I thought I'd give you a surprise. You should have seen old Watkin move!' Cranston's voice boomed like a bell. 'I never knew the tub of lard could skip so quickly!'

'Take it off, Sir John.'

The coroner struggled and lifted the mask. His great, red face was bathed in sweat and wreathed in a wicked smile.

'The Drapers' Guild lent me it,' he declared, holding the mask up appreciatively. 'What do you think, Father?'

'Even the Lord Satan himself would be envious, Sir John.'

'Good, I thought you would say that.'

Cranston went and sat at the foot of one of the pillars. He put the candle down beside him and beckoned Athelstan to join him.

'Come on, priest. I am not only here for pleasure; there has been another murder.'

Athelstan sat beside him and stared at the flickering candle flame. He felt a tingle of excitement in his stomach and knew the prior was wrong; he would never exchange this for some dry, dusty schoolroom.

'There's been a murder,' Cranston went on, 'in an alley just off Walbrook. At the Golden Magpie – a fine tavern with a boisterous landlord. To cut a long story short, earlier today mine host was found in a cellar with his brains dashed out, yet the door to the cellar was locked and no one saw anyone go in or leave.'

'And you have begun questioning already, Sir John?'

'Yes, I have. Now, tell me, Brother, how can anyone get into a cellar, dash a man's brains out, yet the door be locked from the inside? There's no sign of forced entry. No one saw anyone go anywhere near that door.'

Athelstan scratched his chin. 'But that's impossible, Sir John.'

The coroner began to shake with laughter. 'Of course, it is. I made it up.'

Athelstan nudged him vigorously in the side. The coroner threw his head back and roared with laughter.

'No, no, Brother, we have had murders enough. The only business that concerns me is that Alice Frogmore has brought a fresh bill of trespass against Thomas the Toad. Have I ever told you about Thomas the Toad?'

Athelstan sighed and got to his feet. 'No, Sir John, you have not. But I have a dreadful feeling you are going to!'

'That's right, monk, we are off to see that one-armed pirate in the Piebald tavern. We are going to have a jug of claret, a dish of fried onions, two of his beef pies, some fresh manchet bread then we'll come back here and rehearse this bloody play once and for all! And, if there's any more trouble between God the Father and God the Holy Ghost, I'll knock their heads together!' Cranston lumbered to his feet and picked up the demon mask. 'Do you think it suits me, Brother?'

'Yes, but don't show the poppets or they'll scream.'

'Oh, I have. They thought it was funny, but the dogs flew under the table. I gave a hell of a fright to that idle bugger, Leif.' Cranston put the mask on. 'Come on, let's frighten old Watkin!' He swaggered towards the church door.

'Sir John,' Athelstan called. 'Perhaps it's best if you didn't!'

'What do you mean, monk?'

'I am a friar, Sir John, and poor old Watkin has been frightened enough.'

'Ah, I suppose you are right.' Cranston's voice sounded muffled behind the mask. He tugged at the horns but the mask was stuck.

'Oh, bloody hell!' Cranston groaned. 'Brother, the sodding thing won't come off!'

Athelstan now tugged at the mask but it wouldn't move. Shaking with laughter, he stepped back.

'What are you bloody well laughing at?'

'Sir John, you had best kneel down.'

Cranston obeyed but, pull as he might, all Athelstan got was a stream of filthy curses from Cranston, who claimed his ears were being torn off.

'There's nothing for it,' Athelstan concluded. 'We'll

have to stop off at Basil the blacksmith's and see what he can do!'

So the friar gently took Sir John's hand and led him out of the church. Even as his parishioners scattered, Athelstan knew he was entering the legends of Southwark as the friar who captured a demon and took it to a blacksmith to send it back to hell.